FREDDA BUTTLER

AND THE LEFT-HANDED PEOPLE

*To Julie
I hope you enjoy
Fredda and her
Friends...
C R Manske*

C. R. MANSKE

COVER ILLUSTRATED BY C. R. MANSKE
BACK COVER AND ART DESIGN BY CELIA M. OLIVA

Text copyright © 2012 by C. R. Manske

Cover Illustrated by C. R. Manske copyright © 2012 by C. R. Manske

All rights reserved.

Book Design by

C. R. Manske: Author

Celia M. Oliva: www.photoartbycelia.com

Book Edited by

Claire Raio

ISBN-10: 1479337439
ISBN-13: 978-1479337439

LCCN: TXu 1-817-374

TO ALL LEFT-HANDED PEOPLE IN THE WORLD

C. R. Manske weaves a fantastic tale for all ages in the first of her Fredda Buttler series.

Fredda Buttler's parents have gone missing. She now resides with her only known relative, Great-Aunt Annora, a former teacher at the prestigious International Academy boarding school. Confined to the academy, she finds herself the victim of prejudice, harassed by teachers and a gang of bullies, because of her "awkward, clumsy" left-handedness.

Burning to discover the whereabouts of her parents and a place without prejudice, she hatches a plan to escape. But before she can, an unexpected ally arrives, seemingly to her rescue, and draws Fredda into a whirlwind journey filled with danger, magic and intrigue. She is joined by her friends and thrust into a strange new world and dimensions she never knew existed. The more Fredda explores the paths she might choose to find her roots and the more secrets she unlocks, the more confusing, challenging and dangerous her search to find the answers she so desperately desires becomes.

CONTENTS

ACKNOWLEDGEMENTS - I

CHAPTER 1
THE ESCAPE - 1

CHAPTER 2
THE MYSTERIOUS PRESENT - 27

CHAPTER 3
BLUE - 48

CHAPTER 4
RULES AND REGULATIONS - 60

CHAPTER 5
THE RIGHT GADGET - 73

CHAPTER 6
THE TRUTH IS COMPLICATED - 90

CHAPTER 7
THE COLOR MATTERS - 116

CHAPTER 8
THE OTHER SIDE - 140

CHAPTER 9
ONLY A LEGEND? - 160

CHAPTER 10
GOING RIGHT TO UNDERSTAND LEFT-190

CHAPTER 11
LOVE SINISSTER - 216

CHAPTER 12
THE REAL DARKKPLACE - 244

CHAPTER 13
YOU GOT IT ALL WRONG! - 267

ACKNOWLEDGMENTS

I would like to express my deepest thanks to the following friends and family for their help and support:

To Debra Tantillo, a righty, thank you for being the first to patiently listen to me obsess about each idea for my book and thank you for your financial support.

To Claire Raio, my right-handed editor, and the first to read the entire story, thank you for your encouragement and support for my writing talents. Were it not for you, this story might still be in the drawer. You not only corrected and improved my book, but understood what I wanted to say and "translated" my second-language English into the way it reads today.

To Celia M. Oliva, a right-handed photographer, thank you for giving life to the cover of my book.

To my family and close friends, who knew that I was writing a book but had no knowledge of the title or content of the story, thank you for being so patient and for not asking any questions.

To my mom, even though she is not here with us anymore, I truly believe you would have loved reading my story as much as I loved writing it. Thank you, Mom, for letting me be leftie and for not trying to change who I am.

CHAPTER 1

THE ESCAPE

It was a cold early morning, still dark outside as Fredda woke up to the sound of an ambulance siren. The fire still glowed in the fireplace illuminating parts of the bedroom. Fire light fell on her friend, Tildda, still in bed.

Fredda got up and walked to the window, and with her pajama sleeve, cleaned the foggy glass so she could see outside. None of the students were up yet because it was too early. However, the faculty was out there. She could see them standing under the soft light of the lamp post. *Something must have happened. There are a lot of people outside the main building of the teachers' quarters,* Fredda thought. Disturbed, she stood at the window watching until the ambulance took off and disappeared behind the school buildings.

International Academy was one of the best boarding schools in the country. Perhaps, even one of the best schools in world. It was a highly prestigious school for wealthy children from all over the globe. The students of International Academy were sons and daughters of the very rich and famous. They were the type of people who had no time to deal with them because of their busy schedules. So, the best way for solving the parents' problems, was to leave their children at International Academy. Here where they were assured their progeny would be treated spectacularly with the best care.

Fredda climbed back into her bed, but couldn't fall back to sleep. The incident kept her wide awake. She stayed in bed just staring at the ceiling, and thinking until the bell rang. *It must be 6:00 a.m.,* Fredda thought.

She went back to the window. It was a gray morning and exceptionally cold for this time of the year. Fredda looked up, her warm breath clouding the window glass. But through it, she saw the big school bell up in the tower swinging back and forth to ring in the new day. Lights began switching on in other bedroom windows.

Fredda headed to the bathroom where she followed her morning routine. She then went to the closet and took out her uniform. She reached for her worn out black shoes sitting next to Tildda's crisp shiny ones.

Fredda donned her own white knee high socks, pleated knee length dark gray skirt, white long sleeved shirt with a square pocket on the left side. Sewn on the pocket was a big light pink number six which meant she was in the sixth grade. For the finishing touch, she put on a light pink bow tie. Boys on the other hand, wore a blue bow tie. Other than that, everything else was the same … except the pants, of course! Fredda grabbed her winter coat.

Dress code was extremely strict at International Academy. Some of the *don't* rules were: do not roll the sleeves up; do not undo the tie; do not undo the neck button and do not roll down the socks. These were just a few of the rules with regards to their uniform. There were also some restrictions for clothes on weekends. Such as, no inappropriate clothes like mini-skirts, shorts, sleeveless blouses, low cut pants, flip-flops, no hair color, no nail polish and definitely no heavy makeup.

Fredda remained for a while gazing at herself in front of the mirror.

"Fredda?" a voice came from behind her shoulder.

Fredda jumped.

It was her friend, Tildda. She was a tall, thin girl, with long blond silky hair and beautiful blue eyes.

Fredda wasn't as tall as her friend but she was also thin. Her brown hair fell to her shoulders and her big dark brown eyes often reflected a deep sadness. But when she smiled, with her amazing pair of dimples, she dazzled.

"What are you doing staring at the mirror? You never like to see yourself in the mirror."

Fredda always thought that mirrors were trying to tell her something she wasn't sure she wanted to know.

"And why didn't you wake me up?"

"Oh! Don't worry, you're not late. I'm very early this morning," said Fredda, who normally stayed in bed longer after the bell rang.

"Ah! That's better, I don't want to be late again," said Tildda, yawning, and stretching her arms up in the air.

"Are you okay, Fredda?"

"Yeah, I guess so."

"You look worried."

"Do I?"

"Yes, you woke up very early and you're all dressed and staring in the mirror. I think that's enough evidence that things aren't okay with you."

Fredda went back to the window and waited for Tildda to dress so they could go to the cafeteria and have breakfast together. Fredda couldn't wait to tell her friend about the ambulance.

During breakfast, Fredda noticed that none of the students talked about this incident. She thought maybe they didn't know anything yet because whatever had happened occurred so early.

But, Fredda knew something was going on when she spied the teachers talking animatedly among themselves in their dining room. Teachers and students shared the same place at meal time. However, the teachers were separated by a glass enclosed room equally beautiful to the students'. They also sat on plush chairs at polished mahogany tables covered with fine white linen tablecloths. Hand-blown, hand-painted vases filled with fragrant white lilies and red roses decorated each of the tables.

Fredda whispered secretively to Tildda about the ambulance while they were having breakfast. But, Tildda was more interested in her breakfast and didn't pay much attention to her.

"So, how do you know about the ambulance again?" said Tildda yawning, rubbing her eyes with her knuckles and still thinking about her cozy bed.

"As I told you before," whispered Fredda, "I saw it from our bedroom window."

"Uh! And where was I?"

"Tildda, are you kidding me? Are you paying attention to this conversation?"

"Oh, I'm sorry, Fredda, I'm very tired. You know, I'm not an early bird and I feel that my mind isn't here yet."

"Well, you better come back to this planet where we're all living because in a few minutes we're going to start class, and we all know what'll happen if Mr. Numericoss sees you sleeping in his classroom again."

Mr. Angullus Numericoss was their math teacher.

"OH! YOU'RE STILL UPSET WITH ME ABOUT THAT DAY, AREN'T YOU?" shouted Tildda. Several students turned their heads to see what was going on.

"Oh! Now I got your attention, didn't I?" replied Fredda. "I'm not upset about that day, Tildda, but lots of other students are. They still won't talk to you because of that. And besides, I'm still here, aren't I?"

"I'm sorry, Fredda," whispered Tildda. "This issue is still very fresh in my mind."

"I know it is and I'm sorry I brought it up."

They had breakfast in silence. Fredda didn't eat much because her mind kept drifting to the ambulance.

The students started walking out of the cafeteria.

"It must be time to go," said Tildda. Both of them grabbed their backpacks and headed towards the classroom. "So, you were saying that you heard an ambulance this morning, right? And it was still dark, right? And you think that something happened. What do you think happened?"

"No idea. But when an ambulance comes, it's because something bad happened," said Fredda who remembered when her Great-Aunt Annora was taken from the same place by an ambulance and never came back.

With that thought, Fredda stopped walking momentarily. Tildda stood in front of her. Fredda, with a furrowed brow, began walking again as Tildda walked backwards facing her.

"Yes, you're right Fredda. An ambulance only comes if something bad happens."

"Miss Freddarika Buttler and Miss Matildda D'Rof," shouted a powerful voice from behind them.

They froze. The air got so thick that it could be sliced several times. As they turned around to see who the voice belonged to, they realized that it was a teacher. However, not one of their own and not only a simple teacher, but Mrs. Marga Maufrodezza, the most feared teacher in the entire school.

Her face showed her advanced age. Her tall skinny body was draped in a well-made dark dress. Every dark hair on her head was in place. She adjusted the glasses perched on her very pointy nose, as she waited for their response. Up until this day, Fredda and Tildda had never spoken to Mrs. Maufrodezza, but they knew her reputation for being a horrible person.

Fredda and Tildda looked at each other and answered at the same time, "Yes."

"Well, well, well … What do we have here?" With a smirk on her face, Mrs. Maufrodezza said, "The wealthy and the poor walking side by side. Ah! How ironic!"

"Excuse me?" said Tildda

"Oh! Nothing, I was just thinking out loud."

Fredda and Tildda glanced at each other, but didn't say anything. Tildda could see that Fredda was very uncomfortable. They had heard very clearly what Mrs. Maufrodezza had said, and both of them knew the meaning of that sentence.

Tildda again looked at Fredda, but this time, Fredda wasn't looking at her. She was looking nowhere, into space ... as if she wasn't even there anymore.

Tildda came from a very well-known, wealthy and powerful family. Her great-grandparents were famous and were the founders of one of the biggest companies in the world.

Fredda, on the other hand, didn't come from a famous or wealthy family, yet was allowed to be a student at International Academy only because of her great-aunt, Mrs. Annora Buttler. She was a former teacher, who had full custody of Fredda. This allowed Fredda to have all the privileges as if she were Mrs. Annora's daughter. Although her great-aunt never had any children, Fredda had become her own. The school had rules and regulations allowing the teachers' daughters and sons to get their education there for a tuition reduction as part of their employee benefits plan. However, she was the only student at the present time to take advantage of this plan. The other teachers at International Academy were too old to have children in school or didn't have any children at all.

The girls' backgrounds were extremely different, but not different enough to be a problem for them. They had become very close friends.

"You know that you are not supposed to use this path to go to your classes. This path is out-of-bounds for the students," barked Mrs. Maufrodezza.

"Oh! We didn't realize we were using a forbidden path, Mrs. Maufrodezza," said Tildda quickly, before Fredda could say something to put them in a compromising situation, such as detention.

"So, you know what to do, don't you, Miss D'Rof?" said Mrs. Maufrodezza angrily.

"Yes, we do." Tildda grabbed Fredda's hand bringing her back to the present, and pulled her out of the off limits area. Moving their feet as fast as they could, they reached their classroom, smoothed their hair and uniform as they peeked through the little window on the door to see if Mr. Angullus Numericoss was inside.

Fredda stood on tip toes, but wasn't tall enough to see. "So, is he in?" asked Fredda, teetering on her toes.

"I don't see him in the classroom."

They ran into the classroom and sat in their seats with a thump. By this time, they were very hot from walking so fast that the cold morning didn't bother them anymore.

"I'm so glad we aren't late," said Tildda.

"Me too," replied Fredda.

Some of the students looked at them with frowns on their faces. The students could smell trouble coming from these two.

On the other hand, Olliver said, "I'm glad you two aren't late."

"We are too," replied Fredda.

Olliver Nolland was shy, chubby and as clumsy as a twelve year old could be. His classmates always tried to avoid him, except for Fredda and Tildda. Sometimes Olliver was able to share his study time with the girls.

Mr. Numericoss entered the classroom and everybody stopped talking. Mr. Angullus Numericoss had straight-backed posture and a statuesque stride. His three piece suit fit his slim body perfectly. His slick black hair, thin mustache and chiseled features made him the most handsome teacher at school.

Sometimes, while in the corridors, one could hear girls talking about him ... "Too bad he's already married," and, "His wife is very lucky to have him as a husband," and other comments like that. But what the female students didn't know, in reality, was that Mr. Numericoss wasn't actually married.

Students assumed that he was married because of the ring he wore on his left hand. He was a very private person in class and also outside of school. Not even his colleagues knew much about his private life. The only thing they knew was that he was extremely devoted to math. Everything about his life revolved around math, everything. Time, numbers, graphics, codes, lines, more numbers and codes, everything that contained a number interested him.

However, today, he entered the classroom charging like a furious bull. He even forgot to check his gold pocket watch to see the time, as he usually did. "Open your book to page two hundred and thirteen and leave your homework on your desk," he began. "Here is the latest test and I can assure you that you will have to study harder ... a lot harder if you want to pass this class and continue your education. Nevertheless, some of you did well, others unbelievably poor as usual. I will call the failing grades first. Come here and pick up your test," said Mr. Numericoss sternly.

"How can he be so handsome and so mean at the same time? And I bet you that I'm one of those unbelievably poor grades as usual," whispered Tildda.

Fredda looked at Tildda and smiled. It seemed these days, only Tildda could cheer her.

"BUTTLER!" Numericoss spat out. "YOUR TEST!" he shouted.

"You don't have to distort geometry, Miss Buttler. Mr. Isaac Newton has already done this job for us in physics and also in math. Just follow the rules and you won't have any problem. I cannot understand how you can be from the same family as Mrs. Annora Buttler, a genius like her," said Numericoss, sarcastic again.

All eyes in the classroom focused on Fredda. Mr. Numericoss had never talked to a student like that before. He was always somewhat insulting when students didn't do well in math, but never as much as he was being with Fredda now.

It seemed that Numericoss was disgusted with her and in his distorted mind, people should be related by IQ rather than by blood.

She grabbed her test and saw Attos Azzar and his two friends, Eddra Boggs and Luggos Durmellus, laughing at her.

Numericoss continued calling out the poor grades, and the list was not short! The test had been extraordinarily difficult and even Tildda's name and some other good students, who never thought their names would be called, were also on the list. Still, Numericoss had only mocking words for Fredda.

It seemed that today was not going so well for her. First, the ambulance woke her up early in the morning, and she still didn't know what had happened. Then, Mrs. Maufrodezza caught them in the out-of bounds area of the school and made a nasty comment to Fredda. And now, here was Mr. Numericoss with his criticism and his sardonic way of making a comparison between Fredda and her genius great-aunt. Can you imagine, it was only the first class of the day?

Fredda sat down and looked at her test to avoid looking at other students' faces. It was easier to look at her paper than to face the students whose minds, she imagined, were probably still thinking about the comparison of a genius great-aunt and her stupid great-niece.

The class was boring, with some new material for the finals, and more homework than usual.

There were only two weeks left in the calendar year for this semester before summer vacation started. International Academy was the last school in town to discharge its students because it was a private school. It had its own rules and regulations about almost everything. The last day of school was July thirty first, and Mr. Numericoss needed to finish the math book way before then.

"For those of you who scored very poorly on your test, you can, perhaps, regain some points if you do extra homework from pages one hundred ninety nine through two hundred twelve. I will collect the extra homework next class," said Numericoss.

Finally the bell rang. Fredda was free from math that day or so she thought. But then, she heard Numericoss bellow, "Remember! Math is the way to progress in life. Without math you are nobody! And I shall say it again! No calculators are allowed. Class dismissed."

"We have to do this homework to get some extra points, don't we?" said Tildda rolling her eyes.

"Yes, we must," responded Fredda.

"But we don't know much about this chapter, do we?" Tildda frowned.

Olliver was passing by and overheard the conversation.

"I … I can help you, I … I mean if you need some help."

"Really?" said Tildda smiling again.

"Yes, of course I can help you," replied Olliver excitedly.

"Okay! How about the library today after our last class?" asked Tildda.

"Okay," Olliver grinned.

Fredda was always amused by how easily Tildda could get her way.

"What do we have next?" Tildda asked.

"Uh, let me see our schedule," said Fredda.

"We have history," replied Olliver quickly.

The three of them moved on to their next class together. As they stepped from the school building where their math class was held, they were hit with an icy rain. They didn't have any other choice but to go to the next class using the long way through the buildings instead of the short cut through the beautiful garden.

"Well, at least Mrs. Lagarttus is nice," said Fredda still thinking about that horrible math class.

Mrs. Lotta Lagarttus was called a human encyclopedia, among the students. Although she was elderly with sagging skin and wrinkles lining her face, she remained elegant and well-bred. She enunciated her words clearly, sat with legs crossed at the ankles, and her table manners were impeccable. No matter how angry she became, she never raised her voice.

As the trio approached the history classroom, they saw Attos, Eddra and Luggos at its door. They blocked the entranceway so that Fredda, Tildda and Olliver had to stop.

"So, if you have such inclination to distort things, maybe you could distort the rain and make it sunny," said Attos with a wicked smile.

Eddra and Luggos, who were taller than Fredda, crossed their arms forming a wall in front of the door.

Attos Azzar was thin and freckle-faced with dark hair and dark eyes. He was as tall as Tildda, but his ego was bigger than an elephant.

Eddra and Luggos stood silently glaring at them. Eddra was a tall, robust girl with long black hair. Her pal, Luggos, was a large black haired boy with a strong bulldog face. They both looked down at Fredda.

However, Tildda couldn't contain herself and challenged, "Well, why don't you distort the weather today, if you're so clever!"

Attos stared nastily at her.

"I don't understand why you and Olliver hang out with this low class friend of yours!"

But before the conversation could become ugly, Mrs. Lagarttus arrived on the scene and smelled trouble. "What has been going on? Why is everybody outside of the classroom?"

Nobody said a word.

"Well, every one of you should be in the classroom right now," she said very politely as usual.

The six of them stared at each other once more and began walking. One by one, they made their way into the classroom quietly. The rest of the students, who were already waiting for Mrs. Lagarttus outside the door, just followed the six of them.

For the majority of students, history was the most boring class of all. Even though Mrs. Lagarttus tried her best to teach the class with enthusiasm, it seemed that the students weren't very interested in history. Other subjects such as science: taught by Mrs. Gerdha Lerddus; geography by Mr. Ottello Banguehlla; art by Mrs.

Violetta Sarnna; music taught by Mr. Vincent Violla and even culinary taught by the principal, Mrs. Cellestin, were more interesting than history.

The morning passed slowly and the weather was brutally cold now. It seemed to be a winter's day although it wasn't supposed to be so frigid. Actually, it was supposed to get warmer as the summer vacation was approaching. The weather was quite unusual.

Fredda, Tildda and Olliver went to the cafeteria for lunch, which wasn't supposed to be called the cafeteria, but the school restaurant.

"I'm starving," said Olliver.

"Me too," said Tildda.

However, Fredda didn't say anything. She just kept walking as fast as she could toward the school's restaurant.

Inside was cozy and warmed by the lit fireplaces. The restaurant was elegant. Today, the students could hear the music coming from the piano next to the glass room. Whenever the piano was playing, it meant that it was a special lunch day. Lunch and dinner were served every day in a finest fashion. On the other hand, breakfast was served in the small room adjacent to the formal dining area. The students called it the cafeteria. However, the school faculty preferred it to be called the breakfast room.

The school emblem, a dragon symbolizing wealth and power, was embroidered on the dining room's white table cloths and cloth napkins. This symbol was also imprinted on the fine dinner plates, glasses and silverware. One thing, for sure, the students all agreed that International Academy provided superb meals every day.

Abruptly, the pianist stopped playing, and the walls of the glass room started to rise. All four sides lifted at the same time, which made the private room not so private anymore. The teachers were all sitting together with the students in this big restaurant.

The vice principal, Mr. Vallentino Kaffona, swung a golden bell back and forth over his head. Everyone stopped talking and their eyes locked on him. There he stood, a powerful man with a shiny head and a thick mustache. His voice boomed with no need of a microphone. However, what most students remembered about Mr. Kaffona wasn't his bald head or his robust built, but his fashion sense. Orange was his favorite color and today he had on an orange plaid suit with an orange tie.

And so, he began, "Today I have two announcements to make."

"Where is Mrs. Cellestin?" whispered Fredda.

"As you all already know, every month a chef comes to our school to prepare an extraordinary lunch or dinner for us. The meal today is prepared by a very famous chef, Mr. Jean Pierre De La Mancca," said Mr. Kaffona twisting his lips to pronounce the chef's name.

Tildda and Olliver peered at Fredda and shook their heads to let Fredda know that they didn't know where Mrs. Cellestin was.

"I hope you all enjoy the meal and thank you once more, Mr. De La Mancca, for this opportunity you are giving us to taste your fabulous culinary expertise," completed Mr. Kaffona.

Then, Mr. De La Mancca waved to all the students and shuffled off directly to the kitchen.

But, Mrs. Hilda Camerron, a large woman with a thick neck and her two assistants, Mr. Nepttune, an extremely thin and fragile looking man and a short skinny young fellow named Grillo, weren't very happy about Mr. De La Mancca being the guest chef today. Mrs. Camerron was the official cook or *chef* as the faculty preferred to call her. She'd been a chef for many, many years and whenever anybody stepped into her kitchen you could be sure that she would remind you that the kitchen was hers, and nobody argued the point with her.

"It seemed that today someone has a bigger mustache than Mr. Kaffona," said Olliver referring to Mr. De La Mancca's. Tildda smiled at Olliver and he smiled back.

"The second announcement I have for all of you is that, unfortunately, the principal, Mrs. Cellestin, had to be taken to the hospital early this morning and she will remain there for the rest of the semester."

"No," Fredda whispered desperately.

Tildda and Olliver just turned to each other confused.

"I will be taking her place as principal for the moment, and I am promoting Mrs. Marga Maufrodezza to vice principal. Also, Mrs. Maufrodezza will be the substitute teacher for English and culinary lessons until the end of this semester. Thank you, and enjoy your lunch," he finished.

Students spied Mrs. Maufrodezza looking at Mr. Numericoss.

"No wonder! Now I know why Mr. Numericoss was so irritated today," said Tildda. Her words tumbled out so quickly that Olliver couldn't understand how she came to that conclusion.

"And why do you think that Mr. Numericoss was so irritated?" asked Olliver.

"Don't you know?"

"Don't I know what?"

"That Mr. Numericoss always wanted to be the principal and now he had a great opportunity to become vice principal and he lost it again to Mrs. Maufrodezza."

"Oh, No!" exclaimed Olliver.

"What now?" Tildda asked.

"If Mrs. Maufrodezza is going to be the substitute teacher, then she'll be our English teacher," said Olliver frowning.

"Not only that!" completed Tildda, "She'll be our culinary teacher also," Tildda had the same disgusted expression on her face as Olliver.

Meanwhile, Fredda wasn't participating in their conversation. She seemed to be in another world.

"Are you all right, Fredda?" asked Tildda.

Fredda scratched her head and said, "I guess so."

At International Academy the students were served by attendants during lunch and dinner. At breakfast, they were free to serve themselves. The waiters and waitresses started coming to serve the students dressed in formal tuxedoes, looking like penguins. Actually, the one who was serving Fredda, Tildda and Olliver looked just like one. He was very skinny, had a big head, a short thick neck, pointed nose and his eyes were set far apart.

"Good afternoon, Mademoiselles, Monsieur," he began. "We have a choice of soufflé of chicken, fish or beef, and all the entrees are accompanied with vegetables. As you already know, this is a French dish," the waiter told them and then he turned toward Tildda.

"Chicken, thank you."

"And for you, Mademoiselle?" looking at Fredda. But Fredda didn't answer.

He cleared his throat and asked again, "And for you, Mademoiselle?"

"Fredda?" now Tildda called her.
"Oh! Yes," said Fredda.
"Chicken, fish or beef?" Tildda repeated.
"Chicken, please," replied Fredda softly.
"And for you, Monsieur?" asked the waiter.
"Beef, of course! Thank you," said Olliver.
"I can't believe that we're going to have Mrs. Maufrodezza until the end of this semester. We were supposed to have her next year. She's supposed to be very tough," Tildda whined.

Olliver's mouth was slightly open in anticipation as he looked at the plates. The waiter, with a penguin face, arrived to serve them. The presentation of the plates was stunning and the savory aroma was to live for.

"I hope it's as tasty as it's beautiful," said Olliver almost drooling on the table.

After the waiter served Fredda and Tildda, he stood silently, plate in hand, looking down at Olliver.

"OLLIVER!" shouted Tildda.
"What? What did I do now?"
"The elbow," replied Tildda, a bit annoyed.
"Oh! Sorry, Tildda."
"How many times do I have to tell you about your elbow on the table?"

Olliver took his elbow from the table and put his hands to rest on his lap so the waiter could serve him.

Tildda and Olliver devoured their meals like vultures. They also had chocolate mousse for dessert. Fredda, on the other hand, ate very little and very slowly. It seemed that the announcement of Mrs. Cellestin's hospitalization had greatly disturbed her.

"We should have time to take a nap after lunch," said Olliver, holding his protruding belly like it was going to fall off his body.

Fredda didn't say anything and Tildda rolled her eyes and shook her head disapprovingly.

"We have two more classes and then we're done for today," said Tildda breathing deeply.

"Not so fast, Tildda," said Olliver, "you still have to do extra credit for math."

"Olliver, why do you have to spoil the moment?" asked Tildda.

"Well, I was just reminding you! That's all," continued Olliver insulted, "And besides I don't need the extra credit, I'll just be helping you."

Before Tildda could say anything else to get this conversation to go badly, Fredda said, "Yes, Olliver we're very glad that you can help us, aren't we?" Fredda gave Tildda a warning look.

"Oh yes, we're very glad that you can help us, Olliver," said Tildda sweetly.

The rest of the classes came and went that afternoon, yet the weather continued to be colder than the morning, forcing Fredda, Tildda and Olliver to move speedily from the last class to the library across the courtyard.

The library of International Academy was the most beautiful library in town. It was even more impressive than the city library. Mahogany shelves, from floor to the high ceiling, were filled to bursting with books and more books. The shiny wooden floors reflected them. On the walls, were pictures of famous former teachers and students. All was extraordinarily placed in perfect harmony.

At the entrance hall, hung huge portraits of the most famous teachers of all times. Fredda's great-aunt, Mrs. Annora Buttler was among them.

They rushed by the portraits in the direction of the main room. They found a table, sat down and opened their math books to page one hundred and ninety nine.

But before Olliver could start saying anything, a young boy approached their table and said almost in a whisper,

"Excuse me. Ah ... well, I was wondering if I c..." and the voice disappeared.

"Well," said Tildda impatiently, "if you stop whispering and mumbling at the same time, perhaps we can understand what you're trying to say."

"Well, I ... I was wondering if I could join you with the math homework because it seems to be a bit complicated, and it seems that you're on the same page," the boy's neck stretched to see if the page matched his book, "as me." He then retracted his neck.

"Well," said Tildda, "I don't have any problem, but Olliver is the one who's going to help us with this awful math. So, Olliver, what's it going to be?" asked Tildda.

"I'm okay," said Fredda before Olliver responded to Tildda's question.

"Oh! Yes, if it's okay with you, Tildda, and you, Fredda, it's okay with me," completed Olliver.

"My name is Noell Segat," said the boy avoiding their eyes. He was very timid and very small for his age. He had very dark hair and beautiful blue eyes.

"Yes, we all know who you are," said Tildda, "You always sit in the back of the classroom and you don't talk to anybody because you're very shy." The boy turned as red as a cooked lobster.

"But here, we all talk, and we all speak the truth to one another," said Tildda looking at Noell, "Even if the truth hurts."

Fredda and Olliver couldn't contain themselves and started laughing loudly. The laughter was contagious and Tildda and Noell joined in.

The librarian, Mrs. Nickelleta, glared at them and they tried very hard to compose themselves. Mrs. Nickelleta was a fat lady who looked as old as the books in the library.

"Well, let's start with our latest test because the latest test has to do with our homework," said Olliver. Everyone took their last math test from their backpack.

"Let me see your tests. Let's start with Tildda's," said Olliver. Then he talked about what she'd done wrong and he did the same with Noell's. It seemed that they both understood their mistakes. They also asked some questions and Olliver was able to answer them.

"Now let's see your test, Fredda," said Olliver. He took the test from the table and he turned the page to the right, then he turned the page to the left and then he turned it upside-down. He scratched his head. Fredda, Tildda and Noell eyed each other questioningly, as Olliver continued scratching.

"So what's going on?" asked Tildda who had no patience whatsoever.

"Well ah … ah well, I think, maybe ah … ah, the drawing of this geometric figure seems a little bit ah, um kinda, well, sorta, ah … ah, it looks distorted!" said Olliver, eyes downcast.

"Distorted?" said Tildda angrily, "You sound just like Mr. Numericoss. Let me see it!" She grabbed Fredda's test from Olliver's hand abruptly.

Fredda and Noell joined her. The three of them stared at it and Olliver asked, "How did you manage to draw it three dimensionally?"

"Oh c'mon, I didn't draw it three dimensionally. I only smeared ink all over the paper," answered Fredda, snatching the test away from them.
"And how come nobody else had the problem of smudging ink all over the paper like Fredda?" asked Tildda.

"It's because Fredda is left-handed," offered Noell, who was quiet until this moment. "Left-handed people have the tendency of smearing the ink on the paper when they write or draw," and he continued, "My father is a lefty and he also does it sometimes."

Fredda was pleasantly surprised to know that she was not the only person who smeared ink on paper. If there were more people like her around, she wouldn't feel so awkward. Fredda hadn't had the opportunity to meet another lefty at school yet.

"So funny, I never noticed that you were a lefty, Fredda," said Tildda.

"Yes, I am and this is the only way I can write. I've tried to write with my right hand because my great-aunt insisted I learn. She worked really hard with me to change my writing hand, but I just couldn't! Great-Aunt Annora finally gave up and told me that I must be a true lefty. I really didn't understand what she meant by that. I guess I have to find a way of being more careful next time I draw, or otherwise, I'll get in trouble again in math."

"Yes, I guess you have to be more careful next time," said Olliver.

The time passed quickly and Olliver proved to be a great help. They finished half their homework and decided to come back tomorrow to finish the rest. One exercise per page … a total of thirteen pages of that *awful* math book, as Tildda called it.

As they were leaving the library, they again passed in front of the huge portraits of the famous teachers. But this time, Fredda stood in front of the portrait of her great-aunt. Fredda had stood in front of that painting appreciating it so many times. However, today Fredda took a deeper look at it. She had mixed feelings about her famous great-aunt. She didn't know if she should be proud to be her great-niece or if she should be annoyed by the fact that everyone was trying to make a comparison between the two of them.

Tildda stared up at the painting and then at Fredda. "Is there a problem?" she asked, concerned about her friend.

"I don't know yet," Fredda answered.

"This is your great-aunt, isn't she?" Noell, looked up at the portrait.

Fredda, not taking her eyes from the painting, nodded.

"My father told me that she was the best teacher he ever had," said Noell. The others stared at him.

"I didn't know your father was a former student!" said Tildda surprised.

"Yes, he was, and he also said that the school owes Mrs. Buttler big time."

"How come?" asked Fredda, even more interested to know about her great-aunt now.

"Well," continued Noell, "Dad told me that she earned a lot of awards for the school and with the awards came a great deal of money which she donated to our school. Dad also told me things about you. That your tuition was already prepaid and had nothing to do with the fact that your great-aunt was part of the faculty. He said that your great-aunt had paid for your studies a long time ago. He also said that with the money your great-aunt received from the awards, she could have paid for your studies not once but many times over."

Each word that Noell offered was like history being told for the very first time. Fredda's big brown eyes widened, as did Tildda's. Both were astonished by what they were hearing.

It was the first time Fredda had ever heard anything about her great-aunt other than her being a genius. She didn't know much about her great-aunt's past even though she'd lived with her. Her great-aunt never told her much about anything. The only thing she knew was that Great-Aunt Annora was brilliant.

"My father also told me," Noell went on, "that she could have had any job she wanted. Maybe working for a university or a big company or even for the government, but she loved the school and never left. Well, until that fateful day when she got sick."

"Do you know anything else?" asked Tildda anxiously.

"No, not really," replied Noell.

Fredda turned again to look at the painting once more and thought for a moment about what else her great-aunt might not have told her about herself and about her family.

Then, they tore themselves away from the portrait so as not to be late for dinner.

It had been quite an interesting day for Fredda so far.

However, the information she'd gotten from Noell about her great-aunt was unbelievable and made Fredda wonder even more about the principal, Mrs. Cellestin, not being at school. And why had no one ever told her about her great-aunt's awards money? Fredda had known about the awards but not about the money attached to them.

Fredda, Tildda, Olliver and Noell raced from building to building trying to avoid the rain and to avoid being late for dinner.

Dinner was superb as usual and afterwards, the four of them headed to the dormitory.

Being at International Academy was like being at a luxurious hotel. There was a great restaurant, awesome food, bedrooms with their own bathrooms, a gorgeous library, stunning gardens and study rooms all over the place. The classrooms were extremely comfortable with fireplaces in each. The only difference was that at a luxury hotel people relaxed and had fun and at International Academy students had no fun and were never relaxed.

Fredda, Tildda, Olliver and Noell said good night to each other. The girls headed towards the left side of the building while the boys took a right to go to their rooms.

"I'm exhausted," said Tildda

"Me too," responded Fredda.

The two girls walked to their room slowly. It was the first time, after a long exhausting day, that Fredda had a chance to think about everything that had happened. She had dozens of questions on her mind. However, so few answers. *Why do some teachers dislike me so much? Why didn't anybody tell me more about my great-aunt's past, the only family I have left?* And on and on.

The two of them entered their room. It was warm and clean as usual. The cleaning staff came during the day to change the bed sheets, collect the towels and dirty clothes.

Tildda jumped into bed, stayed there for a little while and closed her eyes for a moment while Fredda paced back and forth in front of their beds.

Then Tildda went into the bathroom to change into her pajamas. When she came back from the bathroom, Fredda was still pacing. Tildda couldn't hold it anymore and said, "What's going on, Fredda?" Tildda was uneasy.

"I have to tell you something," said Fredda, calmly but still walking. "But I don't know exactly how to start."

"How about you stop pacing, so I don't have to follow you with my head like I'm watching a tennis match!"

"Oh, yes, of course."

Fredda sat on the end of her bed. Tildda was already sitting up on her own and Fredda began, "I have to talk to Mrs. Cellestin about my great-aunt. But I know, Mr. Kaffona and Mrs. Maufrodezza, won't let me leave to go to the hospital. With all the rules," and Fredda paused, "the only way I can do it is if I escape."

CHAPTER 2

THE MYSTERIOUS PRESENT

"ESCAPE?" shouted Tildda, bolting out of bed. Her rapid fire of questions followed. "Are you out of your mind? Did you lose it completely? Do you have any idea how dangerous things are outside? And, what about the security guards? You know they're the best guards in this entire city." Now Tildda was the one pacing back and forth in front of their beds.

"Not really," said Fredda, shaking her head, "I don't go outside that much."

"EXACTLY! YOU DON'T KNOW!" screamed Tildda.

"You don't have to shout at me, Tildda," responded Fredda, slightly trembling and apprehensive. She realized that telling Tildda about her plan might not have been such a good idea.

"Sorry, Fredda, but just the fact that you want to escape is scary, very scary. And besides you could be expelled. No, you're going to be expelled for sure! You'll be the first student to attempt to escape from here. No student has ever made any attempt to escape. You'll be in the history books of the school, do you know that?" said Tildda, peering into Fredda's eyes. "And then, what are you going to do? How're you going to survive? Where are you going to sleep at night? Where are you going to study? Who's going to take care of you? Where are you going to eat?"

So many questions, so fast! How? What? Where? Who? Fredda didn't even remember the first one.

"Calm down, Tildda, I'm still here, okay. And besides, don't place me in the history books before it happens. Let's go to sleep. We've had enough for one day, don't you think?"

"Yes, maybe that's a good idea," said Tildda, beginning to calm down. "Maybe you'll go to sleep and forget this horrible idea of escaping," Tildda jumped back into her bed.

The next morning, both of them were extremely tired since neither of them had a good night's sleep. Both were out of bed before the bell. They got ready but said nothing to each other until Tildda, who couldn't resist the temptation of not talking, asked Fredda a question.

"How do you plan to escape if you *were* to escape from here?"

"Do you really want to know?" smiled Fredda.

"Yes, of course," Tildda smiled back conspiratorially.

"Well, if I were to escape from here someday …"

Fredda went to her side of the closet and took out a box with some books and papers. She put the box on her bed and started pulling things from inside of it. She took out a very well-worn leather book. From inside the book, she pulled out a bunch of papers and spread them on her bed. Then, she grabbed a thick rectangle of folded paper.

"What is it?" asked Tildda excitedly.

Fredda opened it. "It's the school's map."

"How did you get this?" asked Tildda in shock.

"Well it's a long story but I'm going to try to tell you very fast or we'll be late."

"Please!" said Tildda, more impatient than ever.

"Do you remember that I told you I attended school from first to fourth grade here at International Academy?"

"Yes," said Tildda with her big blue eyes widely open.

"Okay, you know where the building is located, don't you?"

Tildda nodded her head.

"When I was in fourth grade, after school was over for the day, the students went home because, you already know, that only when you're in fifth grade you become a resident at International Academy. But I didn't go home. I had to wait for my great-aunt until she was done with her classes so I could go to the teacher's quarters, which is located in the back of the school. That's where I used to live with my great-aunt, and students are not allowed to go to that area by themselves."

Tildda's head continued to bob up and down encouraging Fredda to go on.

"So, after school, I usually went to the school restaurant to get some snacks from Mrs. Camerron, the cook, and after that, I used to go to the library. It was there at the library that I got hold of this map."

"And the map was just lying there?" said Tildda disbelievingly.

"Yes, it was."

"And you want me to believe you, Fredda?" Tildda stood, her hands on her waist and her head tilted in question.

"You don't understand. Let me explain."

"Yes, because I'm thinking that you stole it!"

"Well, maybe I borrowed it from the library. Well, what I'm trying to say is that I made a copy for myself."

"Yeah, it looks like a copy and it looks like you used pencil," said Tildda, examining the paper.

"Yes, I used pencil because I was afraid of smeared ink all over my drawing. The map was lying there open on the table. The library was under renovation at that time so the workers left the blue print, as the workers called it, lying there for weeks. I made a copy for myself when they weren't around. I didn't steal it, did I?"

"Well, not really, you only made a copy for your personal use," said Tildda, trying to make some sense of this news. "But I still don't understand how this map can help you to escape. And besides, I still don't think that's such a good idea!"

"Well, we have to go now, Tildda, I'll explain more to you later."

"Yeah, let's go, I don't want to be late."

Fredda put her map back inside the old book and put the book inside the box and the box inside the closet and they left for breakfast.

The weather was still very chilly, and it also seemed that it would be another rainy day.

On their way to the breakfast room, they met Olliver and Noell. The four of them sat at the same table, and breakfast, like lunch and dinner, was a pleasant occasion for the majority of students.

Mrs. Camerron was back in her kitchen with her two assistants, Mr. Nepttune, and the young fella, Grillo.

The students served themselves from a large orchestrated table with all variety of foods and drinks. Breads, omelets, pancakes, waffles, cereals, veggies, fruits, cold cuts, pastries, yogurt, coffee, tea, milk, hot chocolate, juices and water. Olliver returned several times to the buffet table to sample different foods. Fredda, Tildda and Noell couldn't understand how he could eat so much.

"How can you eat so much?" asked Tildda.

"I'm hungry, Tildda," replied Olliver.

"Yeah, you're always hungry, aren't you?" said Tildda smirking at him. But Olliver didn't say anything. He was too busy eating his delicious breakfast.

"Well, summer vacation is almost here," smiled Noell, "Where're you going on vacation, Tildda?"

"Ah! I think my mother wants to go to France this year. We like to spend some time with Grandma."

"And you, Olliver, where're you going?" asked Noell.

"I believe my father wants to go to Africa," said Olliver, still chewing. "And what about you, Noell," asked Olliver, "Where will you be going?"

"Well, my family wants to go to Egypt or Greece."

"What about you, Fredda? Where're you going this summer?" asked Noell.

There was a pause. Tildda and Olliver looked at each other and then at Fredda. Noell, at this point, was staring at the three of them.

Fredda took a deep breath and without looking at anybody but her plate said, "I'll not be going anywhere, Noell. I'll be at school, as usual."

Noell turned to Olliver. He was confused.

Tildda opened her mouth to explain, but before Tildda could say a word, Fredda cut her off, "Thank you, Tildda for trying to explain it to Noell, but I think I can handle it myself."

"Okay," said Tildda snapping her mouth shut.

"I won't be going anyplace, Noell, because I don't have anybody to call *family* except my great-aunt, Annora. But, as you already know, she's now living at the nursing home, and besides, she doesn't even remember me. So, I'll stay here at school, as I do every year."

"You've never been any place other than here?" asked Noell, amazed to hear about Fredda's vacation plans.

"That's right, Noell. I've never been to any place my whole entire life. I mean, other than the nursing home to see my great-aunt and the field trips around the city," responded Fredda.

"How's that possible?" questioned Noell.

"Oh, please! Don't be stupid, Noell!" replied Tildda, "Fredda told you that she doesn't have anybody, what part of, *anybody*, don't you understand?"

"I'm sorry … It's just because I never met anyone who doesn't go any place during vacation." Noell was having difficulty computing the information Fredda had given him.

"Well, now you've met one, right here, Noell. Let's move on and let's go to class," Tildda redirected.

Noell and Olliver started walking ahead of Fredda and Tildda, toward the building for their first class of the day.

The weather was still vicious and the students couldn't understand how it could be so cold when it was supposed to be getting warmer.

Fredda and Tildda walked slightly behind Olliver and Noell, and Tildda remarked to her, "I didn't know that your Great-Aunt Annora, doesn't know who you are. Fredda, you never told me."

"Well, last time I went to see her, when Mrs. Cellestin took me to the nursing home, my great-aunt was not herself. She was talking to me as if it was the first time she'd ever seen me. She didn't know my name. She didn't know that I was her great-niece. She didn't remember who Mrs. Cellestin was. She didn't even remember who she was *herself*. My great-aunt was talking about things that didn't make any sense to me like, *'The thing in the sky was the greatest thing I have ever seen in my life!.'* She talked about finishing an equation. Stuff I couldn't comprehend. You know that she was a great mathematician, so I think she still thinks she's working on some kind of project like when she was a teacher here at school."

Tildda just nodded her head as they continued walking towards the classroom. Fredda went on, "So Mrs. Cellestin told me that I shouldn't see my great-aunt anymore. And she told me that from now on, she'd be taking care of me in regards to my school stuff and she also told me …"

But before Fredda could tell Tildda what else Mrs. Cellestin had told her, Olliver and Noell stopped in their tracks. They stepped backwards to stay protectively close to Fredda and Tildda. Olliver accidentally stepped on Tildda's foot, "Ouch that's my foot, Olliver, and you're kinda heavy!"

"Sorry Tildda, but I'm a man and I'm supposed to be heavier than you!" said Olliver whispering and not taking his eyes from the person approaching.

"Excuse me, but as far as I'm concerned, you're still an ongoing project of a man. You're a boy and there's a huge difference between a man and a boy," completed Tildda, looking down, still preoccupied with her foot.

"We can finish this conversation later. Okay, Tildda?" Olliver's eyes were riveted on Attos Azzar nearing them.

Olliver knew that Attos was going to say something awful about Fredda, as he always did. And this time proved no different.

"So Noell, what're you doing hanging out with this low life? Does your father know that you're hanging out with Buttler?" said Attos Azzar, the worst thing that had happened to Fredda's life at school.

Attos was accompanied by his two best friends, Eddra Boggus and Luggos Dumerllus, who just stood in front of Olliver and Noell being silently intimidating. Tildda, who wasn't afraid of Attos, stepped in front of Olliver and Noell to respond.

At the same moment, a door on Tildda's left burst open, rapidly cutting off Tildda's view of Attos and his friends. Tildda stepped back. It was Tildda who, this time, stepped on Olliver's foot. But, he said nothing. His eyes and everybody's eyes were fixed on the door.

Mr. Numericoss came through it furious. He stopped in front of them and snapped at Fredda, "What are you looking at? You are supposed to be in class instead of being behind the door eavesdropping on my conversation!"

The door slammed closed and the four of them no longer saw Attos, Eddra and Luggos who had probably fled the scene as soon as they heard Numericoss' voice.

Numericoss hadn't seen them either.

The door swung open again. This time it was Mrs. Maufrodezza, eyes blazing with anger. She spied the four of them, but fixed those dark eyes on Fredda and shouted, "WHAT IS GOING ON HERE? AREN'T YOU SUPPOSED TO BE IN CLASS?"

"They were eavesdropping on our conversation." Numericoss glowered at Fredda.

"Why is it that every time I see you, Miss Buttler, you are doing something against the school's rules and regulations? Mrs. Maufrodezza stared venomously at Fredda.

Fredda said nothing, as neither did Olliver, Noell nor Tildda.

Then the door burst open one more time. This time it was the principal, Mr. Kaffona, dressed in orange, of course. "What is going on here? Aren't you supposed to be in class?" He looked at the frightened students standing there, "And you, Mr. Numericoss, and you, Mrs. Maufrodezza, aren't you supposed to be in class also?" said Mr. Kaffona, "Well, what are you waiting for children? Move! Fast!" ordered Mr. Kaffona again, not giving Mr. Numericoss or Mrs. Maufrodezza any chance to speak.

They left, as fast as they could, glad that Mr. Kaffona had shown up at that particular moment.

Olliver's and Noell's faces were sheets of white. They'd never experienced this type of situation. Fredda and Tildda on the other hand, weren't as shaken. They were more used to this kind of treatment, especially Fredda.

"Olliver, stop shaking!" said Tildda, "And you too, Noell, everything's okay now."

"I thought we were gonna to be expelled!" said Olliver dramatically.

"Oh please, Olliver! How could we be expelled? We didn't do anything wrong! We were just walking, not even running!" replied Tildda firmly.

"You know what I'm trying to say, Tildda. It'll be their word against ours."

The day had barely started and the four of them had already been in trouble.

"The semester will be done in less than two weeks and we can't afford to be in trouble now before our finals," said Olliver, still trembling.

"I think we need to get to class now or we're going to be late," said Tildda.

"Yes, we should go," said Fredda.

"To which building? What class do we have?" asked Tildda.

"Ah! Let me think," said Olliver opening his notebook to look at their schedule, still disoriented.

"Science," he said, "science and then geography ah … and then music and … no math."

"I hate math," said Tildda.

Olliver continued, "We have English, last class of the day, with Mrs. Maufrodezza, our new English teacher," completed Olliver.

"Oh! Not Mrs. Maufrodezza again!" cried Noell.

Throughout the day, the quartet stayed together and tried to avoid Mrs. Maufrodezza and Mr. Numericoss.

They made it through science with Mrs. Lerddus, geography with Mr. Banguehlla, and music with Mr. Violla. To the groups' relief, none of them had given homework since those teachers felt that their students needed the time to study for finals.

Finally, the last class of the day arrived. Fredda, Tildda, Olliver and Noell were worried. They thought Mrs. Maufrodezza would bring up what had happened early in the morning.

Not wanting to be late, they speed-walked to the next building. Just the thought of being late was enough to put Olliver and Noell in a frenzy.

"Faster, please, can you walk faster?" said Olliver to the girls.

"We're walking as fast as we can, Olliver," said Tildda, out of breath, "Maybe, we should run."

"No running, please," said Noell, "Imagine if someone sees us running! For sure, we'll be in more trouble."

The only time running was allowed anywhere at school was in physical education class.

Not even the hard weather bothered them at this point. Class would begin in five minutes and they'd be there in the same classroom with the most feared teacher in the entire school! Mrs. Maufrodezza wasn't supposed to be their teacher until next year, when they'd be in seventh grade!

They got to the classroom on time. The four of them took seats in the back as the other students were already in class, including Attos, Eddra and Luggos, who stared at them.

Suddenly, the door opened and the object of their fear stepped in, carrying a briefcase in her right hand and a black book in her left. She put the briefcase and the black book on her desk and positioned herself in the middle of the classroom, between the blackboard and the desks.

As she was about to speak, a loud noise came from outside. "Bang! Bang! Bang!" as if something had fallen next to the classroom.

The student's eyes fixed on their new teacher. Most likely, they were waiting for Mrs. Maufrodezza to say something. She looked at them, sending a message through her black teacher's eyes. Nobody moved. The students knew not to ask questions, not even to breathe.

Mrs. Maufrodezza hovered over her students looking even taller and skinnier than ever. Her long pointy nose looked even longer today! Her hair, always pulled up so she could better hear conversations between students, seemed more perfectly neat than ever. No one ever dared talk in her classroom unless called upon first.

Mrs. Maufrodezza's personality was reflected in the expensive, conservative clothing she always wore.

She approached the classroom door and pulled it open to check what had happened. The students could hear the conversation in the hallway because Mrs. Maufrodezza had left the door open wide.

"Oh! It is you again, Guerdha," barked Mrs. Maufrodezza.

Mrs. Guerdha Lerddus, the science teacher, was a tiny woman, actually so small that sometimes she was mistaken for a student. On her pruned up face, slipping from the bridge of her nose, was a pair of huge round bottle thick glasses. Her hair stuck out messily from her head. She wore a bright dress with flowers printed wildly all over it. She loved flowers, and usually wore clothing patterned with them. She spoke very softly and slowly.

And whatever she lacked in style, she made up in knowledge.

"HOW MANY TIMES DO I HAVE TO TELL YOU NOT TO CARRY THIS STUFF ALL BY YOURSELF?" Maufrodezza yelled at Mrs. Lerddus.

"I am so sorry about the noise, Marga," responded Mrs. Lerddus, in her soft, slow voice. "I know that I should have had someone help me, but I could not find anyone available."

"You are so clumsy, Guerdha! Pick up the mess you have made and do not dare make any more noise!"

"Oh, yes, yes, do not worry, I will be very careful. And I am again, so very sorry to have disturbed your class, Marga."

Mrs. Lerddus bent down to pick up all the books, broken glasses, boxes full of plants and more books spread all over the hallway, being very careful not to make any noise this time.

Meanwhile, inside the classroom, nobody dared move a finger. As Mrs. Maufrodezza entered the classroom slamming the door closed, she resumed her position in front of the blackboard.

"I am Mrs. Marga Maufrodezza." Like no one knew?

"And I will be your new English teacher. Mr. Kaffona told you yesterday, when he publically promoted me to vice principal."

The students could see the pride Mrs. Maufrodezza had when she talked about being vice-principal.

She continued, "I understand that we will not have many classes together, as the end of the school year is very close. I will also be your English teacher next year when, hopefully, all of you move on to seventh grade."

The students remained silent, planted at their desks.

"I have a very different way of teaching my classes. Very different from Mrs. Cellestin. English is an extremely important subject. And for all of you, the *keyboard generation*," and she made a quotation with her fingers, "who like to use computers, I have news for you. Computers are not a magic solution for education. They actually cause you to be slow thinkers. Not even to mention that your generation wants to change the language with all this texting back and forth. Chopping the words of our beloved English language and creating your own sub-standard vocabulary!"

Mrs. Maufrodezza looked directly at Noell. She knew that Noell's father was a big name in the computer business. Fredda, Tildda and Olliver also turned to Noell who looked even smaller than he already was.

She continued, "Think about not having access to a computer or any other gadgets. What will you do if you do not know how to write without a keyboard? You will need to know how to use a pen and paper. Computers will be banished from this point on in my classes. I will also write to the principal, Mr. Kaffona, about banishing these gadgets from the entire school. Mark my words!"

She grabbed a piece of blank paper and a pen, and displayed it to the class.

"These are the tools for the magic of education. Everybody will have to turn in their papers the old fashioned way. And now for the best part of the class, get your papers and pens and start writing an essay. The title is, 'My Year in School', so I can become familiar with you and your writing skills. The essay should be ready by the end of this class. I require two completed pages, at least, no less than that." Her presence seemed almost threatening. Mr. Numericoss and Mrs. Maufrodezza were running a close race for being most frightening.

Fredda was relieved since she didn't have a computer. Besides, the computers at the library had the mouse on the right side which made it difficult for her. She was used to writing most of her papers by hand, not like the other students who had their own personal computers.

"WHAT ARE YOU WAITING FOR?" shouted Mrs. Maufrodezza, her voice shaking the student's desks.

The students scrambled for their pens and papers. Mrs. Maufrodezza snapped open her black book and began eagerly writing, while her students agonized over their essay.

Tension hovered over the classroom as the class scribbled their thoughts on paper.

Fredda was glad that she and Mrs. Maufrodezza were blocked from each other's view by students between them. Her mind eased somewhat as she tackled a subject she enjoyed – writing.

Time seemed to pass quickly on the big clock ticking over the blackboard.

Mrs. Maufrodezza rose and began walking back and forth between the desks.

Suddenly, Mrs. Maufrodezza screamed in horror, "WHAT ARE YOU DOING, MISS BUTTLER?"

Fredda jumped out of her seat as the pen in her left hand accidentally smeared fresh ink on her essay.

The other students' heads shot up from their papers and focused on Fredda.

She flushed red. It took her a few moments to somewhat recover. "I … I… was writing the essay … as you told us to do."

The venomous shouting continued, "AND WHO TOLD YOU THAT YOU HAD PERMISSION TO WRITE WITH YOUR AWKWARD, CLUMSY, HANDICAPPED LEFT HAND!"

Attos laughed with Eddra and Luggos while the rest of the class whispered and joined in the laughter.

Maufrodezza went to her desk, got a wooden ruler from her briefcase. Holding the ruler in her right hand and smacking it against her left, she said, "In my class, students will obey. In my class, there will be no student who will use the wrong hand to write or do anything else. In my class, you are going to conform to the right side, if you like it or not."

She approached Fredda's desk and continued hitting her left hand with the ruler.

Now standing in front of Fredda's desk, she said angrily, "Give me your hand!"

Trembling, she held out her right hand to Maufrodezza.

"Trying to be smart with me, Miss Buttler?"

Fredda looked at Mrs. Maufrodezza, pulled her right hand back and rested it on her desk.

"GIVE ME YOUR HANDICAPPED HAND!" Maufrodezza shouted again.

Fredda hesitated. She knew why the ruler was there.

Maufrodezza screamed again, "YOUR CLUMSY HAND! AND I AM NOT GOING TO ASK AGAIN!"

At this point, Maufrodezza was furious. The entire class held their breath and watched them both.

Fredda looked at her left hand, the hand she was born to use swiftly and competently. She looked at Mrs. Maufrodezza and extended it towards her with the palm up and open.

"I'm going to teach you something today that you will never forget. You will be using the correct hand from now on."

Maufrodezza held Fredda's left hand with her own left hand and with her right, in which she was holding the ruler, she elevated her arm high.

Fredda squinted her eyes closed and grimaced in anticipation.

But at the moment Maufrodezza was ready to slam the ruler on Fredda's left hand, someone knocked at the door.

Every student turned toward the knock. Maufrodezza looked at Fredda and the knocking continued.

Maufrodezza hesitated, lowered her arm, walked furiously to the door and pulled it open.

"I am sorry to interrupt your class, Mrs. Maufrodezza, but Mr. Kaffona is demanding the presence of Miss Freddarika Buttler in his office," said Mrs. Utilla, Mr. Kaffona's secretary.

"I have some business to finish first with Miss Buttler," said Maufrodezza superiorly.

"Mr. Kaffona said that she should go immediately and he cannot wait for the end of the class."

"Well, it must be urgent then," said Maufrodezza impatiently, "MISS BUTTLER!" Maufrodezza shouted once more. "The principal wants to talk to you now. I wonder what you did this time?" said Maufrodezza still holding the punishing ruler.

Fredda let out the breath she'd been holding, grabbed her school bag, left the messy paper on her desk, walked rapidly to the door and left with Mrs. Utilla.

Out of one terrifying situation and possibly approaching another, Fredda wondered why Mr. Kaffona had called her.

Fredda wondered, *Why did Mr. Kaffona call me? It was probably because of this morning. Maybe Mr. Numericoss made a complaint about us.*

She walked silently alongside Mrs. Utilla, a chubby lady whose jaws hung like a hamster's. Fredda's heart still beat rapidly after her escape from Mrs. Maufrodezza.

Fredda had thought she hated Mr. Numericoss, but now she knew she hated Mrs. Maufrodezza even more. It was true about her reputation of being the most terrifying teacher in the whole entire school.

She continued to the principal's office with Mrs. Utilla in silence. They arrived at the main office of International Academy.

The main office was located on the second floor which looked like a lobby of a luxurious hotel. It had gorgeous marble floors, a centerpiece of fresh colorful flowers on a round table, high ceilings and sturdy columns to sustain the stunning structure.

Fredda had been to the main office several times when Mrs. Cellestin was the principal, but this time she saw that there had been some redecorating. Mrs. Cellestin's name was still on her door, but the vice principal's name was gone from his room and a new one hung on another door now reading, Principal, Mr. Vallentino Kaffona.

"Please this way, Miss Buttler," said Mrs. Utilla. Fredda followed the secretary.

She opened a door that Fredda was not familiar with, and was told to take a seat and wait for Mr. Kaffona.

The room was striking, with a huge half-moon window from which she could see the entire main garden of the school. There was a lovely single pink orchid in a wooden basket on the mahogany table next to his desk. Books were organized in mahogany cabinets like the ones in the library and a thick file lay on his desk.

The door burst open and Mr. Kaffona entered, wearing his favorite color, orange, of course.

Fredda stood in front of the huge window admiring the garden.

"Oh! Yes, Miss Buttler, please take a seat," he said, gesturing toward a chair where she should sit. He sat in the plush leather chair behind his desk.

"I have some questions to ask you, Miss Buttler."

"Yes," responded Fredda. It was a bit difficult for Fredda to concentrate on Mr. Kaffonas' words. His head was so shiny and distracting.

"Have you been in contact with your great-aunt, Annora, Miss Buttler?"

Fredda shook her head. "No."

"Have you been in contact with anybody outside school, Miss Buttler?"

Fredda shook her head again.

"Do you know anybody outside the school, Miss Buttler?

And the head shaking *no* continued.

"Well, I went through your entire file to see if I could find something about your," and Mr. Kaffona paused, "family, and I found nothing." He opened Fredda's file.

The big book, lying in front of Fredda's eyes, was *her* file, and probably, her entire life was in it. She would give anything to have access to that book.

While Mr. Kaffona's eyes were lowered as he studied it, she craned her neck, trying to read the information that was in it too.

Mr. Kaffona snapped the file closed and met Fredda's eyes.

"Well, Miss Buttler, this morning we have received a package addressed to you!"

"To me?" said Fredda intrigued.

"Yes, to *you*, Miss Buttler. The note said, 'To Miss Freddarika Buttler,' and as far as I am concerned, there is only one Miss Freddarika Buttler in this entire school. But the most interesting thing is that there is no sender's name on the note. No signature whatsoever."

"And where is it?"

"Oh yes, of course!" said Mr. Kaffona and he stood up and grabbed the beautiful pink orchid and handed it to Fredda.

"A flower?" said Fredda, a bit disappointed.

"Not only a flower, Miss Buttler, a very rare orchid, if I may say."

"And who would send me a flower? I mean, an orchid?"

"That is the question, isn't it, Miss Buttler? Who could possibly have sent you a rare orchid?"

"I have no idea," said Fredda, becoming more intrigued by the minute.

"So you don't know, Miss Buttler."

Fredda just shook her head again.

He opened Fredda's file once more and glanced at it.

"I have here, written in your file, that you received a package last year from Miss Matildda D'Rof, in August to be more precise." He closed the file again.

"Yes, I received a birthday present from her."

"Are you sure you did not ask your friend, Miss D'Rof, to send you this orchid?"

"Why would I ask Tildda, I mean, Matildda to send me a flower? If I could ask for something, sir, I would've asked her for a pair of sneakers which I need more than a flower," said Fredda, scratching her head.

"Very well, very well, if you do not know anything about this orchid then you may go now, Miss Buttler."

Fredda stood up, grabbed her backpack and was leaving, when Mr. Kaffona called, "Aren't you going to take your flower? I mean, your orchid, Miss Buttler?"

"Oh yes, my flower, I mean, my orchid, of course."

"And don't forget to water the plant. Plants like water. Otherwise, they will die," said Mr. Kaffona, already opening the huge file and reading it again.

She grabbed her flower, her backpack and left the office in a hurry. She didn't understand anything that had just happened.

Confused and distracted, she continued walking rapidly and found herself in the main garden. *What should I do now?* She took a look at the big clock on the bell tower and realized classes were over, but she remembered her math homework and headed to the library.

CHAPTER 3

BLUE

Fredda hurried. Her math homework was due tomorrow and she hadn't yet finished it. She was having a terrible day so far. *Why would someone send me a flower when I'm in need of new clothes, shoes and maybe a new rain coat?*

Holding her flower, with her heavy backpack thumping against her, Fredda walked rapidly. She was in such deep thought that the cold weather didn't even bother her.

Finally, she arrived at the library. At the main hallway, she stopped and stared at her great-aunt's huge portrait and said aloud, " Great-Aunt Annora, do you have anything to do with this flower?" Of course, the picture didn't respond and Fredda said, "What am I doing talking to a picture? I must be out of my mind."

"Fredda?" It was Tildda calling her.

Olliver and Noell were with her.

"Ah! I'm so glad to see you here," said Fredda, still holding the orchid.

"Did you start the homework already? Did I miss anything?" asked Fredda.

"We only got here a few minutes ago, and we've been talking about you and what happened earlier with us and Mrs. Maufrodezza," said Olliver.

"And did she give any homework for next class?" asked Fredda.

"Yes, loads," said Olliver, "She told us to read the whole next chapter for next class before the finals."

"What's with the flower?" asked Tildda.

"It's not just a flower. It's an orchid," corrected Noell.

"And how do you know that it's an orchid, Noell?" retorted Tildda.

Fredda, Tildda and Olliver awaited Noell's answer.

"I know, because my father told me. Besides, my father sometimes gets them as a present or sometimes he gives them as a present."

"Really?" asked Fredda. Noell nodded.

"And who gave you this orchid, Fredda?" asked Olliver.

"I have no idea."

"Wait a minute," said Tildda, "That was the reason Mr. Kaffona wanted to see you in his office immediately?"

Fredda nodded her head.

"To give you this flower? I mean, this orchid?" said Tildda surprised.

"Yes, to give me this stupid, *rare* orchid, as he referred to it. Can you believe it? I need so many other things in my life more than this orchid," cried Fredda.

"But we thought that we were gonna be in trouble because of what happened this morning. Remember the eavesdropping situation? I thought we were gonna be expelled," said Olliver.

"I guess we're not, Olliver," replied Fredda.

"We should go back to the math book, if you know what I mean," attempted Noell.

They all agreed and returned to that *awful* homework. Olliver proved again to be a great help.

The time flew, and they finally finished, according to Tildda, who couldn't stand math. They felt more confident now after spending a few hours in the library doing homework. Fredda, Tildda and Noel thanked Olliver for his help.

It was dinner time, and the students always loved to meet at the school restaurant. The four of them headed there.

Fredda still carried her new present, the *stupid flower*, as the wet weather once again interrupted the fastest way to the restaurant.

At the entrance of the restaurant, Fredda, Tildda, Olliver and Noell saw Attos, Eddra and Luggos.

Of course, Attos, who couldn't keep his mouth shut, nastily said, "What's up with the flower, Buttler? Did you decide to be a gardener?" Attos smirked.

Eddra and Luggos laughed.

"It's not only a flower, clever boy, don't you know? It's a *rare orchid*," said Tildda with a bigger smirk on her face and her hands on her hips.

Now, it was Fredda's, Olliver's and Noell's time to laugh.

"Don't call me boy! I have a name!" said Attos enraged.

"Oh! Maybe I should call you a project of a man. That's what boys are, projects of a man!" said Tildda crossing her arms over her chest.

Fredda, Tildda, Olliver and Noell snickered.

"Wait until I tell my father that you're hanging with these low class kids, Noell!" Attos said furiously.

He turned and strode away. Obviously, Eddra and Luggos followed their master.

"Why did he want to tell your father, Noell?" asked Tildda.

"Because my father and his father do business together!" answered Noell, looking at Attos and the others leaving the scene.

After dinner, students were able to retire to their rooms or watch one hour of TV. One hour per day was the maximum the school allowed. Of course, the channels were very well selected by the school administration. There were several TV screens placed around the huge school, so students could be sure to find a program that they liked.

Olliver and Noel decided to watch TV after dinner, while Fredda and Tildda went to their rooms. After all, Fredda had had a horrible day, even worse than yesterday, when Numericoss had made a comparison between her *genius great-aunt* and her *stupid great-niece.*

The fireplace was lit, clean sheets were on the bed, clean towels in the bathroom and a note on the nightstand saying that the uniforms were ready to be picked up at the school cleaners.

One interesting aspect about International Academy was that the students were there to study and not to do chores, such as cleaning their bedroom and bathroom or doing their own laundry. Those kinds of jobs were considered unimportant. At International Academy, students were there to learn the skills with which to achieve wealth and power.

Tildda changed, while Fredda placed her pink orchid on the windowsill and stood at her favorite spot in front of the bedroom window.

The rain beat on the glass as the thunder and lightning lit the sky. Fredda stared at the flower and thought over the past couple days. She yearned to escape from school and search for her family, despite not knowing anybody else other than her Great-Aunt Annora. But the arrival of the flower sparked hope in Fredda. Maybe there was someone other than her great-aunt who knew her.

Why would someone send me a flower?

Tildda came back from the bathroom in her pajamas and saw Fredda mesmerized by it.

"Who would send you a flower, Fredda?"

"I have no idea, but I was wondering the same thing."

"I guess maybe there's someone out there who knows you after all."

"You know, I was going to tell you something before we got caught by Mr. Numericoss this morning," remembered Fredda.

"Oh! Yes, I completely forgot about it," said Tildda, absolutely surprised that she could forget something as important as that.

"Well, last time I saw Mrs. Cellestin, she told me that she was going to take care of me and my school stuff. She also told me that she would give me something that was left to me by my great-aunt, but only after my thirteenth birthday. And that's coming soon."

"After thirteen?" said Tildda, a bit amazed.

"Well, she told me that I'd be more mature at thirteen and I'd be able to handle things better. I really didn't understand that part," said Fredda.

"And what is it?" Tildda questioned, impatient and curious as usual.

"I have no idea. I asked her, but she told me she couldn't say anything more than that. That's the reason I have to go to see her at the hospital, so she can tell me what it is that my great-aunt wants me to have."

"Now I understand why you want to talk to Mrs. Cellestin so much. You weren't making any sense to me before, Fredda."

"I know, I've been thinking about the last conversation I had with Mrs. Cellestin for a long time," said Fredda looking at her orchid again.

"And you think you're going to get your answer from this flower?" asked Tildda sarcastically.

"Not really," said Fredda, her eyes still fixed on it.

"Then, don't stare at it …"

"Meow, meow … . Meow."

"What's that?" asked Fredda startled, "It sounds like a ca…"

"A cat," responded Tildda quickly.

"A cat in our bedroom!"

"Meow, meow." The sound came again.

"Where is it?" asked Fredda.

"I think it's coming from under the bed," answered Tildda, and at the same time, she dove at the floor and peered under the bed. "It's not under the bed, Fredda."

"I think I know where it's coming from. It's coming from inside the nightstand," said Fredda.

"Inside the nightstand? Then let's open it."

Tildda ran quickly to open the nightstand door. "It's locked, the door is locked," said Tildda more annoyed than ever.

The meowing continued.

"The top drawer of the nightstand!" said Fredda excitedly, "There's a key, try it!

The noise continued.

Tildda found the key, opened the large nightstand door, and suddenly, a cat sprang from inside it, landing on Fredda's bed. It just sat there.

The cat was slender, with a silky smooth dark gray coat. His golden eyes were as piercing as a panther's. It was royal and commanding.

"This cat belongs to someone," said Fredda staring at it.

"And how do you know that?"

"The cat has a leather collar," replied Fredda calmly.

"Yes, it does," said Tildda looking at the gorgeous cat.

The cat moved towards Fredda and sat near her.

"Well, I guess the cat likes you, Fredda."

"Wait."

"What?" responded Tildda.

"There's something written on its collar," said Fredda, surprised.

"What does it say?"

"Call me Blue," read Fredda.

"Call me Blue!" repeated Tildda.

"Yes, his name is probably Blue. He's most likely a boy, otherwise his name would have been Pink," chuckled Fredda, her dimples punctuating her smile.

"Blue, ah! I like it," said Tildda smiling also.

"Me too!"

However, keeping the cat would be a problem. The rules and regulations for having a pet at school were as severe as the uniform rules. No pets allowed. Ever! Not even a gold fish or a hamster.

But the rules and regulations didn't take the excitement away from Fredda and Tildda having fun with their new little friend, Blue. He was comfortable and the girls pet him as he purred, asleep.

"What are we going to do with Blue?" asked Tildda.

"I'm not sure yet," responded Fredda and she continued, "We should probably let him go out in the morning. Otherwise, we're going to be in trouble, deep trouble!"

"But, we still don't know how Blue got in here. How did he end up inside the nightstand? And how did Blue get locked in? Do you think someone put him inside?" asked Tildda suspiciously.

"Do you think that someone put Blue inside the nightstand and locked him up to make it look like we brought him here so we'd be breaking the rules and regulations?" Fredda expanded on Tildda's suspicions.

"It's possible."

Rolling thunder was followed by lightning cracking the sky.

Blue leapt from Fredda's bed and ran inside the open nightstand. She tried to grab him, but he was faster than she. Fredda bolted after him but he was gone.

"He's gone!" said Fredda.

"How can he be gone?" responded Tildda. "He's only a cat, not a magician."

"I'm telling you he's gone! Wait! There's a hole in the back of the nightstand and also a hole in the wall," said Fredda shocked.

"A hole? Let me see it." They pulled the nightstand from the wall and looked behind it. "You're right! There is a hole. Maybe I can go after him. Let me see if I can get through it."

"Wait, Tildda, let me get my flashlight." She went to her closet, grabbed the flashlight and lit the way for Tildda.

The hole was a tunnel big enough for a person their size to pass through.

"What's this place?" asked Tildda.

"This is the part that I was going to tell you about this morning. About the map."

"Did you know about this passage?" asked Tildda surprised.

"Not this one, the only one I know of, is the one in the library in the girls' bathroom."

The girls followed the curves of the stone tunnel looking for Blue.

"Wait!" said Fredda.

"What?"

"I think we should count our steps and the left or right turns we're making. Otherwise, we could get lost. Okay?" Fredda suggested.

"That's a good idea. You count the steps and I'll count the turns," responded Tildda.

The tunnel branched off into others and the girls continued on, making their turns by gut instinct. They saw nothing but stone walls until they spotted some light ahead coming from above.

"What do you think this place is above us? What do you think that light is from?" asked Tildda.

"No idea," responded Fredda.

There was silence from the spot of light above, filtering in through the spaces between the iron grating. The girls stood under it, listening, until Fredda broke the silence.

"Let's try to move the cover so we can see where we are. Then we can go back to our room. Okay?"

"Okay," said Tildda.

The ceiling was fairly low at this point in the tunnel, so the two of them had the leverage to lift the wrought iron cover together.

They climbed up and found themselves inside a bathroom. However, not a familiar one. It looked like the girls' hallway bathroom on the left side of the building. But, the color was light green instead of light yellow.

"Okay, we should go now," said Fredda.

"Yes, I think that's a good idea." But before they could make it back into the tunnel, someone opened the bathroom door. The girls froze.

Several thoughts spun around in Fredda's mind. *How many rules and regulations have we broken already? I'll be expelled for sure! Not only me, but poor Tildda, who came with me to look for the mysterious cat. Now she'll also be expelled.* Fredda was sure of the worst.

"What's going on here?" Olliver appeared in front of them embarrassed and horrified that he had entered the wrong bathroom.

"Quiet, Olliver," whispered Tildda.

"What are you two doing in here?" he asked confused. He spied the cover moved from the floor. "And what's this on the floor? It seems like a hole," he asked more astonished.

"We can explain everything, but not now, Olliver," whispered Fredda.

"We better go now. Tomorrow we'll explain everything to you. Okay?" Fredda whispered again.

"O… Okay," he stammered.

As Tildda was about to drop into the opening in the floor, the door broke open again. Fredda's heart beat so intensely, it seemed that it was going to jump out of her mouth. Tildda's blue eyes widened and Olliver's mouth dropped open. They held their breath for a moment.

Then, another familiar face entered the bathroom. It was Noell.

"Oh! I can't take it anymore," said Tildda throwing up her hands.

"What are you all doing in here?" asked Noell.

"Please … we don't have time to explain," whispered Fredda. "Tomorrow we'll tell you all about this bathroom business."

"But?" Noell began to ask.

"There's no time for but, how, what or why … we'll tell you tomorrow, we promise. Please, Noell, we have to go now!" said Tildda firmly.

The girls took off. The boys helped put the cover back, and then they just stood there stupefied.

Fredda and Tildda sped to their room trying not to make any noise. They squeezed back in through the same opening in their bedroom and there, sitting on Fredda's bed, was Blue.

"Blue!" whispered Tildda trying to keep her anger at him under control. "You have no idea the night we've had so far because of you! We were very close to being expelled!"

Blue stretched himself, turned away from them, found a very comfortable position, and just dozed off like nothing had ever happened.

"Do you realize that you're talking to a cat, Tildda?" commented Fredda, shaking her head.

"Yes, I think I'm losing it! Now I understand why you asked me to send you a flashlight and batteries as a birthday present. It was an odd request, but now it makes a lot of sense."

They pushed the nightstand back to its original place.

Fredda went inside the closet, got her box of old books, grabbed the map and started drawing in the new tunnels.

This side of the tunnel connected their room to the bathroom on the other side of the building. This was a spectacular find for Fredda and even more intriguing for Tildda, as she hadn't known anything about the tunnels at all before this evening.

Now that Tildda knew, tomorrow Fredda would have to reveal her secret that she'd been keeping since fourth grade.

"Well, what're we going to do with our hairy friend, Blue?" Tildda asked Fredda.

"I've an idea. We can leave the little door open on the nightstand and maybe Blue will be gone by morning. If not, we'll have to put him outside in the corridor and we have to be very careful not to be seen by anyone. Okay?"

Tildda nodded in agreement.

The two of them gathered their books and homework for tomorrow, put everything in their backpacks and got ready for bed.

It had been a heck of a day for the both of them. Fredda hoped tomorrow would be better.

However, when she was organizing her books, she realized that she would be in the presence of the most feared teacher at school again. Maufrodezza would be teaching culinary class.

Fredda would have math with Numericoss, the most handsome teacher in the whole school ... however, also the most sarcastic.

She was no longer so hopeful that it would be better tomorrow.

CHAPTER 4

RULES AND REGULATIONS

The bell clanged loudly from its tower. It was 6:00 a.m. and the girls groggily dragged themselves up from a short yet deep sleep.

Fredda opened her eyes first, looked around and to her relief, Blue was gone. She closed the nightstand door, locked it, then put the key inside its little drawer.

Afterwards, she got ready and waited for Tildda.

The weather continued to be icy cold and drizzly.

They left for breakfast, and sure enough, Olliver and Noell were waiting and eagerly waving to the girls to join them at a corner table in the breakfast room.

Olliver had already start eating, as usual, but Noell was more interested in asking questions about the night before.

"So, are you going to explain to us what happened last night," questioned Noell.

"Of course, we promised you, remember?" said Tildda.

Fredda told them about the map and the tunnels, and how she'd gotten hold of the map. She also told them about Blue.

"A cat?" cried Olliver horrified.

"Shh!" said Fredda putting her left index finger over her mouth.

"Do you know how many rules and regulations you've both broken so far?" worried Olliver.

"Probably a bunch of them," said Tildda not very concerned at the moment. "But if you don't say anything to anyone, we won't be in trouble, right? Promise me you won't tell anything to anyone."

"Yes, of course, I promise. I won't tell anyone," responded Olliver quickly.

"Me too, I promise I won't tell anyone either," Noell added.

"Can we have a nice breakfast, now? I'm starving." Tildda ended the discussion.

Fredda could see Mrs. Camerron in the kitchen giving orders to her staff. The students were all eating and lively chatting about their summer vacation plans. Fredda could see that the teachers inside their glass room seemed cheerful as well, except for Maufrodezza and Numericoss, who glared hatefully at each other.

After breakfast, the four of them shuffled along as classes were beginning. The weather continued to be chilly, even though the drizzle had finally stopped.

"What classes do we have today?" asked Tildda.

"We have history, with Mrs. Lagarttus. Then we have P.E.," said Olliver.

"But I thought we were done with P.E. for this semester?" said Tildda, apparently surprised.

"Well, maybe you girls are done, but we still have one more class today," said Olliver.

"Oh! Good, so we'll have some free time before lunch," said Tildda.

"Then, we have math, and last class of the day will be culinary with Mrs. Maufrodezza," finished Olliver.

"What a day! Numericoss *and* Maufrodezza! We must be cursed!" said Tildda.

They all cracked up laughing.

The history class proved to be as boring as usual, even though Mrs. Lagarttus tried her best to keep the students awake. But, between her calm, gentle voice and the boring subject matter, Fredda found her eyelids drooping.

The good news was that Mrs. Lagarttus gave no homework so that they'd have more time to study for their upcoming finals.

After history class, the boys went to P.E. Fredda and Tildda headed to the cleaners to get their uniforms and after that dropped them off at their room.

The girls decided to spend some free time in one of the beautiful rooms at school. The red room was warm and there were well arranged bouquets on the side tables next to the leather couch. Overstuffed silk pillows on both sides of the couch made it even more comfortable. Hot tea was set atop an elegant table in the corner. There were matching lamps on each end of the couch behind the flowers, and some books and school magazines on the coffee table. This room was close to the restaurant, so they'd be able to see when Olliver and Noell were done with their class, and then go enjoy lunch together.

They had become close friends over the past few days and it seemed they really enjoyed spending time together. They also felt stronger as a group to defend themselves against Attos, Eddra and Luggos.

Fredda and Tildda burrowed into the couch. Tildda who couldn't contain herself said, "So, let me ask you a question, Fredda. Do you spend all your summer vacation time exploring the tunnels trying to find a way out of school?"

"Yes, when nobody is here. The students and most of the teachers and faculty are gone, so it's very easy to explore. I've been doing it since fourth grade. But this summer, it'll be more interesting because I'll be able to explore at night. Now that I know there's a connection from our bedroom, it'll be easier. You know, as I told you before, I could explore the tunnel only from the girls' library bathroom. So I wait for Mrs. Nickelleta, the librarian, to open the library in the morning and I stay there most of the time. She often falls asleep because the library is so empty all summer long. So, it gives me time to go down the tunnel and draw on my map. But so far, I haven't found any way out. Maybe, this summer I'll find something. I really need to see Mrs. Cellestin."

"Maybe you should ask Mr. Kaffona. Maybe he'll take you to see Mrs. Cellestin!" said Tildda trying to find a solution for Fredda's problem. "Ah! I know! I can ask my mother to take you to see Mrs. Cellestin at the hospital when she comes to pick me up for summer vacation. She can ask Mr. Kaffona," said Tildda excitedly.

"Really?" Would you ask your mother to do that for me?" Fredda's smile beamed in anticipation.

"Of course!" Mom'll do it! Don't worry."

"That would be great!" A spark of hope lit in Fredda. *Maybe this would be an easier solution than escaping from school.*

Tildda mirrored Fredda's thoughts, "So, you don't have to escape and then you won't be expelled, and I won't be left alone here with Olliver and Noell. I won't be able to survive here alone," Tildda moaned dramatically.

Both of them laughed so hard that the other students turned to them and stared. Only Tildda could make Fredda forget about the horrible week she was having at school.

"It's almost lunch time and where are they?" asked Fredda.

"Don't worry, Fredda, Olliver's never late for lunch or any other meal." Tildda stuck out her belly and rubbed it as she imitated Olliver's, "I'm *always* hungry!"

The duo burst out in giggles which grew into hearty laughter. The other students stared at them again curiously.

"There, there ... Can you see them?" pointed Fredda, "The boys."

They waved to them and the boys waved back. They gathered in the corner of the dining room again feeling more free to talk about their secret there.

The waitress came, took their order and moved on to the next table. Today there seemed to be a variety of choices from the sea. Fredda and Tildda's choice was flounder. Olliver ordered shrimp and Noell chose lobster.

A few minutes later, the waitress came back with their plates. Noell's lobster drew their attention, as the presentation was superb.

Then, the waitress handed a note to Fredda. Curiosity caused her to rip it open quickly and read it to herself. The note said:

Dear Fredda,

Come to see me when you are done with lunch.

Hilda Camerron,
The Chef

"Who wrote you a note?" asked Tildda, a busybody as usual.

"It's from Mrs. Camerron. She wants to talk to me after lunch."

"Do you know the cook?" asked Olliver.

"Yes, I mean, my great-aunt knows her."

"And what does she want with you, Fredda?" asked Tildda, very interested.

"I really don't know yet. I'll see her and then I'll let you know."

They ate their delicious lunch, and then Fredda hurried to the kitchen to talk to Mrs. Camerron.

"Ah! There you are, dear Fredda!" said the cook with a smile.

"Hi, Mrs. Camerron, how're you doing?" said Fredda, politely.

"Hi, dear Fredda, I'm doing all right and how are you doing?"

"I'm doing okay," responded Fredda, not telling Mrs. Camerron about the horrible time she was having this week.

"Well, I guess you got my note, didn't you?"

Fredda nodded her head.

"Well, dear Fredda, I know that summer vacation is around the corner and I also know that Mrs. Cellestin," and she paused, "is not going to be here when the vacation starts and I really don't know when she'll be back. I wanted you to know that you don't have to worry about your meals because I'll be here this summer to take care of the people who will be here at school all summer long, like you. So, you will get food from me every day, same time as usual breakfast, lunch and dinner. And if you would like, you can eat here in the kitchen with me so you won't feel so alone," said the cook sweetly.

"Oh! Thank you very much, Mrs. Camerron, I really appreciate that. I really didn't even think about that until now. Because you know, Mrs. Cellestin always took care of it for me. I mean, before, it was my great-aunt who took care, but now that she's not here anymore, you know."

"Yes, I know, dear Fredda, don't you worry about summer," said Mrs. Camerron. "Go now before you are late for your class."

"Thank you again," said Fredda, "Bye now."

Fredda took off in a hurry so as not to be late for Numericoss' class. She ran to the classroom despite the fact that she knew she was breaking more rules. She was huffing and puffing when she got there, but no one noticed. Everybody else was talking among themselves while waiting for Mr. Numericoss.

Fredda rushed into the classroom on time before him.

Of course, Tildda immediately questioned her. "So, what did she want with you?"

Mr. Numericoss uncharacteristically rushed into the classroom. Lately, it seemed that he was always in a hurry.

"Later," responded Fredda, and Tildda nodded.

Olliver and Noell glanced at Fredda whose eyes sent the message that she couldn't say anything at that particular moment. They received it.

"The homework and extra credit, put them on my desk," said Numericoss arrogantly.

Fredda, Tildda, Noell and everybody else who wanted a chance to get a better grade, placed their extra credit work on his desk.

"Today is the last class before our final test. We will be reviewing the chapters so you will be able to study. For those of you who got a horrible grade on your last test, I suggest you study more, a lot more," he said looking at Fredda.

"We are going to need some volunteers for this next lesson of the day! I am going to give you some exercises on the blackboard and you will have to solve them. Any volunteers?" asked Numericoss.

Some students shot their arms up, including Olliver, who really enjoyed math.

Numericoss' eyes darted back and forth around the room like a cannon full of balls searching for its target.

"I do not see many students wanting to do this assignment today … MISS BUTTLER, TO THE BLACKBOARD!" he shouted cruelly.

Fredda jumped. She stood up hesitantly, walked very slowly towards the blackboard and stopped in front of it.

Numericoss approached her and wrote the exercise on the board. "Do it, and don't leave this board until you prove to me that you understand what you are doing."

Fredda lifted her left hand, took a stick of white chalk and looked at the board. She knew how to solve the problem because she'd done the exercise at the library with Olliver and the others. For the first time, she felt sure that she could prove to him that she knew the subject well.

A huge scream resounded from the back of the classroom where Numericoss stood. His voice bounced back and forth off the four walls and finally stopped.

"WHAT DO YOU THINK YOU ARE DOING, MISS BUTTLER?"

Fredda stammered, "I'm … I'm … I'm trying to solve the problem," she finally spit out.

"And since when you are allowed to use …" and he screamed, "YOUR LEFT AWKWARD, EMBARRASSING HAND ON THE BOARD?

"Since, Ah! Always," she said puffing up her cheeks and squinting her eyes.

The students burst out laughing.

"QUIET!" screamed Numericoss again.

"You think that is funny, don't you, Miss Buttler?" Numericoss spewed furiously.

Fredda didn't say a word.

"Take a look at this classroom, Miss Buttler. Take a very good look and tell me if you see anybody here writing with the wrong hand. Even the place to put pens and pencils are arranged diligently on the right side of your desk," said Numericoss superiorly.

Fredda surveyed the classroom and all she could see were students holding their pens with their right hands, even the naughty Attos, Eddra and Luggos who were slyly smiling at her. Not a single student in her classroom was holding their pen or pencil with their left hand.

Fredda knew about the little hole in the desks in which to place pens and pencils, but always used her left hand to put them in it. Fredda's face flushed crimson. She was the only one in her class who was lefty!

She was still gripping the white chalk with her left fingers and she was still looking around when Numericoss snarled, "Did you see, Miss Buttler? You are the only one in this class who holds the chalk with your wrong, handicapped hand! International Academy is a very prestigious and respected school in this country. I do not want you to embarrass this school when it is time for you go to out there and apply to a university. That is, if you qualify to attend at all! You are nothing but a disappointment!" He continued boring into Fredda with his furious eyes.

Fredda looked at the white chalk as her left fingers exchanged it for her right. As she did so, she thought to herself, *This is the wrong hand for me. It feels so awkward, weak and unnatural.*

She looked at Tildda, Olliver and Noell for some kind of support, but they couldn't do anything to help her.

Fredda looked around the classroom one more time. Every single student was still holding their pen with their right hand and their eyes remained fixed on her.

Without knowing what to do first, she turned towards the blackboard again, totally lost for a moment. Then, her determination kicked in. She looked at the problem written on the board, took a deep breath and holding the white chalk with her awkward right hand, she started solving the problem and torturously trying to write the numbers on the board. They were far from perfect but at least they looked correct.

She finally finished and turned around to face the class.

She stood there while Numericoss asked the class if the result was right. To her astonishment, and Numericoss' disappointment, the class agreed that the result was correct.

"You may sit down now, Miss Buttler," Numericoss seethed.

She exhaled.

But the class didn't get any better. Every time Numericoss had a nasty comment about something, he looked directly at Fredda. It was obvious that he disliked her, not only because of her genius great-aunt, but because she was the only lefty in his class.

However, Numericoss was not the only one.

The bell finally rang and class was finally dismissed.

Thankfully, there would be only one more time this year when she would need to see Mr. Numericoss. The final test next week.

She didn't move from her chair. She sat there while all the students filed by and looked at her. Tildda, Olliver and Noell stayed, apparently trying to support their friend.

"I really don't understand why only *now*, Mr. Numericoss, and even Mrs. Maufrodezza, hate the idea of you being lefty," said Tildda perplexed. "It seems that all of a sudden these two teachers are making their own rules and regulations."

"But this behavior started right after Mrs. Cellestin was taken to the hospital," said Noell, trying to grasp a thought.

The three of them turned immediately towards him.

"You're right! Noell," responded Fredda. "Everything started changing the day Mrs. Cellestin was taken away from school!"

Tildda and Olliver agreed.

"But the question is, *why*? Why are they behaving this way?" said Tildda.

"Well, I guess we won't be able to answer that question right now and besides we have to get going. We have one more class to attend. Our last class before our finals next week," said Olliver. "And we better hurry up. Otherwise, we're gonna be late for culinary."

They couldn't afford to be late. With large steps, not talking to each other, but only feeling the cold air hitting their faces, they finally arrived on time. Curiously, all the students were outside elbowing each other out of the way, trying to read a note posted on the locked door.

After a while, Fredda, Tildda, Olliver and Noel reached the door and read:

Dear Students,

Due to a broken pipe in our main kitchen, the culinary room is unavailable and the class will be rescheduled for Saturday morning at 7:30 a.m.

Thank you,

Marga Maufrodezza,
Vice Principal

The students could hear the crews cleaning the room and fixing the pipe in the main kitchen.

"Saturday was supposed to be our first day off before our finals next week," groaned Tildda. "I was looking forward to sleeping a bit longer and taking a break from this exhausting week we had," she continued whining like a spoiled brat.

"But at least dinner will be served on time because the pipe is fixed!" a voice came from the kitchen. It was Mrs. Camerron, the cook.

"Hello, dear Fredda," said Mrs. Camerron.

"Hi, Mrs. Camerron."

"Thank you, Mrs. Camerron," said Olliver, "I'm so happy that dinner will be served on time."

CHAPTER 5

THE RIGHT GADGET

Fredda opened her eyes. The clock next to her bed on the nightstand read 7:00 a.m. She bounded from her bed not even realizing where she was for a moment. The only thought that went through her mind was that she and Tildda wouldn't be able to make it for the 7:30 a.m. class with Mrs. Maufrodezza.

She looked at Tildda's bed and saw Tildda sleeping like a baby. Fredda went to wake her, very gently so as not to scare her.

"Hey, Tildda wake up," said Fredda almost whispering.

"You have to wake up. Otherwise, we're going to be late for class."

But, Tildda, mumbled some scrambled words, turned over and went back to sleep.

Fredda thought for a moment, went to the window, looked at her orchid which she'd forgotten to water, as Mr. Kaffona instructed her, and looked outside.

The morning was gray. It seemed that it was going to rain again.

She looked at the tower, but didn't remember hearing the bell this morning. However, Tildda must not have heard it either. She was still sleeping.

Fredda went back to Tildda's bed.

"Wake up, Tildda, you have to wake up, " she said louder.

"Okay," said Tildda.

"What time is it anyway?"

Fredda looked at the clock again and said, "It's 7:02."

"WE'RE GOING TO BE LATE!" shouted Tildda jumping off her bed, now terrified.

Very calmly, Fredda said, "Do as I say, Tildda. Put on your uniform and brush your teeth. We have to go. Okay?"

Tildda did exactly as Fredda told her to do. Fredda did the same.

They stopped by the breakfast room, which looked emptier than usual, quickly grabbed some fruit and then rushed to culinary class.

The door was open and the students were already waiting for Mrs. Maufrodezza inside.

The room was a replica of the kitchen but on a miniature scale. It even included a dining area which resembled the main restaurant. A baby grand piano sat in the middle of the dining room. There were two fireplaces and beautiful red curtains covered the huge windows on the dining side.

Fredda looked around the classroom for the boys. She couldn't rely on Tildda.

Tildda was still thinking about her comfortable bed.

"There!" said Fredda, "In the back of the room, the boys are there."

As they walked to the back, many students looked at them with dislike as they passed by.

When they saw Tildda, they remembered the time when she fell asleep in Numericoss' math class. Because of her, Numericoss assigned pages and pages of homework not only to Tildda but to the entire class. They had all spent the entire weekend unhappily doing math work. Tildda plus Fredda meant double trouble to them.

Each table accommodated four students and was equipped with kitchen utensils and a small stove burner.

Fredda and Tildda joined Olliver and Noell. The boys had saved them seats.

"We thought that you girls were gonna be late," said Olliver.

"Thanks to Fredda, we're not," responded Tildda. "We didn't hear the bell this morning."

"Don't you know about the bell?" asked Noell.

"What about it?" replied Tildda.

"No bell today, remember it was supposed to be our day off? Today is Saturday. The whole school is still sleeping while we're here," Olliver yawned.

"No wonder the school seemed so deserted," said Fredda.

At the same moment that Fredda finished her sentence, Mrs. Maufrodezza strode inside the classroom holding her briefcase in her right hand and her black book in the other.

The students froze. There was a silence. Mrs. Maufrodezza had a way of imposing fear on others only by her presence.

She positioned herself again in the middle of the class facing the students, as she did in English class and she began, "Listen well! For those of you who think that this is boring, dull, dreary, tedious, tiresome, mind-numbing," and the words rushed out, "lackluster, monotonous, uninteresting, unexciting, uninspiring, platitudinous, repetitive, wearisome and humdrum, you had best think differently."

The students' mouths were agape at the tirade of vocabulary that had spilled from Mrs. Maufrodezza's mouth. It would have taken most students a whole afternoon to memorize all those words.

Mrs. Maufrodezza continued, "This class is vital for you. Not only will you learn about food and how food is prepared, not to become a chef, of course, but to be aware that exquisite food exists out there. You will also be taught how to dress for various occasions and how to behave at the table. Many multimillion dollar deals have been made at fine restaurants all over the world. Acquiring refined tastes and table manners are essential for your life," and she looked directly in Fredda's direction.

"Miss Buttler," said Mrs. Maufrodezza with her superior tone. "Have you taken a look at yourself in the mirror this morning? It looks like you came from …" and she paused, "… from a cat fight."

"No, I didn't," responded Fredda, not sure why she'd said that, thinking that now she'd be in trouble.

The students started laughing, which was not common in Maufrodezza's class.

"QUIET!" shouted Maufrodezza irritably.

"You think you are so funny, don't you, Miss Buttler?" said Maufrodezza with her fiery black eyes fixed on her.

"It's because we didn't hear the be ..." said Tildda, but Maufrodezza cut her off.

"Quiet, Miss D'Rof, you are not in any shape to explain anything! It seems that you are following the *wrong* leader!"

Not that Tildda looked any better than Fredda! They actually both looked very sloppy this morning. Both had crooked ties, sleepy faces and their hair stuck up in several places.

"Just to let you know, Miss Buttler, your group will not be able to get the highest grade even if your group delivers the assignment correctly. Grades in this class also take into account the dress code and cleanliness," said Maufrodezza viciously. Maufrodezza turned back to face the students.

Fredda turned to look at Tildda and the boys, realizing that they would also be penalized if they were in her group. She felt guilty.

Maufrodezza went back to her favorite position in front of the class between the blackboard and the students' desks, took a deep breath, and opened her mouth to speak, when a strident voice was heard from outside the classroom.

"IF I CATCH THIS HAIRY THING AGAIN AROUND MY KITCHEN I'M GOING TO KILL IT!" someone shouted.

Maufrodezza stared at the classroom door with her mad black eyes and strode outside to check the yelling.

Not only one person was outside the classroom, but also Mrs. Lerddus, Mrs. Camerron, holding a big knife,

Mr. Nepttune, holding a broom and the young fella, Grillo, holding a big wooden spoon, all searching for something.

"IT IS YOU AGAIN, GERDHA! MAKING NOISES AS USUAL!" shouted Maufrodezza.

"I did not say anything, Marga. I was only trying to save the poor cat's life, before they kill it." Mrs. Lerddus looked at the kitchen workers with a horrified face.

"The cat belongs to someone because I can see it has a brown collar," said Mrs. Lerddus, her voice trembling.

"The cat is a …" and Mrs. Lerddus looked at the hallway again to see if she could get a last glance at the cat, "… a Russian blue, a beautiful Russian blue! And besides, the cat passed in front of Mrs. Camerron and went towards her right side, that means, it is good luck!" she finished.

"If this gray cat shows up again in my kitchen. I'll kill it in a heartbeat if I see it stealing food again! It doesn't matter if the cat belongs to someone or it is gray, brown, white or if it is bad or good luck, I'll kill it!" said Mrs. Camerron fiercely wielding a big knife in her hand.

"I think they're talking about Blue," whispered Fredda.

"Yes, I think so. Gray cat with a brown collar," replied Tildda.

"Shhh," said Olliver, "Nobody should know about the cat. Nobody should know that we know about the cat."

"Well, I guess everyone knows about the cat now, Olliver!" chimed in Tildda.

The conversation continued outside the classroom.

"If, and when, you find this gray cat, Mrs. Camerron," said Maufrodezza superiorly, "I hope you do not serve it as a meal to us."

The group was shocked at Malfrodezza's repugnant comment. Even the students sat with mouths ajar.

Maufrodezza continued, "Now, if you do not mind, I have to go back to my classroom and I hope I can get the quiet I need to continue my class." She strode quickly inside.

"That might not be a bad idea, cat soufflé! Even Monsieur De La Mancca would be proud of me!" whispered Mrs. Camerron.

Her assistants smiled. Mrs. Lerddus was appalled.

"Take it easy, Gerdha," said the cook, "I'm just joking about the soufflé. And besides I'm not a superstitious person, but this thing about the cat passing by and going to the left or right side would only work if the cat is black, don't you think?"

Mrs. Lerddus thought about saying something, but she thought again … *Some things are better left unsaid.* She left without saying a word.

Back in the classroom, Maufrodezza positioned herself again at her favorite spot and started the class once more.

"This assignment requires," she paused, took a look at the classroom with her dreadful eyes and continued, "four students per team and I can see that you are already divided in teams of four, so no student should move from their table. Look at your colleagues at the table. They are going to be your teammates. Each student needs to complete a task in order for your team to complete the assignment. So, in other words, every single one of you needs to do your part, by yourself, to help your team. And when I say by yourself, I mean it! You do the task you are assigned and let the next task be done by another member of your team."

Students surveyed their team's members and without saying a word, turned back to the front of the class to listen to the rest of the rules for the assignment.

"In front of each of you, there is a little number on the table."

Students looked down for a moment and Fredda saw a little number one in front of her. Tildda read off the number two.

Maufrodezza continued, "Now, that you all know your numbers, you can start the assignment. There is a box underneath your table and all the ingredients you need. I am going to write the instructions for this task on the board."

Olliver bent down on his knees, got the box and brought it to the center of the table. Tildda opened it and started taking out all sorts of stuff from inside. There was a bowl, a can, four aprons, four pairs of gloves, eggs, sugar, gelatin and other ingredients to make what seemed to be a sweet dessert.

On the blackboard, students read the instructions for the assignment written in a very neat, uniform hand writing. The instructions said:

All students must wear gloves and aprons for this assignment.

Student number one – Open the can, mix half of the contents of the can with the gelatin in the bowl.

Tildda gave the can, the bowl and the gelatin to Fredda. Tildda and the boys continued reading the instructions on the board. Tildda knew that she would be the next student in line to complete the next task.

Fredda gathered all her items and said, "I need a can opener."

Fredda Buttler And The Left-Handed People

Noell helped her find the opener, from among all the well-organized utensils.

A shiver ran through the class, as thunder rumbled and a storm's heavy lightning flashed outside the classroom window.

Finally, Noell found the can opener. He handed it to Fredda so she could proceed with the assignment. She took a look at the utensil and realized that she had never used a can opener before. She had never needed to cook for herself and the culinary classes had so far been mostly lectures. Next year, students would be assigned real cooking assignments. She looked at the opener again. It looked like a tool used to fix a car rather than a utensil for the kitchen, but she pulled her mind back to her task.

She got the can and held the opener with her left hand and tried to figure out how to open it. She wasn't really sure how this device worked. It seemed that the gadget didn't fit the can properly. She continued trying while Tildda and the boys read the rest of the instructions.

Fredda thought that something must be wrong with the opener. But she persevered, not wanting to let this problem affect their poor grade even more.

Afraid to ask any questions to her friends because it could cost them, Fredda studied the instrument and thought for a moment – *this opener seems to be for a person who's right-handed. Everything is for a right-handed person lately!* So, Fredda switched the utensil to her right hand and the opener fit the can perfectly. But she still couldn't open it because she had no strength in that hand.

Tildda noticed the struggling Fredda from the corner of her eye and whispered, "What's going on, Fredda?"

"Well, I'm having some problems with this ridiculous can opener."

"I can see."

"If I can't open this stupid can, we won't be able to continue our task," said Fredda, frustrated.

Their conversation drew the attention of Noell and Olliver as well.

Their voices drifted to the front of the class and Maufrodezza straightened up, craned her neck and shouted, "WHAT IS THE PROBLEM IN THE BACK OF THE CLASS?" Nobody said a word as usual.

The four friends glanced at each other. Attos, Eddra and Luggos turned their heads, like busybodies as usual, and Attos smirked at Fredda. His face reminded her of Numericoss.

Back to the can opener problem now, the four of them whispered, trying to find a solution for their problem.

They thought about letting Tildda, who was sitting next to Fredda, try to open the can but this would be too risky.

For sure, the trio, Attos, Eddra and Luggos, would report them to Maufrodezza and then they would have even more of a problem.

Fredda worked as hard as she could to open the stupid can but without success. The clock was ticking and ticking. The other students were ahead, way ahead of them!

Olliver became more nervous. Noell, whispering, made an effort to convince him that things were going to be all right.

Fredda was now sweating and the weather outside didn't make it easier. The storm seemed to be stronger and stronger. The thunder louder and louder with each crack.

Fredda Buttler And The Left-Handed People

Most of the students were on step three of the assignment and some of them were on step four. Tildda could see them from the back of the classroom.

"What're we going to do?" whispered Olliver to Tildda.

Tildda perplexed, just rolled her eyes upward as she threw her arms out and shrugged her shoulders. Fredda was still fighting with the can and the opener. She was really trying her best but no results came from the fighting.

Tildda seemed lost between them, not really knowing what to do to help her friend. If she tried to help Fredda, they could get into more trouble. So doing nothing seemed to be the best option at the moment.

Momentarily, the time would be up and the inevitable would happen. The zero grade was closer with each tick of the clock.

Tildda, Noell and Olliver looked at Fredda, still struggling to get that silly can open as best she could. She knew that this time her friends were going to pay because she was lefty!

"Time is up!" Maufrodezza spat the words out of her mouth.

Maufrodezza rose from her chair and walked around the class, and at the same time said, "Leave only your final product on the table and put all the utensils back. Place the box under the table." She continued walking until she reached Fredda's table.

"Well, well, well. What do we have here?" said Maufrodezza crossing her arms and looking straight at Fredda. Her black eyes were terrifying.

Olliver was shaking like a tree in the wind.

The sky lit up with lightning and thunder followed.

"Miss Buttler, I will be glad to give your group a very special grade for this assignment. Unfortunately, I cannot give your group a negative grade. It is against school rules," said Maufrodezza intolerantly.

None of the students moved from their place or laughed at Fredda. The class was silent and the only noise that could be heard was the horrible weather outside.

Tildda saw Attos with a self-satisfied smile, contemplating their misfortune.

Finally the bell rang but nobody moved.

"Read the next three chapters of your book. These are very important chapters. Now, class dismissed!" Maufrodezza said angrily.

The students knew that no class would take place next week. The reading of the next three chapters of the book were a hint for the finals.

Each student filed out of the classroom quickly and wordlessly. Nobody even made eye contact with Maufrodezza.

But the four of them remained. They sat in silence. There was nothing else to say. Finally, Tildda said, "A negative grade! I've never heard such a thing!"

"A negative grade means, after a zero, a negative one, a negative two and so forth and so on!" said Olliver who seemed to be perplexed. "This is the first time in my life that I got a zero as a grade! I can't believe it. I got a zero in culinary. What am I going to tell my dad?" he cried.

"WELL, AT LEAST YOU HAVE A FATHER!" shouted Fredda furiously.

Tildda and Noell couldn't believe what Fredda had just said. She continued, "It seems that you live on the right side while I'm living on the left. Everything is easy for you! You don't have to worry about anything, do you? I, on the other hand, have to bend myself out of shape like a pretzel to fit your side. That's not normal to me! I'd like to see you doing everything with your left hand just for a day! I hate living in a right-hander's world," Fredda looked directly into his eyes.

Tildda and Noell looked at each other and didn't say a word. Olliver didn't know what to say either and bolted from the classroom.

Inside, there was silence once more, but the thunderstorm exploded noisily outside.

Then, Tildda, asked, "Noell? You seem to be okay with a zero grade."

"Yes, I am. It's not every day that you get a zero as a grade." Noell smiled weakly at Tildda and she returned one.

"I'm glad that the two of you think that this is funny! It may not be a big deal for you, but honestly, I want to open that stupid can like everyone else," said Fredda annoyed.

"Well, what do you want us to do? We already got a zero as a grade along with you! There's nothing else we can do!' said Noell bravely.

"C'mon, Fredda," said Tildda. "What can they do? Give us detention because you couldn't open that ridiculous can? We're okay with the grade and we're still here with you. Only Olliver's upset because he thinks his father will be furious. And besides, his father shouldn't blame him."

"Yes, his father shouldn't blame him. He should blame *me*!" responded Fredda with anger.

"You're being very harsh on yourself, Fredda," Tildda countered gently.

"No, Tildda, I'm being realistic."

This was the last straw! She had been taking everything that happened this week lightly, but now she was angry at being lefty and living in a world designed for right-handed people. She said to herself, *I wish I could live in a world where everybody is lefty.* She continued thinking, *Why wasn't this leftie issue a problem before? Why now? Actually, since Mrs. Cellestin left school, it's become an immense problem. Why did they allow me in this school since I was in first grade and only now the teachers feel it's a huge problem?"*

Then it occurred to Fredda that she couldn't be the only leftie in the entire school! "We have to find out who else is a leftie in school." Fredda lit up.

"What?" asked Tildda.

"She said that we have to find out who else is a leftie in school," repeated Noell.

"I know what she said, Noell, but why?" asked Tildda.

"Because most likely if there're more student lefties in school, they're having the same problem as I am," answered Fredda.

"That's a great idea!" said Noell.

"From now on we're going to observe the students everywhere. And when we find them, we're going to ask them if they're having any problem. Okay?" said Fredda.

"Okay, we'll be observing from now on," responded Tildda.

"We have to find Olliver and tell him about the observation," said Noell.

"I doubt if he's going to help us after today," remarked Tildda.

"We have to try to find him at least, and let him decide if he wants to help us," said Noell.

"Okay," Fredda agreed, a little more composed and less angry at them and at herself.

"By the way, what were we trying to make this morning, anyway?" asked Fredda.

"Pineapple dessert," said Tildda and Olliver together.

And Fredda thought, *All that commotion for pineapple dessert!*

Finally, they were free from classes for the year. But finals were next week. The weather still proved to be a challenge. More rain poured outside like it was winter all over again. They hadn't seen the sun for days. Summer was just around the corner, but it looked more like the season had a mind of its own.

"What's next?" asked Tildda.

"Well, next is lunch and then the schedules for the finals are going to be posted in the library hall," Noell answered.

The three of them went to the restaurant which was located next door to the culinary class. It seemed that the whole school was inside the restaurant. It was packed. The warmth of the lit fireplaces felt comforting. Noell looked for Olliver, while Tildda tried to find a table for them.

"Over there!" pointed Tildda, "There's a table in the corner and it's empty."

They rushed to the table and sat down. Noell was still searching for Olliver, but he couldn't find him anywhere.

The atmosphere was celebratory as the year was almost over. There would be only another week and after that vacation!

However, for Fredda, Tildda and Noell, the zero grade hanging over their heads dampened their moods and the table seemed to be empty without Olliver, who could eat like a bull and make Tildda crazy.

Lunch came and went and they headed to the library hall to get their schedule for finals. When they were almost at the entrance to the library, a voice came from behind them. "Miss Buttler, please, Miss Buttler?" It was Mrs. Utilla, Mr. Kaffona's secretary.

"Hello, Miss Buttler," said Mrs. Utilla. "Mr. Kaffona would like to see you immediately."

Fredda questioned, "Now?"

"Yes, now," said the secretary irritably, holding a big umbrella.

So without another word, they left.

Tildda said, "I bet you that it's about the zero grade."

"Most likely," responded Noell.

Mrs. Utilla and Fredda walked together under the big umbrella without saying a word. Fredda wondered what Mr. Kaffona wanted to talk to her about today. *Most likely, it was because of the zero grade. It was all my fault.*

They arrived at his office and the door was open. Mrs. Utilla and Fredda stepped in. Mr. Kaffona said, "Oh, yes, Miss Buttler, take a seat, please."

"Thank you, Mrs. Utilla. That will be all." The secretary left.

Fredda saw the huge file on his desk and thought it was probably hers. She remembered the last time she was in his office.

"Well, Miss Buttler," said Mr. Kaffona. He continued, "I have your file here and I have been trying to find some important information about you," as he was flipping the pages and fixing his glasses to see better. "I cannot find the name of a responsible person to sign these papers for you."

Because of his shiny head and his outrageously colorful clothing style, Fredda was having difficulty following his words. She cleared her throat and said, "Excuse me, sir. I don't understand."

"These papers need to be signed," said Mr. Kaffona.

"Sign ... what papers?"

"The trip of course! The annual trip at the end of the year. All the students are going to different places around the city and your class is going to …" He paused, took a look at another paper that was lying on his desk and said, "The Museum of Art and History."

Fredda had totally forgotten about the trip. After the past few days, things had happened so fast and hadn't been in her favor, that her mind wasn't very clear.

"Well, Miss Buttler, I know that Mrs. Cellestin had always signed for you in the past, but under the circumstances I cannot sign anything for you, as I am not your guardian or any member of your family. So you will not be going on the trip tomorrow."

"But …"

Mr. Kaffona cut her off.

"I cannot do anything for you, Miss Buttler. These are the school rules and I cannot change them for you or for any other student. You know we have to follow the rules and regulations at all times."

Fredda thought, *It's always about the rules and regulations!*

CHAPTER 6

THE TRUTH IS COMPLICATED

Fredda wasn't sure if she was upset with the bad news that she had just received from Mr. Kaffona or because she had forgotten about the annual trip. However, she wasn't the only person who had forgotten. Perhaps, it had slipped Tildda's mind, too, as she hadn't mentioned it this week either. The trip would be the only chance she had to get outside school. And she hadn't been outside the school for a long time. Last time, she remembered, was when she had gone to visit her great-aunt.

She stood outside the main office for a while appreciating the dreadful weather which mirrored her day at International Academy.

It seemed that all the unpleasant news that could've come into her life had arrived in just one week. *How much worse could it get?* She asked this question to herself over and over again.

Fredda stood there for a long time thinking about her life - the family she didn't have; the vacation she had never taken; her great-aunt, Annora, her only family and she was in a nursing home; Mrs. Cellestin, the only person Fredda could trust; and the most horrific week at school she had had so far.

After a while of contemplating, Fredda realized that she wasn't supposed to be outside the main office. According to the school rules and regulations, no student was supposed to be in that area wondering about life, especially Fredda. She grabbed her backpack and took off towards the free areas where students were expected to be.

Fredda didn't know where she would find Tildda and Noell. The school was huge and with so many places to look, she decided to go back to the library hall. Any room was better than standing outside in the wet weather. Last time she had seen Tildda and Noel, they were looking for the schedule for next week's finals. Fredda hadn't had the opportunity to get a look at it.

So, she passed by the blue lounge heading toward the library. Tildda and Noel were there sitting very comfortably on one of the many couches.

"Fredda!" yelled Tildda. "Where have you been? We were so worried about you! What did Mr. Kaffona want with you? It was about the zero grade, wasn't it? I'll bet it was about that stupid class!" finished Tildda edgily.

"Tildda, let Fredda breathe!" said Noell annoyed.

Fredda sat down on the couch, and dropped her backpack on the floor. She faced the crackling fireplace. Noell and Tildda could see the reflection of fire on Fredda's wet face. Fredda took a deep breath and said, "No, it wasn't about the grade in that stupid class."

"No?" asked Tildda.

"Nope," replied Fredda.

"Then what was all that about?" asked Noell, surprised.

"It was about the annual trip tomorrow."

"Oh! The trip," said Tildda. "I completely forgot about it."

"Me too," said Noell.

Fredda was relieved to hear that she wasn't the only one who had forgotten about the trip. Fredda told them about the conversation she had had with Mr. Kaffona and all the rules and regulations around it.

"This is awful," said Tildda, not pleased with the news.

"Remember last year! We had a great day. It's not going to be the same without you," whined Tildda.

"I don't even remember the trip last year," said Noell.

"It's because you had no friends last year, remember?" said Tildda. "It's no fun when you have no friends!" she added.

"Yes, it's no fun at all." replied Noell.

They stayed in the blue room for the rest of the afternoon trying to just relax.

The week seemed to have rushed by. The next morning came very quickly. The buses were aligned in the parking area and the spirit of this early morning was vibrant around school. The rain had stopped. However, the dark clouds obscured the sun and blue sky. Not what the students expected for that time of the year.

Uniforms were a must for this trip and all the students looked impeccable so as to uphold the school's reputation out there today.

Fredda's spirit was crushed. She had also worn her uniform not because she wanted to, but because she had no other clothes to wear. Perhaps, today it was a plus to be wearing her uniform, so she wouldn't have to explain why she wasn't going on the annual trip. She blended well in the restaurant with the other students.

The three of them sat at the same table, but the table seemed empty without Olliver who sat by himself not very far from them.

"Fredda, what are you going to do today?" asked Tildda.

"Well, I don't know yet. Maybe I'll go to the library to see if I can find any books about," and Fredda whispered, "left-handed people."

"Oh! Yes, we should be observing other students, shouldn't we?" said Tildda.

"Yes, we should," said Noell.

They scanned the room for other lefties, but they didn't have any luck.

"I think I should be having breakfast with Olliver," said Noell.

"I think it's a good idea, so Olliver won't feel left out," responded Tildda.

Noell went to have breakfast with Olliver. The girls noticed how Olliver brightened when Noell sat next to him.

As everything else good about the school, breakfast didn't last long. They heard the whistle blowing outside. Most likely, it was Mr. Boneless, the P.E. teacher, using his whistle. It was time for the buses to move out.

Fredda and Tildda slowly walked together to the bus. The majority of students were already inside them. Tildda looked for bus number thirteen when she saw Noell waving from bus thirteen's window to get her attention. She hopped inside and took a seat, way in the back, with the boys.

Noell opened the bus window and called to Fredda, "Don't waste your time today looking for any particular book at the library. Olliver already tried and couldn't find anything related to the subject in question. He's been observing everyone all week and couldn't find anyone else with your *skill*. We don't have to look any further. Fredda, there's no one else like you."

Fredda looked at Olliver and he smiled at her. She smiled back. It seemed that the exchanging of smiles was proof that the incident that had happened yesterday was over. And, the information that Noell had gotten from Olliver was extremely important.

Fredda waved goodbye and the bus took off. She walked to the front gate, waved goodbye again and waited for the two well-starched security guards to close the gates. The iron gate clanged shut with her still behind them. Fredda felt as if she were in jail rather than at a highly secured school.

She grabbed the bars and rested her chin on the flat part of the cold iron. The air from the other side caressing her face, felt different from the air on the school side of the gate on which she stood. It seemed fresher. She watched people passing by and thought about what Noell had just told her, *'There is no one else like you ...'*

No one like me? Why? Fredda asked herself.

While she was gazing straight ahead and thinking about the words that Noell had said to her, a figure, seemingly out of nowhere, popped up directly in front of her. Fredda, startled, jumped backwards so fast that she tripped over her own feet.

The figure was a tall, old skinny man whose face and hands were smudged with dirt and whose clothes were worn and ripped. He smelled like garbage. He held a newspaper under his arm pit and muttered something.

Fredda remained sprawled on the ground in dismay. Her attention was drawn to the old man's teeth, the deep yellow-green of which she had never seen before. It looked as if he hadn't brushed his teeth for months, maybe years.

He stuck his withering face between the gate's bars. This action prompted the guards to immediately rush over and pull Fredda to her feet and asked if she was ok. Then they turned and said, "Excuse me, sir, you cannot grab the gates. This is private property. You will have to step aside. You may stay in front of the gates but you cannot touch them."

As if he didn't hear the guards at all, he continued talking with his fingers grasping the bars.

"The thing in the sky was the greatest thing I have ever seen in my life," he repeated over and over, crazily.

The guards tried to unglue his hands. "Sir, you have to step aside. Please," repeated one of the guards.

However, the man held on tightly and didn't budge. His strength was surprising. His eyes fixed on Fredda. And then, her breath caught in her throat and her heart picked up its beat as his sentence registered in her brain. *These are the exact same words Great-Aunt Annora said to me the last time I saw her!*

"Please, sir, you have to move aside," the guard patiently ordered once more.

"If you don't let go, we'll have to call the police, sir!" said the other guard losing his patience.

He finally let go of the bars and stepped away from the gate. But, his eyes were still fixed on Fredda. The guards composed themselves and straightened their immaculate uniforms without taking their eyes from this strange visitor.

"The thing, remember the thing!" The elderly man, once again, pointed to the sky. However, there were only dark gray clouds there.

Although there was nothing to be seen other than scary clouds, Fredda looked up at the sky and saw that the clouds were very dark indeed. It seemed like rain. Again, the wind kicked up.

He stuck his head between the gate's bars and said clearly, "I was a student at this school once and I …" But before the man could finish, the guards screamed at him. "THAT'S IT, SIR! WE ARE GOING TO CALL THE POLICE!"

"UGGOSCHNAPPS! UGGOSCHNAPPS! UGGOSCHNAPPS! UGGOSCHNAPPS!" the man screamed over and over. Then, as suddenly as he had appeared, he ran away.

The guards told Fredda that she should return to the school's main area in case the strange man returned. "Crazy man, that one!" one of the guards said. "And he thinks that he was a student here at this prestigious school."

"I believe he's drunk," Fredda overheard.

Fredda was still trying to process what she had just heard. She said aloud, "How can it be? That filthy man said exactly the same words my great-aunt said to me not long ago!"

Fredda stopped and looked up at the sky once more. It was steel gray and she felt the rain drops falling on her face. It was cold, very cold. The sky opened and the rain poured out. She ran towards the main building and found a safe place where the rain couldn't get her. Fredda checked the sky again. It seemed that the clouds were revolving and twisting back and forth. The movement absorbed Fredda's attention and she heard nothing else but the wind.

Suddenly, a hand touched her shoulder.

"Fredda!" a voice accompanied the touch, startling her.

Fredda thought, *I'm in trouble now!* But to her surprise, it was Mrs. Camerron.

"Hi, Mrs. Camerron, you scared me."

"I am sorry, dear Fredda! But, what is going on? You are all wet and your uniform is all dirty!"

"Oh," Fredda noticed that she was indeed wearing a dirty uniform. "Well, I fell down."

"Were you running again?" asked Mrs. Camerron. "You know, dear Fredda, no running at International Academy," Mrs. Camerron continued sarcastically. "Rules and regulations. We all know about them, don't we?" She wasn't very pleased with them either. A slight smile turned up the corners of her mouth.

Fredda wasn't sure if she should tell Mrs. Camerron about the mysterious old man she had just encountered. But instead, she answered, "Oh no! I wasn't running. I just fell down as I was looking at the sky. I wasn't paying attention and I lost my balance."

"I know, the weather has been horrid lately. I think you had better go now and take a hot shower and change your wet clothes, dear Fredda. Otherwise, you might get sick or even worse, if someone else sees you like this you'll be in trouble!"

"Yes, Mrs. Camerron, I think it's a good idea. Thank you and I'll see you later."

Fredda was now shivering and sped toward the dormitory while still watching the sky.

"Don't forget to come to lunch early today," said Mrs. Camerron. "Remember the students are not in today, so I can get you an early lunch, dear Fredda."

Fredda got to her room without anyone else seeing her in the dirty uniform. She entered and took her shoes off so as not to track the floors with dirt from the rain. She started toward the bathroom when her eyes zeroed in on the windowsill. She yelled, "DEAD FLOWER! Oh no! I should have listened to Mr. Kaffona about watering this stupid flower. I completely forgot about it. Now it's dead! Totally dead!" The orchid's vivid pink petals had faded and their tips were brown and limp.

She wasn't sure what to do with it at this point. She grabbed it and ran to the bathroom, put the flower under the faucet in the sink and showered the orchid with fresh water, "I hope you survive! But I think you're dead, really dead." She placed the flower basket back on the windowsill and looked at the ragged flower sadly, "I'm so sorry! I don't think I have a green thumb."

Fredda thought, *Here I am again, talking to an object. The other day, I was talking to a portrait. Today I'm talking to a flower. I'm really losing it.*

Fredda took a long hot shower. She put on an old but clean uniform, and a really worn pair of shoes. The other pair was soaked with rain.

She sat down on her bed and was brushing her hair when another scream came from her mouth, "YOU'RE ALIVE! I DIDN'T KILL YOU!" Dropping the hair brush on the floor, she ran to the window and there sat a vividly bright pink orchid reaching for the sky.

"Oh, I'm so happy that I didn't kill you! You know I'm not very good at taking care of things, especially live things like you, but I promise that I'll be more careful.

I'll water you often. I'll follow the advice that Mr. Kaffona gave me. I promise!" Then she chuckled to herself, *I'm still talking to a flower. I'm definitely losing it!* She smiled.

Fredda lit the fireplace to warm herself. She took a seat on the windowsill close to the pink orchid and pondered the bad weather. Looking at the sky, so dark that someone could confuse it with the beginning of night, Fredda realized she had never seen such a horribly rainy and cold beginning of summer. Now the room felt cozy. However, it was almost time to go see Mrs. Camerron for lunch.

Today, school was a peaceful place. Almost every soul was out on a school trip except for a few faculty members. Today, Fredda could feel how it was going to be this summer. She'd be roaming around the school by herself, just as she had since she came to live here. But, there was one more week to go before the emptiness of the corridors would give Fredda the feeling of solitude.

Fredda left the fireplace on so that when she got back to her room she wouldn't have to suffer from the cold. She went to have lunch with Mrs. Camerron.

When she arrived at the restaurant, it was so empty that she could hear the wood crackling in the fireplace. Sure enough, Fredda heard Mrs. Camerron calling her.

"Here, dear Fredda, come over here in the kitchen."

Fredda sat down. From this small corner table, she could look through a half-moon window and see the entire restaurant. Mrs. Camerron asked Fredda what she would like to eat from the menu today. Chili soup, corn bread, salad, mixed vegetables, mashed potato and beef stew.

Fredda considered it for a moment, looked towards the restaurant windows and answered, "Chili soup with corn bread, please."

"Very good choice, Fredda, on a day like this, it's good to be warm," responded the cook.

A couple of minutes later, Mrs. Camerron came in with a great bowl of chili and a basket full of small corn breads not only for Fredda but also for herself. The cook sat down at the table with her. Fredda saw Mr. Nepttune and the young fella, Grillo, already eating at another table on the other side of the kitchen.

But before she started eating the delicious chili, she decided to ask Mrs. Camerron a question.

As soon as Fredda opened her mouth, someone called the cook.

"Mrs. Camerron!" boomed from the restaurant.

"Yes," responded the cook, "I am coming. Fredda, don't wait for me. Just start eating because they will call several times."

Fredda could see, from the half-moon window, that some of the teachers and the faculty were arriving for lunch.

Fredda reconsidered, and decided that maybe it wasn't such a good idea to ask or tell Mrs. Camerron about all the things that had happened to her this week, including seeing that stranger this morning. Mrs. Camerron came often to the table and tried to eat her meal with Fredda, but had to leave to attend to the faculty members.

After lunch, the weather was still the same. Fredda decided to stay in for the rest of the afternoon. She went to her cozy room and tried to organize herself for the final week. She cleaned up her messy backpack, put away some books, took a look at the finals schedule that was on

Tildda's desk and saw that there were a lot of subjects that didn't required a final test. PE, music and art were some of those subjects. *Good news!*

Fredda even had time to take a nap. The nap became a dead sleep and Fredda only woke up with the noise coming from the corridors made by the students, which meant they were back from the field trip.

Fredda couldn't believe that it was so late so soon. Tildda burst inside the room.

"Hi. So, how did you do today?" asked Tildda almost without a breath.

"I did okay," responded Fredda, spleepily rubbing her eyes.

"And how was your day?" asked Fredda.

"Boring, boring!" said Tildda making funny faces. "It was very cold and without you things weren't the same. I don't have to go to a museum, I'm living in one. Noell and Olliver were with me all day, and you know, I couldn't take it anymore."

Fredda only smiled and said, "I'm starving." It wasn't very often that Fredda said something like that!

"Oh! Fredda you sound like Olliver, he's always starving. I want to know what you really did all day. Your day was probably better than mine."

"I'll tell you over dinner, okay?" Fredda got out of bed.

The four of them met again for dinner. Noell chatted a lot, telling Fredda about the great day he had with Tildda and Olliver. Olliver was quieter than the others.

"Okay, Noell, enough about our day," said Tildda somewhat bossily. But everyone knew that Tildda could get bossy at times.

"We want to know what Fredda did all day."

"You mean *you* want to know what Fredda did all day?" said Noell jumping in.

"Well, probably her day was better than ours. We were in and out of that bus. The weather was awful and it was freezing most of the time. The lunch was nothing like Mrs. Camerron's food and the art was horrible," said Tildda.

"Wait a minute, Tildda. The art was great. *I* really appreciated being there looking at the most glorious world of art painted by those famous people. Do you know how many people would've loved being there today?" said Olliver.

Tildda ignored him. "So?" She asked Fredda.

"Okay, Tildda, something happened today," she whispered.

"I knew it! I knew you had a more exciting day than us!" Tildda was always enthusiastic about a good story.

"Shhh," said Fredda, "It doesn't mean that I had a better day than you. Well, I followed the bus this morning, until the guards closed the gates in front of my face. Remember? So, I was there looking through the gates and thinking about actually being outside, when this crazy, filthy man appeared out of nowhere, jumping in front of me on the other side of the gates. The guards fought to get him away."

"Well, I was thinking about something more exciting than a filthy man jumping in front of the gates. I was thinking maybe you had time to explore the tunnels," Tildda murmured.

"Well, but this isn't the whole story," responded Fredda. All their eyes looked at her expectantly.

"Not the whole story? So, tell us," Tildda said frustrated.

"The man just stared at me at first and then the words that came out of his mouth were, 'The thing in the sky was the greatest thing I have ever seen in my life!' And he pointed at the sky."

"And what's so impressive about what the man *said*?" asked Tildda.

"That was exactly what my great-aunt said to me the last time I saw her! And *she* also pointed to the sky," Fredda completed.

"And then what happened?" asked Tildda itching for an answer.

"Then, the man said that he was a student once at International Academy, and after that he started shouting a word something like, 'Uggoschnapps!, Uggoschnapps!, Uggoschnapps!' And then he ran away."

"Ah! Probably a loony! I thought that we were going to hear a great story." Tildda was disappointed.

Meanwhile, Olliver who was drinking the rest of his glass of water, spit out the whole sip and sprayed all over the table.

"OLLIVER!" shouted Tildda. "What's the matter with you? Where are your table manners?"

"I'm so sorry, Tildda! But I couldn't help myself when I heard what Fredda said. It's not Uggoschnapps!" said Olliver wiping his mouth with the back of his hand.

"What do you mean it's not Uggoschnapps?" asked Tildda more annoyed than ever and trying to dry herself and the table.

"His name is Uggo Schnapps and he was a student here at International Academy a long time ago."

Now, all their eyes were fixed on Olliver.

"How do you know that, Olliver?" asked Fredda totally absorbed.

"*His* portrait's also at the library entrance, but on the opposite side of your great-aunt. That's why nobody pays much attention to his portrait," responded Olliver. And he continued, "He was not only a *student* but also a *teacher*."

"A teacher?" Noell piped up. "And how come he's homeless now?"

"Are you sure, Olliver?" asked Fredda.

"Yes, I'm absolutely sure."

"Tomorrow I'll go to the library. I'd like to see if he's the same person we're talking about," Fredda said to them.

"I want to see it, too," said Tildda still drying herself.

"Me too," said Noell.

Sure enough, the next day they were all at the library checking out the portrait.

"So, what do you think, Fredda?" Tildda asked eagerly.

Fredda took a long look at the portrait. It was somewhat difficult to see the fashionable young man as the same disheveled man she had seen.

But there was something about the man's eyes that no matter clean, filthy, old or young, Fredda would have recognized him.

"Yes, this *is* the same person!" Fredda was more intrigued than ever.

"So, he *was* a student!" said Tildda.

"Not only a *student*, but a *teacher* at this prestigious school," said Olliver.

"And how did he manage to become a bum?" asked Noell, fascinated.

"I have no idea, Noell," responded Fredda staring at the portrait.

"Well, I guess we're not going to get any answers by staring at this painting. We've got to ask someone about him," said Tildda.

"No, I don't think we should ask *anybody*," said Fredda. "I don't think it's a good idea. And besides, I don't want anybody to know what we know about this Uggo Schnapps."

"Okay," said Tildda. Olliver and Noell agreed.

Finals week came and went in a flash. The only hard tests were math, and, of course, English. The culinary final proved to be a little confusing as all the questions seemed alike to them.

Friday afternoon the final scores were posted on the big cork board at the library entrance.

Students searched for their names. Elated cries rang out, "Yes, I passed! Vacation now!" It was like being at a big party.

Fredda was probably one of the last students to check her grades. Not because she wasn't interested, but because even if she hadn't passed any of the subjects, which to her surprise she did, she would have to remain in school, anyway. She had no other place to go. For Fredda, the summer was a totally different experience from the others. Tildda, Olliver and Noell also passed.

After the grades, the students headed to their dormitories to pack. This evening would be special. It would be the last dinner together before summer vacation, and besides, the students wouldn't have to go to bed early.

For Fredda, it would be the beginning of the worst time of the year. She hated summer. Nothing exciting ever happened. It was depressing for her to be at school without her friends, imagining everyone else having so much fun out there.

At dinner that night, the students were more relaxed, no uniform needed, except for Fredda who didn't have any other clothes. Students were expecting Mr. Kaffona's long end of the year speech, but to their astonishment, he just rang that golden bell over his head and announced, "Have a nice summer and enjoy the meal," and then he sat down to eat. The students applauded appropriately by International Academy standards. But, of course, clumsy Olliver had already spilled water all over the table!

Tonight, bedtime was also pushed up so students would have more time to enjoy the night. The atmosphere at school was party-like. Students were chit-chatting and laughing. Even Fredda tried not to think about tomorrow and she enjoyed the company of her friends. They saw Attos and his two buddies, Luggos and Eddra, in a corner apart from everybody else, not mixing with the other students as usual.

Like everything good at school, the party didn't last too long and it was soon time to go to bed. Slowly they all left for their rooms.

Tildda was all packed. She was excited, but at the same time, a bit sad because Fredda would have to be at school by herself.

"Don't worry, Fredda," said Tildda, "When my mom gets here, I'll ask her to talk to Mr. Kaffona about you going to see Mrs. Cellestin."

"Thank you, Tildda," said Fredda gazing through the window.

Tildda lay down on her bed and quickly fell asleep, but Fredda didn't. She stayed awake thinking how nice it would've been if she had a family and she could go with

Fredda Buttler And The Left-Handed People

them tomorrow. Her eyelids finally gave up on her and she slept.

Next morning, there was another uproar. The media knew that the academy required parents, grandparents and guardians to pick up their children in person. Parents and guardians were not required at any other time but emergencies during the school year. Several reports from prestigious newspapers, photographers from well-known magazines, radio and TV stations were crowding around outside. Tomorrow the world would be informed of the powerful and famous people who had been at International Academy to retrieve their sons and daughters.

After breakfast, most of the students waited for their parents at the main entrance, where a prominent marble statue of a woman stood. She stood in the middle of the horseshoe with her left hand reaching toward the universe, and her right hand holding something that wasn't quite visible. Her long dress covered part of her hand and the object she was holding.

Parents were due to start arriving at 10:00 a.m. No uniforms were requested that day, so colorful fashionable clothing was worn.

It was almost 10:00 a.m. when Fredda, Tildda, Olliver and Noell stood on the second floor facing all the commotion downstairs. From that particular spot, they would get a bird's eye view of all the celebrities. They weren't alone either. Some male students from ninth and tenth grades were also there talking about the celebrity they wanted to see.

"Well, she's the most glamorous woman in the world," said one of the students.

"I have my camera ready for my best shot," said the another student.

"I'm happy to see her here so close to me," and the comments didn't stop.

The four of them, not knowing what to say about this beautiful celebrity they were talking about, just looked at each other. But Tildda said, "I know who they're talking about!"

"Who?" they asked in unison.

"Gee Ann Allijio, the actress, of course. And she *is* really gorgeous."

"And how do you know that?" asked Olliver.

"Well, I saw her in a magazine."

The caravan of cars crept up the long winding drive to the gates. There were stunning old and new limousines and exotic cars, most of them with their own chauffeur. Each time a car door was about to be opened by one of the spotless guards, the reporters drooled.

Fredda saw Mrs. Camerron and her kitchen crew, hiding behind the bushes. Mrs. Utilla, hid behind the curtains. They weren't supposed to be in the main entrance. Only the teachers themselves who were aligned like soldiers to receive a medal had permission.

Tomorrow, some of them would be on the cover of newspapers and magazines. They all looked meticulous except for Mrs. Lerddus who could never put herself together and look good. Mr. Kaffona was, of course, wearing orange and looked more like an orange tree than a school principal. Mrs. Maufrodezza stood next to him as she was now the vice principal. Mr. Numericcos was on the other end of the line looking very dashing, yet uncomfortable.

A guard opened the door of a long shiny black limousine. An elegant elderly gentleman stepped out. The photographers went wild taking pictures of him.

"Who's that man?" asked Tildda, "He must be important."

"Well, his name is Cat Runey McPal. He's British. I read about him. He used to be in a band which was very famous once." Olliver's eyes were fixed on Cat.

"What was the band's name?" asked Tildda.

"I don't really remember, but it was something related to a bug," responded Olliver.

"Ugh!" Tildda screwed up her face, "A bug? How disgusting!"

He was here to pick up his granddaughter. The boys chattered on about the famous actress who they awaited. A string of important people came and went with their children. The reporters were having a field day.

Yet another black limousine stopped in front of school. The door opened. There she was, the most breathtaking woman Fredda had ever seen. She had long, silky, coal black hair that cascaded down her back in waves. Her figure was an hourglass, outlined by a tight black dress. A pair of large sunglasses perched atop her aquiline nose, even though it was a cloudy day.

She puckered her lush lips, blew a kiss, and waved at the photographers. She smiled as brightly as the camera flashes that wouldn't stop. The photographers and reporters pushed and shoved each other, vying for a photo or a word from Ms. Allijio. They knew they had only a small window of time to get them. But for the young boys ogling her, time was suspended.

That must be the actress, Fredda thought.

"Wow, she really is gorgeous!" exclaimed the ninth grade student.

"She *is* really stunning," said Tildda admiring her.

Gee Ann Allijio waved once more to the photographers and to the teachers, slid gracefully into the car with her sons and daughters and left.

"That was awesome to see her so close. She's even more amazing in person than in magazines," said Tildda all excited.

A few minutes later, it was time for Olliver to go. His father arrived to pick him up. He said goodbye to all of them and quickly left. Most of the students had already left. The school was emptying speedily. However, the reporters and photographers remained.

Now it was time for Noell to go with his father. Noell waved to him from the second floor. The cameras flashed at Mr. Segat, a famous business mogul in the computer field. Mr. Segat waved back to the reporters and to the teachers while Noell said goodbye to Fredda and Tildda. And soon, Noell was gone.

"Well, it's only the two of us now," said Tildda waiting for her mother.

"And soon, there'll be only one," said Fredda looking out in space. Tildda didn't say anything. She didn't know what to say.

The time flew. There were only a few students remaining at the main entrance waiting for their parents. Tildda was one of them.

"My mother is *always* late," said Tildda critically, "I bet you, I'll be the last one to be here waiting for her."

Tildda was right. The commotion was gone along with the photographers and the reporters. It was after 11:00 when Tildda's mother showed up.

"My mother is here, *finally*! She's late as usual," said Tildda, "Let's go talk to her, Fredda."

They went downstairs. The school was so empty that they could hear their footsteps on the granite floors.

Tildda's mother walked over to meet them. She was elegant and slender. Her hair was blond like Tildda's. She wore a beautiful tan matching skirt and jacket with a tan hat and big tortoise-shell sunglasses.

Tildda hugged her and her mother hugged her back. For a moment, Fredda thought, *Nobody ever hugged me like that, ever.*

"Hello," she said, "You must be Fredda. I've heard very nice things about you."

Fredda thought, *That's nice to hear. It seems no one else has anything good to say about me.*

Tildda's mom continued, " My name is Etzzela D'Rof, Matildda's mother."

"Very nice to meet you, Mrs. D'Rof," she smiled.

"My pleasure, Fredda. What beautiful dimples you have!"

Fredda blushed.

Tildda pulled her mother aside to talk to her privately. Her mother turned toward Fredda and smiled. She smiled back. Mrs. D'Rof left toward Mr. Kaffona's office.

"I told you that my mom would to talk to the principal," said Tildda beaming.

A few minutes later, Mrs. D'Rof came back, took her sunglasses off and said, "I'm sorry, Fredda. I can't take you to see Mrs. Cellestin. You know, the rules and regulations do not allow me to take you outside of school." Mrs. D'Rof looked apologetically into Fredda's dark brown eyes.

"Thank you anyway, Mrs. D'Rof, for trying."

"Matildda, we have to go. I will be waiting for you in the car. Goodbye, Fredda, and again, I'm very sorry."

"Well, I have to go now," Tildda said sadly. "I hope you have a nice summer and please don't get stuck inside any tunnels, please," she implored.

Fredda smiled weakly, "I'll see you at the beginning of the new school year. Okay?"

"Okay!" Tildda grabbed Fredda and pulled her in for a farewell hug. They both sighed and let go.

Fredda thought, *I could get used to being hugged.*

Tildda walked off to meet her mother. Fredda stayed and watched all but a few teachers leave.

Her heart felt like the cold, empty pit that the school became for her during the summer. The sky mirrored her mood as ominously dark clouds crept in silently.

Fredda dejectedly returned to her room to get some of the books to return to the library before it started raining again. After that, she would be joining Mrs. Camerron for lunch.

Fredda lifted her overly full backpack with difficulty. She was just about to leave her room when someone knocked.

Fredda opened the door.

"Hi, Mrs. Utilla," said Fredda somewhat surprised.

"Hello, Miss Buttler," said the secretary nervously.

"Mr. Kaffona wants to talk to you immediately!"

Why is it that every time Mr. Kaffona wants to talk to me, he wants to see me immediately?

Fredda and her heavy backpack left with Mrs. Utilla. The secretary trotted in front of her without saying a word. They arrived at Mr. Kaffona's office.

"You can go in, Miss Buttler." The secretary opened the office door and Fredda entered.

"Oh! There you are, Miss Buttler," said Mr. Kaffona nervously. He was not alone. Right there, in the middle of the huge half-moon window stood a refined looking gentleman wearing a dark suit which brought out his straight silver, shoulder length hair and beard. He wore round eye glasses and a pair of unusual shoes, wooden clogs. Fredda had never seen shoes like them before, but they looked interesting on him. He wore a sling around his neck, holding up his right arm.

Fredda saw her big file on the desk.

"Please, Miss Buttler come close. I would like to introduce you to ..." and Fredda moved closer to them. She could see the man's eyes full of water, but he held himself together. Mr. Kaffona continued, "I would like you to meet ..." and he paused again, "... to meet Mr. Buttler, Mr. Albert Buttler, your grandfather."

Fredda's mouth dropped open as she accidently dropped the heavy backpack full of books on Mr. Kaffona's foot! But he didn't say anything. He only cringed. He was more interested in Fredda's reaction, than the pain the books had caused his toes.

"I'm so very pleased to meet you, Fredda," said Mr. Buttler as he extended his left hand to hers.

She thought, *He extended his left hand! Well it's the only hand he has at the moment. The right one's injured. What would Mrs. Maufrodezza and Mr. Numericcos have done if they had seen him greeting me with his left hand?*

Without saying anything, Fredda reluctantly extended her left hand to shake his, as a myriad of emotions played across her face.

Mr. Kaffona's eyes widened. There was silence. Until Fredda said fiercely, her eyes flashing, "Where have you been all these years?"

Mr. Kaffona looked at Grandpa Albert waiting for his answer, as did Fredda.

"Well, Fredda," said Grandpa Albert and he paused, "Would you mind, Mr. Kaffona, I would like to have some privacy here with my granddaughter."

"Oh! Of course, of course," said Mr. Kaffona, but he didn't move. He was hypnotized by the moment, as nobody had ever come to see Fredda, no less a family member.

Grandpa Albert cleared his throat and raised his eyebrows at Mr. Kaffona. "Oh, oh, of course," and he left the room.

Grandpa Albert studied Fredda. "I didn't know about you until a few days ago when I sent you the message."

"Message?"

"Yes, the orchid."

"Oh! The flower, you mean. So, *you* were the one who sent me that flower! But there was no card, so I guess I didn't get the message."

Grandpa Albert hesitated for a moment thinking about what to say next, but it was Fredda who spoke first.

"You said you didn't know about me until a few days ago? What do you mean by that?"

"No, I did *not* know that I had a granddaughter, and I must say a beautiful granddaughter." He muttered to himself, "Dimples like your grandma."

Fredda overheard him, "Where *is* my grandmother?" she questioned.

Grandpa Albert's eyes dropped to the floor, sadness taking over his face. "She's no longer with us. She passed many years ago."

Fredda didn't know what to say.

"Forgive me, Fredda, for not being here for you all those years. I have lost a great deal. You and your grandmother are not the only ones."

"And where *have* you been all these years?"

"Well, Fredda," and he paused again, "What do you know about our family?"

Taking a deep breath, "The only thing I know about my family is my genius Great-Aunt Annora, who is now in the nursing home. And she's the only relative I have ever known. She never told me much about my family. The only thing she told me is that she and I were the last members."

"Oh, I see," responded Grandpa Albert.

"So, are you going to tell me all the things Great-Aunt Annora didn't tell me?" asked Fredda.

"Well …" he responded uncomfortably.

"I want to know the truth about my family. Can *you* tell me the truth?" Fredda looked at him expectantly.

"Well, dear Fredda, the truth …" He took a handkerchief from his pocket, wiped his forehead, paused and said, "The truth is complicated!"

CHAPTER 7

THE COLOR MATTERS

"COMPLICATED! HOW COMPLICATED CAN IT BE?" shouted Fredda.

"I know, it sounds insane, but you have to give me time to explain," he responded.

"I've been waiting for almost thirteen years, *here* in this *school*!" said Fredda looking at him angrily.

Grandpa Albert's eyes glistened with tears. In a raspy voice he said, "And *I* lost almost thirteen years not having you in my life, not even *knowing* that I had you in my life."

Fredda stood there. Time stood still for a moment. Neither of them spoke.

Finally, Grandpa Albert spoke again, "Let's forget about the past. Let's give ourselves a chance to know each other from now on. It was not my fault either, although I've beaten myself up every day since I came back and found out about you."

"Why didn't you ever come back? You may not have known about me, but what about Great-Aunt Annora? She's still your sister, isn't she?"

He took his time to answer the question, carefully choosing the words he was about to say. "Of course, she is still my sister! Well, Fredda, your aunt and I had our differences. We weren't on the best terms, so we didn't speak to each other," he said waiting for the next question.

"You mean you haven't spoken with her for almost thirteen years?"

"Well, a bit more than that," he said expecting the next question.

"And weren't you worried about her?"

"Ah, well, see Fredda, not really. Your aunt had and still has a lot of good friends. This school has been her home and the faculty has been her true family. So, I knew she was in good hands. Otherwise, I would never have left her here alone even though we had our differences. And besides, she would never leave this place, never ever."

Fredda stared at him. She took some time and said, "And what about my parents? Where are they now? Are they dead?"

Grandpa Albert scratched his head, sat down, looked into Fredda's brown eyes, took a deep breath and said, "I would love to give you an answer, but I don't have one. And before you scream at me again, you must listen to what I have to say."

Fredda slowly nodded her head. Grandpa Albert took this as a sign that he could continue, "There was a good reason I left. See, Fredda, one day your mother called. She was so worried that probably she forgot to tell me she was pregnant with you. It was supposed to be the happiest day of her life when she found out that she and your father were going to have a baby, *you*. But instead, your mother told me that your father, my son, the only son I have, didn't come home. So, I promised her that I would find him no matter how long it took. I would find him, I told her."

Fredda's eyes remained glued to her grandfather's. "But I never came back. I had some trouble and I couldn't come back. I never found your father. A few days ago, when I was finally able to come back, I found out about you and also that your mother had disappeared. She had left to find your father and me. So, all this time I have been trying to find your father. I have no answer for you, Fredda. The only person that may have some answers is Annora, but you know that she's not well, don't you?" Fredda just nodded her head.

She walked towards the big window. She looked outside the window as her mind raced with all that she had just heard. She felt guilty about what she had said to her grandfather. All this time he had been trying to find her father and she had been so angry at him.

Grandpa Albert went on, "I know that it has not been easy for you Fredda, but it has not been easy for me either."

There was a silence between them again. Side by side, they looked outside the large window wordlessly. A huge crack of thunder broke their silence. Both of them moved backwards at the same time. It started to rain heavily.

"Well, Fredda, I'll understand if you would like to stay here at school for the summer vacation, but I would like to invite you to come with me and spend the summer together," said Grandpa Albert still looking at the rain.

"You mean you can take me with you?" asked Fredda surprised.

"Of course, I can take you with me. After all, you are my granddaughter, aren't you? And besides, I already signed all the papers. You are free to go if you want, of course."

Fredda took a moment to think. This was so much to digest and things were happening so fast. She had trouble processing that she had a grandpa. She'd be able to go for summer vacation for the first time in her life. Maybe she'd even travel like her friends. She wouldn't have to be by herself at school.

She looked outside at the most beautiful garden in the school. The rain pounded the landscape and more claps of thunder followed.

Grandpa Albert fixed his eyes on her, and finally Fredda responded with a big bright smile, showing her beautiful pair of dimples, "Okay!"

Grandpa Albert was so excited. He was like a little kid talking up a storm without taking a breath. However, Fredda was still so stunned by all the news that she wasn't paying much attention to him.

"Well?" said Grandpa Albert, "What are you waiting for? Go and grab your things!"

"Things?"

"Yes," said Grandpa, "Things! Girls have a lot of things, more than boys, you know *things*."

"Well, I really don't have things, actually I don't have anything."

"What do you mean you don't have anything?" asked Grandpa Albert perplexed.

"I only have a couple of old uniforms and some old pajamas and … another pair of old shoes," said Fredda embarrassed.

"Well, don't worry, Fredda, we are going to buy some new clothes before going home today," said Grandpa Albert grinning, but at the same time, considering this nonsense about Fredda having no other clothes than old uniforms.

Without saying anything else, Fredda just smiled back at him. He stood there admiring her incredible dimples, the same ones that had accented his wife's smile.

Fredda said, "The only thing I have to do is to go to the library and return these books."

Fredda grabbed her heavy backpack and was leaving the room to get ready to go, when Grandpa Albert said, "Fredda! I understand if you don't want to get your things and take them with you. However, please take the orchid I gave you, otherwise it will die. No one is here to water your flower. Remember plants like water. I will be waiting for you at the main entrance."

Fredda thought for a moment, *Grandpa just sounded like Mr. Kaffona*, and she left.

Running to get the books back to the library, Fredda was thrilled about life. She returned the books to the librarian, Mrs. Nickelleta, who gave Fredda a nasty look as she had seen Fredda running through the corridors.

"You know the rules, don't you, Miss Buttler?" scowled the librarian.

Fredda just nodded her head and left quietly. However, once outside the library, she started running again. Before going to her room to get the flower, she passed by the school kitchen and stopped to talk to Mrs. Camerron.

"Hi there, dear Fredda!" said Mrs. Camerron wearing a long white apron over a long dark dress and mixing something in a casserole, probably excellent, with a wooden spoon.

"You are very early today, dear Fredda. Lunch is not ready yet!" she said continuing her mixing.

"No," said Fredda, "I'm not early at all. I just stopped by to tell you that I'm not coming for lunch because I'm leaving with my Grandpa Albert for summer vacation!" The only sound that could be heard was the sound of the casserole dish breaking on the floor.

"Wh… Wh… What did you say, Fredda?" said Mrs. Camerron terrified.

"Are you okay, Mrs. Camerron?" asked Fredda.

"Did you say … your Grandpa Albert?"

"Yes, that's what I said, my Grandpa Albert."

The mix flooded the floor along with the broken pieces of the casserole. Mrs. Camerron didn't move a muscle or even blink.

"Are you all right, Mrs. Camerron?" Fredda asked her, worried.

Mrs. Camerron took a few moments to answer.

"Yes, it's just that I thought that he was d… d…"

"Dead!" Fredda jumped in. "I didn't even know that I had a grandpa. Wait a minute. Did you know that I had a grandpa, Mrs. Camerron?"

"Well, I knew him, but your great-aunt, Annora, told me that he was d-dead," finished the tremulous Mrs. Camerron.

"Oh! But he's alive, very much alive and if you're okay, Mrs. Camerron, I have to go now. I guess I'll see you after summer, bye now."

Fredda took off, running again as fast as she could. School was almost empty and she couldn't wait to get out of that awful place.

She went to her room and got some of her things. She took a look around the room and remembered to take the map of the tunnels which she had drawn. *If someone got a hold of it I'd be in big trouble!*

As she was stepping out of the room, she realized that she had forgotten the orchid, so she grabbed it and rushed out.

Fredda couldn't run anymore. The stuff she was carrying didn't allow her to move very quickly. However, she managed to get to the main entrance in no time.

Grandpa's car was as old as he. It looked more like it belonged in a museum or to a collector, than on the streets. The car was black and all the details were shiny silver. Fredda could see her own reflection in it. Big oval lights in the front, heavy duty bumpers and the spare tire was hung on the back. Grandpa's Albert chauffeur was wearing a black suit, flat hat, shiny shoes to match the car and purple gloves. He was a tall, skinny man, not too old but not too young either.

"Fredda," said Grandpa Albert, "This is my chauffeur and friend, Mr. Gattus."

Mr. Gattus tipped the brim of his hat, swung his left hand in front of Fredda and said, "It's a pleasure to meet you, Fredda, at last."

Fredda was shocked that he was greeting her with his left hand. She looked to her left and then to her right to see if anybody was around. She was expecting someone to shout at her for using the wrong hand!

Mr. Gattus stood still extending his left hand in greeting, waiting for her. Fredda hesitantly extended hers to meet his. "Very nice to meet you too, sir."

The chauffeur opened the door with his right hand and with his left, showed Fredda the way. She hopped inside followed by Grandpa Albert. The inside of the car was spacious. Fredda could smell the leather seats. Everything was in mint condition. The car seemed antique and that nobody had used it for a long time.

Fredda Buttler And The Left-Handed People

Mr. Gattus asked Grandpa Albert, "Where to, sir?"

"Well, we are going shopping!" replied Grandpa Albert smiling.

Mr. Gattus looked at Grandpa Albert from the driver's mirror and said, "Yes, sir."

The car started moving very slowly toward the school's front gates. The guards opened the huge iron doors. Fredda could smell freedom when the car crossed the gates. She noticed Grandpa Albert looking at the shops in front of the school. One of the signs said, Flora Florizeldda's Flowers Shop! Grandpa didn't take his eyes from the sign as the car continued along slowly. When he couldn't see the flower shop anymore, he devoted his attention to her.

Fredda had a great afternoon with her grandpa. Actually, it was the first time in her life that someone had taken her shopping for normal clothes rather than shopping for uniforms.

Fredda wanted to get to know him. She knew behind those round glasses and funky hair style, there was a man who could tell her more about her family than anybody else except her Great-Aunt Annora, who at the moment, was incapable of saying anything that made much sense. However, Fredda didn't ask any questions.

She waited to see if Grandpa Albert would offer information on his own. The wait was in vain as Grandpa didn't say a word about anything other than, "What else do you need?"

They spent almost the whole afternoon shopping.

"Well, Fredda, I guess we're done! How about going home now?"

Fredda just nodded a yes and with her arms and hands full of bags with new things, they went home.

Mr. Gattus drove the car, making a few turns here and there, but Fredda could see that they weren't very far from school. The school tower was distinctly visible from where they were.

After a few minutes, the car stopped in front of a big iron gate very similar to International Academy's. She saw the initials engraved in it. A big letter A followed by a letter T and the last letter was a B.

Fredda thought better than to ask anything at the moment, but she thought maybe the A stood for Albert and the B for Buttler. However, she couldn't figure out the letter T.

Mr. Gattus pushed a car button and the gates swung open. The vegetation was so dense that Fredda couldn't see the house right the way. The house began showing itself after Mr. Gattus drove inside the yard and made a left turn.

It was ancient, however, well preserved. A majestic tower was at the center core. The tower's windows were positioned in such a way that it made the tower seem as if it was observing them, rather than them observing the tower. Fredda imagined the shape of an owl's face in it. She chastised herself, *Here we go again, how can a tower have an owl's face?*

"Oh! I see that you are intrigued by the face, aren't you?" said Grandpa Albert, intrigued by what Fredda's answer would be.

"Face?" responded Fredda, wondering how he could know what she was thinking.

"Don't tell me that you cannot see the owl's face. It was designed as an owl to scare the pigeons because they make a mess. You know they poop all over the place!" Fredda wanted to laugh, but contained herself as Grandpa Albert continued, "The windows were designed to make one believe that they are eyes, not too round not too oval, and the sculptured window trim completes the piercing eye. Magnificent, don't you think?"

Fredda didn't know what to say as Grandpa Albert went on, "No matter what angle you look at the tower from, it always looks back at you with its fascinating eyes."

The tower was so imposing that Fredda almost forgot about seeing the rest of the house. It was a two story pale yellow one, with a porch at the main entrance. The top part of the house wasn't square like other houses Fredda had seen, but had a pointed stone scaled roof with the outstanding tower in the center.

"Shall we?" said Grandpa Albert showing Fredda the way. She grabbed her flower. Mr. Gattus picked up the rest of the bags and they went straight to the main entrance of the house.

Grandpa Albert put his left arm around Fredda as they walked towards the front door and said, "This house has been in our family for many generations and perhaps someday this will be yours, Fredda."

Fredda's mouth dropped. A few hours ago, she had only old clothes and not much to look forward to in her life! Now she had a grandpa who cared about her and someday a house to live in.

Fredda stared at the house. Grandpa Albert opened the door and let her in.

"Welcome home, Fredda," beamed Grandpa Albert.

At the same moment, a woman came from the other room. She looked just like Mrs. Camerron! "What are you doing here? I'M SO HAPPY TO SEE YOU," Fredda shouted happily.

"Oh! No, Fredda! This isn't Mrs. Camerron. This is Mrs. Herta Matrakka."

"But I don't understand, she looks like Mrs. Camerron," said Fredda confused.

"Well, I can explain it to you, Fredda," replied Grandpa Albert eagerly. "Mrs. Matrakka is Mrs. Camerron's twin sister."

"Oh sorry, Mrs. Matrakka, you look just like her," apologized Fredda.

"Yes, I get that a lot. What a curse to be confused with such a person!"

Fredda could hear the bitterness in her voice, and she knew at that moment that the situation between Mrs. Camerron and her twin sister, Mrs. Matrakka, wasn't good at all.

Mrs. Matrakka offered, "And besides she is not one of our kind!"

Grandpa Albert just grunted, making Mrs. Matrakka realize that she shouldn't say anything more.

"Mrs. Matrakka, this is my granddaughter, Fredda," said Grandpa Albert trying to take the conversation in a different direction. "Mrs. Matrakka works for me. She takes care of the house."

"Nice to meet you, Fredda," and her left hand stretched out to Fredda. However, this time Fredda didn't hesitate. She shook with her left hand. Mrs. Matrakka continued grumpily, "As Mr. Buttler said, I am Mrs. Matrakka, not to be confused with my look-alike."

While still shaking her hand, Fredda thought, *If Mrs. Matrakka can cook as well as her twin sister, things will be okay. I'm used to being around grouchy people anyway.*

While Grandpa Albert gave directions to Mr. Gattus, telling him to leave all the bags in the entry hall, Fredda had the opportunity to observe the house. From her position, she could see that it was full of books. There was a tall bookcase in the entrance hall and another in the corridor leading to the back of the house. To her left, there was a French door open and the room seemed to be an office or a mini library with many books and a fireplace.

To Fredda's right was another room. It was the living room. There were more books in small bookcases and another fireplace. Also, towards the right side, Fredda could see the stairs, and it seemed that the kitchen was in the back towards the narrow corridor.

The house was dimly lit inside, but cozy, with lots of black and white pictures hanging on the walls. Fredda was eager to know about all those people in the pictures. Suddenly, a cat came running from the narrow corridor and directly scooted upstairs.

"I know that cat! That's B..." However, before she could finish, Grandpa Albert said, "Blue, yes, Fredda. That's Blue, and he is a handful," he laughed.

Without saying anything, Fredda thought, *Yes, I already know that he's a trouble maker. He almost got Tildda and me in trouble and almost got killed by Mrs. Camerron who wants to cook him.*

"Blue was your father's cat," said Grandpa Albert looking at Fredda, "So, I guess now he can be *your* cat while you are here. I know you cannot have any pets at school."

Fredda was grateful that for a person who had nothing at the beginning of the day, she had yet another acquisition – Blue. And she had also acquired some more information about her parents.

"Well, let me show you your bedroom, Fredda,"

They went upstairs. However, before Grandpa Albert showed Fredda the room where she would be spending the summer, they passed in front of the entrance of the tower. Fredda read, "Observatory Tower."

"Would you like to go up there?" asked Grandpa Albert. Fredda nodded.

"Then let's go," responded Grandpa Albert excitedly.

The steps were built against the wall rather than in the middle of the tower. They climbed to the top and Fredda saw four windows, not too oval not too round as Grandpa had described earlier, and she could observe the city from all four sides. The most impressive monument was the school tower, close by. It was even taller than the tower they were in.

They spent quite some time observing the city. Grandpa Albert told Fredda about the monuments and their locations and some history about them.

After the tower tour, they went back downstairs so Grandpa Albert could show Fredda her room. But before reaching it, Fredda went through the wrong door, stepped in and saw a very organized room. The ceiling wasn't flat, but a pointed cathedral ceiling, which made the room appear bigger than it was. There was an unlit fireplace. The room was cold. A single bed, lots of boys' toys, and books. On the nightstand, there was a series of pictures in a row. A young boy, then a teenage boy followed by another picture of a grown man in a wedding picture with his bride.

"This was your father's room, Fredda," said Grandpa Albert in a shaky voice.

For the first time in her life, Fredda got to see the photo of her father and mother on their wedding day. They looked ecstatic and in love. They peered into each other's eyes with wide smiles. They were so young.

Fredda held the photo in her hands. Her dark brown eyes fixed upon it. She stepped backwards and sat on the bed while Grandpa Albert sat in the rocking chair contemplating Fredda's moment. They stayed there for a long time without saying a word to each other.

The memories of the objects in the bedroom told the story itself. Fredda placed the picture back, but Grandpa Albert said, "Fredda, you can have the picture if you want to. Actually you can have anything in this bedroom. All these objects belong to you now. Your parents were a lovely couple. Roma was a perfect person for Edgard, your father, and vice versa. She was a lovely young lady. They really truly loved each other. I have never seen a love like it."

Fredda grabbed only that picture and left the room. Grandpa Albert led her to a room at the end of the corridor. She entered. It looked like her father's room with the same pointed cathedral ceiling. However, this room had two single beds and the walls were light yellow, almost the same color as the outside walls. A bookcase was packed with books and a lit fireplace made the room cozy and warm. Fredda held the wedding picture close to her heart. She walked between the two beds and placed the photo on the nightstand, perhaps to feel close to them.

She heard a noise and saw Blue coming in from a cat door next to the fireplace which Fredda didn't even realize was there. He made himself comfortable, spreading himself out on one of the beds.

"Well, Fredda, I forgot to tell you that you're going to share the room with Blue. He sleeps here every night when he's not roaming around and creating trouble, if you know what I mean. I hope you don't mind, of course," Grandpa Albert smiled.

Fredda responded, "Not at all, I'm used to sharing my bedroom with my friend. So, I guess that's your bed. Don't worry, I'll take this one, Blue."

"Good, very good, then I'll leave you alone with Blue, and get prepared for dinner. And by the way, Fredda, you should change and put on some of the new clothes we bought together today. I think you might be tired of using this ragged uniform. The bathroom is located next door. See you later." Grandpa Albert was already screaming for Mrs. Matrakka from the upper level

It should have been a happy time for Fredda. She wasn't alone at school anymore. She had someone in her life who loved her, a house to call hers and even a handful of a cat, but Fredda still felt that something was missing. Her parents weren't there to enjoy the moment with her. It was better than staying by herself in that empty school, but it was not totally complete.

Fredda quickly readied herself to go downstairs. She didn't want to miss anything. She heard voices coming from the kitchen.

Fredda entered, and there was Grandpa Albert telling Mrs. Matrakka that the food needed more salt. Meanwhile, Mrs. Matrakka threw back at Grandpa Albert that the kitchen was her territory and he had better learn that. The two battling sisters had one thing in common, they were very possessive about their kitchens.

It was funny to see them arguing. Fredda started giggling and when the two of them saw her, they stopped immediately.

Now that Fredda could pay better attention to the kitchen, it was a welcoming place. The kitchen was narrow and long. At the end, there was a brick stove with pots and pans steaming. It smelled delicious. There was a door next to the stove, a long table in the middle with chairs on one side and a bench facing the fireplace on the other. The walls were a mix of reddish bricks and plaster and a window sat above the brick stove. There was also a full book case in the entrance, more black and white pictures on the walls and Fredda's orchid was used as a centerpiece on the table.

The bell rang. Mrs. Matrakka went to see who was at the door. A minute later, she came back and told Grandpa that the guest was for him.

"Who is it?" asked Grandpa Albert.

Mrs. Matrakka answered, "You had better see with your own eyes. The person is waiting for you in the study." She made a disapproving face, rolling her eyes like Tildda did when she didn't agree with something or someone.

Fredda turned to see if she could see who was there, but as Mrs. Matrakka said, the company was inside the study. Grandpa Albert strode out of the kitchen. Fredda stood under the door frame not knowing what to say or do. "Why are you still there meandering around?" said Mrs. Matrakka with a grumpy face, "Take a seat and have some bread. I don't think dinner will be served on time this evening."

Fredda didn't know exactly if the dinner was going to be served later because Mrs. Matrakka was having some trouble in the kitchen or because the appearance of the company changed the evening's plans. It was disturbing for Fredda to see Mrs. Matrakka in front of her, knowing that this person was not Mrs. Camerron. They looked exactly the same but they were so different.

"I better put a pot of water to boil. This person likes tea," she continued, referring to the company.

A few minutes later, Grandpa Albert returned and said, "Mrs. Matrakka, could you please make some t..."

But before Grandpa Albert finished, Mrs. Matrakka said, "Tea."

"Yes, tea. Thank you!" And he strode back to the library.

When tea was done, Mrs. Matrakka poured some in a flowered porcelain tea pot along with matching cups and strode to the study. Almost at the same time, someone came in from the back door.

Fredda's mouth was full of bread. She swallowed it quickly and said, "And ...who are you?"

He took his hat off and extended his left arm to shake Fredda's hand, and at the same time he said, "Hi, there, my name is Alffo Matrakka and I am Mrs. Matrakka's son. You must be Fredda, Mr. Buttler's granddaughter, aren't you? Nice to meet you, Fredda."

Fredda wanted to say, "Very nice to meet you too." But because she sometimes got distracted by peoples' appearances, she was now distracted by this boy's. He wore a crew cut which emphasized his huge pair of ears and the gap between his two front teeth. He was eighteen years old but he looked younger than his age, much younger. However, her mind snapped back to reality and she shook his left hand. "Nice to meet you, too."

Alffo sat on the opposite side of the table. "Oh! I'm starving." He grabbed a piece of bread and began eating heartily.

Alffo looked at the orchid on the table and with his mouth full said, "Interesting, nobody got the message yet from it. I bet it came from Mrs. Florizeldda's shop."

"What do you mean nobody got the message yet?" asked Fredda, chomping on her bread. She stopped chewing, "And why do you think it came from Mrs. Florizeldda's shop?"

"Well, because Mrs. Florizeldda has the widest variety of orchids in town and because I can see that the leaf in the center is still curled, so the message is still there. I have no doubt."

Alffo wasn't making any sense whatsoever, but Fredda took hold of the orchid and looked to see if the basket said anything about the flower shop. To her astonishment, the name of the shop was on the bottom of the basket in very tiny letters – Flora Florizeldda's Flower Shop. *How could I have missed that? It was the same flower shop Grandpa Albert was staring at earlier today when they left school.*

She placed the orchid back on the table, burning with curiosity about the flower now. She saw the curled leaf in the middle, as Alffo had mentioned.

"Who does this orchid belong to?" asked Alffo.

"It belongs to me!" responded Fredda.

"And why didn't you check the message yet?" asked Alffo intrigued.

"What message? There's no note in the basket. I already checked it!"

"You mean you're looking for a note?" asked Alffo. "A written note?"

"Yes, a note normally is in writing!" answered Fredda looking at the basket again.

"You don't know, do you?" asked Alffo smiling.

"Don't know *what*?" she asked confused.

"How to get the message!"

"There is no message in this basket!"

"It's very easy," said Alffo and he continued, "if the orchid was sent to you and the message is for you – you have to ask a simple question."

"And what is this simple question?"

"The question is – What is the message?"

"That's it?"

"Yes, just ask the question," said Alffo shoving a piece of bread into his mouth nonchalantly.

Fredda looked at the pink orchid, afraid of what would happen next. At the same time, she thought that maybe he was joking with his crazy story about a talking orchid.

She worked up her courage and was about to say something when Alffo said, "It's probably a good message. The color is pink."

"What do you mean the message is good because the color is pink?" asked Fredda with building curiosity, yet still thinking he might be joking.

"Because the color matters!" responded Alffo.

"The color matters?" asked Fredda curiously.

"Of course, the color matters! For example, pink represents love, but not the kind of love you're thinking. It means that someone loves you very much. Red is for love, you know, when people are *in* love. Yellow is wisdom, joy and happiness. Green is the color of nature and also means that you're going to receive good news. Blue is the color of the sky and the ocean, meaning that something big is about to happen. White means peace, a coming together after a fight or such. But, there is one color that nobody wants to receive." Alffo suddenly looked terrified.

"And what color is that?" asked Fredda, with her dark brown eyes wide open, eager to get an answer.

"The black orchid, of course!" responded Alffo tremulously, "The black orchid has a terrifying meaning. It means that someone you are close to is dead or will die or …," and he paused, "… or *you're* going to die." He shoved another piece of bread into his month and swallowed with a gulp.

Fredda had never heard such a thing! Now more than ever, she wanted to know about the message her grandpa had sent her. She took a deep breath and courageously asked the flower, "What is the message?"

The pink orchid sprouted arms of green and plucked the curly leaf from its stem. Fredda couldn't believe what she was seeing. Now, the arms seemed to unroll the curly leaf like a scroll. A voice came from somewhere inside the pink flower, "This message is for Fredda and *only* Fredda. I understand that I haven't been in your life for many years. However, I will be coming to school this Saturday to meet you for the first time. Signed, A.T.B."

The curly leaf disappeared in front of their eyes. Fredda didn't say anything for a while. She couldn't believe what she had just heard nor seen.

"And I thought you were a stupid present! I almost let you die! I even called you *stupid*," said Fredda astonished.

"Yes, you called me stupid a *few* times," the flower responded.

Fredda jumped backward. She was without words at this point. She had no idea why Grandpa Albert didn't tell her about how to get the message.

"I'm so sorry that I called *you stupid* or thought that you were a stupid present or almost let you die because I forgot to water you," Fredda apologized to the plant.

Mrs. Matrakka came in the kitchen from the study already talking up a storm. "Oh! There you are, Alffo, what are you doing here so early?"

"Well, Mom, I w… was fired from my job because I couldn't operate the machine fast enough. You know, the new machines are designed for the righties not for us lefties," said Alffo almost crying.

"I'm so tired of this world being only for the righties. They really don't care about us," hissed Mrs. Matrakka. Mrs. Matrakka's and Alffo's voices rose in pitch and volume as their rant against the injustices done to lefties continued.

Fredda managed to push the orchid back to the center of the table and to get out of the kitchen without anyone noticing that she was gone. She was already overwhelmed by her surprising discovery and the loud voices were too much for her.

As she approached the study, she heard shouting coming from the room where Grandpa Albert was with the *mysterious person*. She went closer and then, she practically glued her ear to the door trying to hear the conversation. At that moment, something touched her waist. Fredda jumped. It was Blue trying to climb on her. He was holding a photo in his mouth.

She took the photo from him and saw two people in it. One person was the younger version of Grandpa Albert. But, she wasn't sure about the other person. The picture looked old. It was black and white, and it seemed that the people in it were dressed for a party. The young Grandpa Albert was wearing a black tuxedo and the woman was dressed in a glamorous gown. The woman looked familiar. It seemed to her that she had seen this woman before.

Blue rubbed himself against the study door. "You're trying to tell me something, aren't you?"

He stretched himself against her legs and tried to reach the photo with his paws. "The people in the photo are the same people inside the library!" Fredda got Blues' message and he purred in agreement.

The doorbell rang. She was startled. She didn't know what to do. Blue ran up the steps. She followed him. She heard Mrs. Matrakka striding from the kitchen, complaining that she wouldn't have dinner ready on time. Fredda stopped at the top of the stairs, positioned herself to see the front entrance and waited.

Mrs. Matrakka opened the door and Mrs. Lerddus, the science teacher, was on the door step.

"Hi, Herta, is it true that he came back?" asked Mrs. Lerddus with excitement.

Mrs. Matrakka pulled Mrs. Lerddus from the outside so abruptly that she almost fell on the floor. The door slammed shut. "What are you doing here? You look awful as usual. Don't you ever comb your hair, Gerdha?"

"I heard that he went to school to get Fredda," responded Mrs. Lerddus, ignoring Mrs. Matrakka's comments about her hair, "He is alive, isn't he?"

"Yes, he is alive and you have no business being here," pointing her finger in Mrs. Lerddus' face.

"I need to talk to him." Her eyes scanned the room to see if anyone else was around.

"What is the matter with everybody? It seems that everyone wants to talk to him tonight," barked Mrs Matrakka.

"She is already here, isn't she?" asked Mrs. Lerddus.

"Yes, unfortunately she *is* already here," Mrs. Matrakka responded grumpily.

Suddenly, the study door opened and Grandpa Albert stepped out. Following him was a woman.

Fredda craned her neck to see. To her astonishment, it was Mrs. Lagarttus.

"Gerdha!" called Grandpa Albert.

"Oh! Albert, you *are* alive! I thought you were ..." she paused, "... dead all these years!" Mrs. Lerddus said in delight and relief. "I really need to talk to you. It's about Annora."

"What is *she* doing here?" asked Mrs. Lagarttus.

"The same thing you are," responded Mrs. Matrakka rolling her eyes, "bothering him!"

Fredda's head started spinning with all this new confusing information. She looked at the photo again. She recognized the second person in the photo. *This is Mrs. Lagarttus when she was young. She looked so beautiful. Why are they all here?*

Fredda hadn't known that Mrs. Lagarttus didn't like Mrs. Lerddus. Fredda knew that Mr. Numericcos didn't like Mrs. Maufrodezza and vice versa, but Fredda had never paid much attention to the two women's dynamics.

"All right, ladies, that is *enough*!" said Grandpa Albert imposing himself. "We are going to have a nice dinner together like a family. I will speak to you, Gerdha, after dinner. Where is Fredda, Mrs. Matrakka?"

"Probably in the kitchen with Alffo," said Mrs. Matrakka looking at the three of them.

Fredda put the photo in her pocket, and decided to go downstairs.

"Oh! There you are!" beamed Grandpa Albert. "We have company for dinner, Fredda, and I assume that you already know these two beautiful ladies."

It seemed that Grandpa Albert was flirting! *Isn't he too old to be doing this type of thing?* Fredda thought.

"Hi, Mrs. Lerddus, Mrs. Lagarttus," said Fredda. "You never told me that you knew my Grandpa."

"Well, Fredda," started Mrs. Lagarttus, very politely as usual, not like she was with Mrs. Lerddus a few minutes ago, "We have known your great-aunt, Annora, and your grandpa for many years. However, we thought that your grandpa was …" she paused and Mrs. Lerddus finished, "Dead." The two of them locked eyes.

"Well, I'm old but not dead, yet," said Grandpa Albert smiling. "Shall we go to the kitchen and have some food, in peace?"

Mrs. Matrakka put the dish cloth over her shoulder and lead the group to the kitchen. The table was already set and everybody sat down. Grandpa Albert sat at the head of the table and asked Fredda to sit next to him. The two teachers sat across from each other, while Alffo and the Mr. Gattus sat at the other end.

Mrs. Matrakka served all of them first and then she joined them at the table. But before anyone could eat, Grandpa Albert said, "Let's make a toast to my return and to my amazing granddaughter. Perhaps now, we can be a family again. I promise you, Fredda, I will not disappear from your life ever again."

Mrs. Lerddus looked at Grandpa Albert with fear in her eyes while Fredda smiled, showing her beautiful dimples.

CHAPTER 8

THE OTHER SIDE

Fredda began to wake from the depths of sleep with the memory of a dream she had had about her family. But as sleep left her eyes and she looked around, it appeared that her dream was a reality. She was in her grandparent's house, not at school anymore. Next to the alarm, which was showing almost 12:00 p.m., was the picture of her parents which Grandpa Albert had given to her.

Blue was sleeping, not on his bed, but on Fredda's. She had never slept so late in her entire life, not even when she was sick. She could hear noises coming from downstairs, people talking.

She got up, took a fast shower and put on one of her new outfits. It felt good not having to wear that awful uniform.

She walked towards the bedroom window and saw the dense vegetation outside soaked with rain. It seemed like it had rained the whole night but the sky looked an even darker gray. She stayed there for a while thinking. But one thing in particular stood out in her thoughts - the talking orchid. *How's it possible that an orchid could talk?* She'd never seen anything like it. *And why didn't grandpa say anything about it?*

She'd love to share this news with Tildda. Perhaps, she should write to Tildda and tell her or maybe not. Tildda would never believe her. She'd think that Fredda had gone crazy. She tried to put herself in Tildda's shoes. If she'd received a letter telling her about a talking flower, she wouldn't believe it either.

She had even more questions now. It seemed that everyone she had been in contact with since she left school was a leftie. She had never seen so many at once. Fredda planned to ask Grandpa Albert about her family, the talking orchid, her problems at school, and even about Mrs. Cellestin. *Maybe Grandpa Albert knew Mrs. Cellestin*, she thought. All of these questions were imprinted in her mind. However, Fredda didn't know where to begin.

She went downstairs to the kitchen. She heard Grandpa Albert's voice as she entered. He stopped his conversation and said, "Oh! There you are! I thought I'd have to wake you up." He smiled. He folded the newspaper and continued, "Well, I think you can skip breakfast. Lunch is going to be served soon."

She didn't see the sling around Grandpa Albert's neck anymore. She wonder why.

The chauffeur, Mr. Gattus, Alffo and Mrs. Matrakka were there as well. Mrs. Matrakka was already glued to the stove.

Fredda didn't want to remember school, but the wonderful smell of the food reminded her of the only good thing about it, the meals. Mrs. Matrakka proved to be a great cook, like Mrs. Camerron, her twin sister.

"Sit down, Fredda," as her grandfather pointed to the seat next to his. "We are all waiting for lunch," he smiled. "The weather seems to be extremely harsh today so maybe we should do something indoors? What would you like to do?"

Fredda wasn't used to be asked what she wanted to do, quite the opposite. She had always followed someone else's directions. She didn't know what to say and it seemed that everybody was listening for her answer.

"Well," started Fredda, "Maybe we can …" but she couldn't think of anything. After all the time she'd spent behind the school's gates thinking about escaping, now that she could go anywhere, she couldn't think of a single place except for the hospital to visit Mrs. Cellestin. *Would that be a bad idea?*

She started again, "Maybe we can go to the …"

Someone rang the doorbell over and over while also banging loudly on the door.

"Oh! I cannot believe it!" said Mrs. Matrakka irritated.

"Since you came home these people are going nuts. They have to see you in person, don't they? The fact that you are alive is not good enough for them. They have to see you in the flesh, don't they?" She rolled her eyes and strode to the front door and at the same time she told Alffo to look at the stove. "And if you let the lunch burn, I'll cook *you* up!" She wasn't kidding.

Alffo got up as quickly as he could to watch the stove so he wouldn't get into trouble.

Fredda Buttler And The Left-Handed People

Everyone in the kitchen could hear Mrs. Matrakka yelling to the person outside the door that she was coming and they didn't have to continue with all the noise.

For a moment, silence took over the house. The doorbell and the knocking stopped.

Mrs. Matrakka came back and looked as if she had seen a ghost. "It's for you, Mr. Buttler," she said in a daze.

"Who is it?" asked Grandpa Albert.

"It is not *who*, it is *what*," she replied.

Grandpa Albert stood up and strode to the front door like Mrs. Matrakka had done before and Mrs. Matrakka and Mr. Gattus followed him. Fredda and Alffo followed behind. Although, Mr. Gattus told them to stay in the kitchen, they continued as far as they could without anybody seeing them.

There it was, a man with a flower in his hand. Not only a flower but an *orchid*. Not only an orchid but the most terrifying color of them all, a *black* orchid.

Fredda wanted to say something, but Alffo put his hand in front of her mouth and gestured that she shouldn't make any noise.

The delivery man said, "Are you Mr. Buttler, Albert T. Buttler, sir?"

"Yes, I am Albert T. Buttler."

"I have a delivery for you, sir."

The delivery man passed the black orchid to Grandpa Albert and stayed there waiting. Grandpa stood shocked, staring at it as did Mrs. Matrakka and Mr. Gattus.

Meanwhile, the delivery man cleared his throat. No one noticed. The man cleared his throat again and Mrs. Matrakka replied, "Aren't you ashamed to be there waiting for something after delivering this horrible thing to us?"

It was Mr. Gattus who reached into his pocket and tipped him. Mrs. Matrakka closed the door and the three of them went into the study.

In the kitchen, Fredda and Alffo looked at each other in horror, thinking about the black orchid. Alffo even forgot about the stove.

"This is bad news, isn't it?" asked Fredda nervously.

"Yes, I'm afraid so. But you have to remember that might be bad news about a friend of your grandpa not necessarily him or …" he paused, "… us."

"But, we might all be in danger," said Fredda, disturbed, "Remember what you said to me yesterday? You said, that it means someone you're close to died, will die or *you're* going to die."

"Yes, I know what I said."

"Maybe this time will be different, nobody will die or no one is already dead," her voice trembled.

"The black orchid is never … wrong. It'll happen or it has already happened. I hate to say that to you, Fredda."

Alffo went back to take care of the stove.

Fredda and Alffo heard the three of them coming towards the kitchen. Grandpa Albert was the first to enter. He came directly to Fredda and looked at her. "I understand if you never forgive me, but I have to break the promise I made to you last night. I'll have to go away and I have no idea when I'll be back. You'll have to go elsewhere because this house is not safe for us anymore, none of us."

"But Grandpa, I want to go with you. I don't want to be apart from you. You're my only family." Fredda begged.

"I understand, Fredda, but you must not come with me! I cannot tell you the details now, but I am in grave danger and I cannot let you and the others stay with me." Grandpa Albert looked into Fredda's eyes sadly.

"Danger?" repeated Fredda.

"Yes, my dear Fredda, *extreme danger*." He hugged Fredda around her shoulders.

She decided not to ask more questions. Alffo had warned her about the black orchid and now she knew that Alffo had told her the truth.

"Mrs. Matrakka, please go upstairs with Fredda and help her pack. Please pack light, perhaps for two or three days at the most. And Mrs. Matrakka, do it quickly, very quickly."

"Yes, sir," she responded.

"Mr. Gattus and you, Alffo, come with me to the study, we have a lot to do and we must move fast."

"What about lunch?" asked Alffo, "I didn't eat yet!"

Grandpa Albert gave Alffo a dirty look. Alffo was the first to leave the kitchen and they all followed.

A few minutes later, Fredda and Mrs. Matrakka joined Grandpa Albert and Mr. Gattus in the study. Fredda carried a light backpack. She noticed that Alffo wasn't there anymore. Perhaps Grandpa had given him something to do already.

"Oh! There you are, Fredda. Let's go through the kitchen," said Grandpa Albert in a hurry. Everybody followed him.

They went inside the kitchen and out the back door which led to a green house full of plants, especially orchids. They went through the green house to the open yard in the back of the house.

Fredda saw the thick vegetation and a narrow pass leading to denser and bulkier green trees. The light was dim. The sun couldn't penetrate the vegetation. The rainy day and the light fog made the passage even darker. Fredda heard sounds of mysterious creatures. However, she wasn't afraid. She had people protecting her. *I'd never come to this side of the yard by myself,* she thought. *Even the tunnels at school are more desirable than this passage.*

Fredda heard the sound of water running. The sound became louder as they approached a sharp left curve where there was a wooden covered bridge. The passage became even darker. The fog threw a dense blanket over them.

Grandpa Albert stopped walking and Fredda bumped into him as she covered her mouth and gasped. She'd never seen a covered bridge before. She looked up. "Sorry, Grandpa Albert," said Fredda.

"It's okay, Fredda. I had the same reaction when I saw this passage and the bridge for the first time."

He went to the edge of the bridge and picked up a lantern that had been left there. He lit it and gave it to Fredda.

"Well, Fredda, now I want you to pay close attention to what I have to tell you. From this point on, you are going to go by yourself."

"You're kidding, aren't you? You want me to go walking over this dark bridge by myself?" she said disbelievingly.

"Yes, Fredda, that is what you are going to do," responded Grandpa Albert.

"And why should I do that?" asked Fredda.

"Because you have to trust me."

Fredda considered this for a moment and said, "I barely know you and you already broke your promise. Why should I trust you?"

"I understand your feelings, Fredda. But you need to know that in life the truth can go in two directions. It can kill you or it can set you free." Grandpa Albert looked deeply into her eyes.

Fredda didn't really understand anything at all. "And if I don't want to go? What are you going to do?" challenged Fredda.

"Well, then I'll have to bring you back to school and you'll have to be there by yourself the whole summer."

Anything sounded better than going back to school. But in this situation, it was between going back to school or going inside that scary bridge. Fredda stopped to ponder her choice.

"Sir, we have to go soon." Mr. Gattus checked their surroundings. Mrs. Matrakka's eyes flitted around nervously.

"Yes, I know Mr. Gattus," responded Grandpa Albert.

"However, I need a moment here with my granddaughter. I can see your point, Fredda. I would also be afraid if someone who I had just met had told me that I have to walk over a dark bridge by myself. So, why don't I walk with you? You give me the lantern and I'll give you my hand."

Fredda, somewhat relieved, passed the lantern to him and he extended his hand to her. She clasped her fingers around it and there they went, into the darkness. Even with the lantern illuminating the way, it was difficult to see.

After a few steps, Grandpa Albert let go of Fredda's hand, but he stood beside her. They looked at each other, and when Fredda turned straight ahead again, there it was - the other side of the bridge.

Fredda saw the light and the vegetation again. She also saw a woman. Fredda looked back and saw the darkness now behind them. She faced Grandpa Albert and was going to say something, but it was Grandpa Albert who spoke, "Fredda, I know that you have a lot of questions about our family and I have a lot of explaining to do, but I really have to go now. I am so sorry that Annora didn't prepare you for this. However, now I understand why she did *not* tell you anything. She was trying to *protect* you."

"Protect me, from what?"

Grandpa Albert ignored Fredda's question and proceeded to say, "I have to go now, Fredda. Over there, that's Mrs. Rutta Theoddora, she'll be taking care of you. You must promise me that you are going to obey her. She is doing me a great favor. One more very important thing, Fredda, always think about the future. Pay attention to the present, and never forget the past, *never*! Just remember that. I will be back and I love you very much." Grandpa Albert turned around and walked away.

Fredda didn't know what to say. She saw Mrs. Theoddora waving to her. Fredda waved back tentatively. By the time Fredda looked back, Grandpa Albert was gone.

Fredda thought for a moment, *What was all that about?* Fredda continued, sadly, across the bridge toward the heavy set old lady with the silver gray braid hanging down her back.

Mrs. Theoddora smiled, "Hello, Fredda, look at you all grown up! Welcome back to Ellivnioj."

"Elliv what?" asked Fredda confused.

"Ellivnioj, of course. Your grandpa did not tell you about it?" asked Mrs. Theoddora surprised and a bit perplexed.

"No, not really. He was in a hurry, had a lot on his mind," she said bewildered. "Excuse me, Mrs. Theoddora, but you said, 'Welcome back?'. I think you're mistaken. I've never been here before. I would've remembered this place for sure."

"Oh, Fredda, of course, you've been here before! You just don't remember. You were too little to remember. Actually you were born here in Ellivnioj," beamed Mrs. Theoddora.

"Born here, in *this* place?" Fredda was now totally lost.

"But I thought I was born in …" but before Fredda could finish, Mrs. Theoddora said, "The other side, The Right Side, as we call it."

"I don't understand, Mrs. Theoddora, Right Side? Is there another side?"

"Of course, there is. This side, The Left Side, is where the majority of people are left-handed like you and me. Welcome to The Left Side. Welcome to Ellivnioj."

"The Left Side?"

"Yes, indeed. The only place we can be free to be ourselves. The only place we can be free to discover ourselves without being pushed by society or being called names."

Fredda thought about the last part of what Mrs. Theoddora said, *'being called names'.* "What names do they call us?"

Mrs. Theoddora looked directly in Fredda eyes, "You really do not want to know about the names they called us, and besides, without left-handed people, life would not be right," she finished with a big smile.

Fredda thought about what Maufrodezza and Numericoss would've thought about the last part of that phrase.

"Shall we go? Our ride is coming." Mrs. Theoddora pointed to the beginning of a narrow path.

They walked toward the dense green vegetation. The fog was as thick as mud. Fredda became flabbergasted as a small building suddenly emerged from it. She looked up and saw a small square tower with circular windows on both sides. The tower was topped with a square based witches' hat roof.

As they approached, Fredda saw a small flight of steps. She carefully walked up to the platform. *No tracks! Can't be a train station then!* Fredda thought. *Can't be a bus station! The road is too narrow for a bus or even a car to fit through!*

Fredda looked around. There was a huge clock on the tower wall. However, all the numbers were in reverse order except for the numbers twelve and six. It was a bit confusing. The clock showed 1:00 p.m. However, it looked like it was 11:00 a.m. Right below the clock, Fredda could read, painted on the wall - Forbidden Words.

She approached the wall and saw a list of words – magic, magician, spell, wizard, sorcerer, sorcery, witch, witchcraft, curse, jinx, enchantment, charm, cauldron, Halloween, incantation, witchery, warlock, wand, crystal ball, broomstick, conjure, coven, potion.

"Mrs. Theoddora, why is it forbidden to say mag ..." and Mrs. Theoddora put her hand over Fredda's mouth, looked to her left and also to her right side to see if anyone was coming.

Staring straight into Fredda's eyes she whispered, "Those words, Fredda, those words were the reason we have a bad reputation. Those words are the reason so many of us were killed a long time ago. You must not say them aloud! Whenever you need to say any of these words, you must s-p-e-l-l them." Mrs. Theoddora looked around again to see if anyone was there, watching them.

Fredda stared at her. In the past two days, she had heard the word *kill* twice. Never before, had Fredda heard such a thing!

Ring, ring, ring. Fredda heard the sound of a bell coming from the darkness. The narrow road was the color of black velvet and the thick fog didn't make it easy to see anything. Fredda approached the edge of the low platform and a man riding a strange vehicle drew her attention. It reminded her of a horse drawn carriage, but it was a bright yellow bicycle pulling a convertible covered carriage, perfect for two people.

"Finally, Mr. Bernno, what happened? You are late!" said Mrs. Theoddora a bit impatiently. She sounded just like Tildda when Tildda got impatient.

Mr. Bernno took a deep breath, "I am so very, very, very sorry. Rutta, I had a flat."

He was a skinny man and looked quite short, but Fredda couldn't tell for sure, because he was sitting on the bike. He wore a funny brown helmet, goggles, like he was going to take off in a rocket, a brown leather jacket, dark pants and high brown boots. He also wore a pair of brown leather gloves, that didn't cover the fingers, only his palms. Mr. Bernno removed his goggles, and Fredda realized that the only clean thing on his face was the outline of the goggles around his eyes. In them, she could see madness.

"To my house, Mr. Bernno, please!" ordered Mrs. Theoddora.

"Yes, yes, yes, Rutta."

Mrs. Theoddora could tell that Fredda was somewhat nervous after meeting Mr. Bernno. She explained, "I know Mr. Bernno may seem strange to you. He repeats words at least three times. However, he is a genius when it comes to fixing bicycles. He owns a bicycle shop in town called Bikes for All. He knows everything about them."

Fredda was slightly relieved as they clambered inside the cart and left. The overgrown vegetation lined the road. Fredda couldn't see much other than the green and the fog. They were on this narrow road for a while.

Much had changed since Fredda had left school a day ago. Still, so many questions, however, so few answers. There was still a great deal Fredda didn't know about her family, her Grandpa Albert and his friends.

The weather didn't look very promising. The vegetation continued to be so green and thick that Fredda could barely see the sky. It was cold and humid for this time of year. She observed her surroundings, but she wasn't sure what to look for. She also wanted to remember the path they were taking from the bicycle station to wherever they might go.

After a while on that road, the surroundings changed abruptly. It seemed they had gone to another planet. Fredda saw the sun shining brightly, and felt the warmth on her face. It was wonderful to see the sun for the first time in weeks.

As they drove along the narrow road, Fredda found herself awash in a kaleidoscope of colors. The azure sky, bright flowers and the verdant green grass on the sides of the road made the place picture perfect. Mr. Bernno zoomed along.

A sharp left curve and boom, the scenery changed again. Now it seemed that they were on a main street. Fredda saw several people riding bikes on its gray cobblestone. The street was charming but became quite congested with traffic. Mr. Bernno began peddling very slowly.

Small, quaint, old buildings, and their window boxes overflowing with collections of gorgeous flowers, decorated each side of the narrow road. People walked along the slim sidewalks in front of them.

Alongside Mr. Bernno's vehicle, were many other riders pedaling a wide variety of bicycles. Old, new, wildly painted, sparkly, single, double and triple seats, high, low, two wheels, three wheels, four wheels, covered, uncovered. One rode by with a large front wheel and a tiny rear one. Fredda had never seen so many bicycles at once. In fact, she realized that she had never ridden one in her life, but she was interested in trying one now.

Fredda was excited and intrigued by the town. Her mind went spinning back to what Mrs. Theoddora had told her when they met, *I was born in this town.*

Mrs. Theoddora noticed Fredda's astonishment, but didn't say anything. There were so many things to see that it seemed for a moment that Fredda had forgotten that Mrs. Theoddora was there by her side.

They passed in front of a small square and there was another big reverse clock like the one in the bike station. Fredda's questions kept piling up in her mind. Suddenly, a house caught her attention. The sign said, Flora Florizeldda's Flower Shop, the same shop's name from which Fredda had gotten the orchid as a present from Grandpa Albert! The same shop's name located in front of her school!

The house was a two story, pointed chalet painted blue, like the sky, surrounded by bright flowers everywhere. All kinds of flowers – tulips, sun flowers, daisies, gingers, bougainvillea, roses, begonias, violets but the predominant ones were orchids. It was by far, the most charming place on that street. Shops and more shops, as they were passing by, and another shop caught Fredda's attention. The sign said, Don't Be Left Out.

Mrs. Theoddora yelled, "Please, Mr. Bernno, could you stop for a moment? I need to buy some things at Don't Be Left Out."

"Of course, of course, of course, Rutta."

Mrs. Theoddora got out of the cart, looked at Fredda and said, "Aren't you coming with me?" Fredda gave her a big dimpled smile. That was exactly what she was hoping for. She was extremely interested to see what the store was all about.

They entered and to Fredda's surprise, there were many things to see, but nothing looked any different from the other stores Fredda had gone into before. Not that she had seen a lot of stores before, but she had been to some in the past.

The first thing Fredda saw was a pair of scissors. She grabbed one and it was like putting on a new pair of gloves. It fit her left hand so well and it didn't feel awkward! It felt like it had been made for her left hand. Next to it was a note about the product. It said, "Better fit & better cut. Please try now!" Fredda took a piece of paper from the pile next to the sign and cut it.

Fredda Buttler And The Left-Handed People

For the first time, she could see the line when she was cutting and she actually cut a straight one.

The next thing that caught Fredda's attention was the can opener. Fredda remembered that painful day, the big zero grade she and her friends had gotten back at school because of this stupid gadget. *It would be nice to have one of those,* Fredda thought.

As she was admiring one of them, Mrs. Theoddora said, "Would you like to have one? I can buy it for you as a present."

"Oh!" said Fredda. "Yes, thank you, Mrs. Theoddora, it'll be very useful."

"I know it will," responded Mrs. Theoddora. She moved back to the counter and continued talking to the person who was helping her with the merchandise.

Meanwhile, Fredda wanted to see everything at once. She kept moving around and found more interesting things like rulers with the number zero starting from the right side followed by the number one. Again, the numbers were in reverse, but easy for her to use. There was a tape measure with the same concept as the ruler, wrist watches, and of course, with all the numbers in reverse like the big clock at the bicycle station. She saw mugs on which she was able to see the decoration when she held it with her left hand. There were card decks with the numbers on the top right side of the cards and the bottom number placed on the left side. Not that it made any difference to Fredda. She didn't know how to play cards anyway. There were numerous tools for the garden, which were very pleasant to hold. Spiral notebooks, where the back became the front. There were many items at this store that Fredda had seen before, but each one that

Fredda grabbed with her left hand seemed like it was made just for her.

Another entrance led Fredda to another side of the store. She read the sign on top of the door frame, Books for Lefties. She was puzzled. *What is a book for lefties?*

It looked like the two stores were connected, even though both stores had its own main entrance. She walked into the bookstore and looked on the shelves. She noticed that all of them had the cover where normally the book ends. Fredda took down one of them, held the book with her right hand, flipped the pages with her left hand and found that they were so easy to flip.

The silence was broken. Mrs. Theoddora was calling her. "I know that you are intrigued by all this merchandise, but we have to go now. Well, come back another day."

They were back on the road with Mr. Bernno pedaling, but they didn't stay on the road for long. He stopped in front of the Windmill Diner. Right below its name in smaller letters it read - Breakfast, Lunch and Dinner.

Fredda slowly looked upwards and saw the most magnificent windmill ever. She could hear the blades above moving slowly. Fredda was fascinated by this piece of architecture. The building was round, made of red bricks, and yellow flowers were placed in wooden boxes in front of each window.

"Like it?" asked Mrs. Theoddora.

Fredda nodded her head. She was still looking up with her eyes open wide.

"Here is where you are going to stay, Fredda. This is my house and the place where I work. It was built by my family many years ago."

Fredda couldn't believe that she was going to stay in such a cool place.

"Hungry?" asked Mrs. Theoddora.

Fredda was still looking up and only nodded her head.

Then she realized she hadn't eaten breakfast. She had awakened late. She hadn't even eaten lunch because of the delivery man, so she answered, "Starving." Then she realized that she sounded just like Olliver. He was always hungry.

Mrs. Theoddora led Fredda inside. The main room was round like the outside, very clean and very homey with checkered table cloths and matching curtains. The walls were packed with black and white photographs and there were lots of books around like in Grandpa Albert's home.

They went all the way back to an adjacent room and there were the stairs leading to the next level. They climbed at least three or four floors.

There it was - her room.

Mrs. Theoddora opened the door and Fredda walked in. The room was neat and painted light green. Through the large picture window, Fredda could see the windmill's blades turning. There were two single beds with a nightstand for each. Placed on the left side of the beds, were lamps and on the opposite wall stood a fireplace. There was a full book case and a clock with the numbers reversed, marking 2:00 p.m. Pleasant landscape paintings hung on the walls. Fredda caught her reflection in an old full length mirror. She saw herself standing in her own room for the very first time.

"Fredda, leave your backpack here and wash up. The bathroom is in the hallway. When you are done come downstairs for lunch."

Because she was so hungry, she didn't hesitate and responded quickly, "Yes, Mrs. Theoddora."

Minutes later, Fredda went downstairs, sat down at one of the many tables in front of the window so she could see the tumult outside. She was excited and also starving. The smell of the food coming from the kitchen was marvelous.

Unexpectedly, a boy appeared in front of her. She jumped backwards in her seat, and the tray with the food that he was carrying almost ended up on the floor, but he managed to catch it before it was too late.

"I'm so sorry. I didn't mean to scare you," the boy apologized.

He was about thirteen years old and was wearing a white apron. He was taller than Fredda, had straight dark hair, dark eyes and he was extremely pale. However, he had a beautiful smile.

"You must be Fredda! My grandparents told me that you're going to be here with us for summer," the boy said smiling, and he continued, "Very good, I hope you like chicken soup, bread, salad and a delicious chocolate cake for dessert. Oh, by the way, my name is Bennjamin Theoddora, but everyone calls me Benn."

He extended his left hand to greet Fredda. With no hesitation she extended her left hand to greet him back. But Benn didn't let go of her hand, extended his right hand, crossing his right arm over their already entwined ones. Fredda paused at first, but brought up her right hand and shook it crisscross style.

Immediately, without even thinking, Fredda asked him, "What is this crisscross shaking all about?"

"Don't you know?" asked Benn, surprised.

"No," responded Fredda.

Fredda Buttler And The Left-Handed People

"This is your first time in Ellivnioj, I guess?"

"Yes."

"Okay, well, there are two ways of greeting people in Ellivnioj. The first is left shake, if you are totally lefty, and it's the most popular one. The other way is the ambidextrous way."

"Wait, the ambi what?"

"Ambidextrous, people who can do things with both hands."

"You mean that you can do anything with both of your hands?" exclaimed Fredda.

"Yes, I can!" said Benn, folding his arms in front of his chest and feeling very proud about it.

The food was still lying on the table untouched. Fredda thought a moment and then asked him, "But if you're left-handed and the other person is right-handed, how do they greet each other?"

"That's very easy! The left always dominates in Ellivnioj, like the right dominates on the other side, The Right Side. Nobody shakes hands with their left in The Right Side, do they?"

Fredda shook her head. However, she thought for a moment about Maufrodezza and Numericoss. *If it were up to them, left-handed people wouldn't even exist.*

"So, aren't you going to eat?" asked Benn worried that maybe she didn't like the kind of food he had brought for her.

"Oh! Yes, I'm going to eat, of course!"

Mrs. Theoddora shouted Benn's name. He said a quick goodbye and ran to the kitchen.

Meanwhile, Fredda devoured the food like there would be no tomorrow. Once more, no matter what side Fredda was on, the food was unbelievably delicious.

CHAPTER 9

ONLY A LEGEND?

Fredda woke up late the next morning, after having difficulty falling asleep the night before. She needed to get used to the sound of the blades from the windmill.

She got up and went directly to the window. It was sunny. Fredda could feel the warmth of the sun through the window glass. She noticed that the chaotic street below was even more frenzied than yesterday.

There was a knock at the door. Fredda, still in her pajamas, opened it and she saw a familiar face with those big ears and the gap between his front teeth.

"Hi, Alffo," smiled Fredda.

"Hi, there," said Alffo taking his hat off. "These are the rest of your things that you left at your grandpa's house."

He carried a small suitcase, "And this is a letter for you from your grandpa."

"Funny. Why didn't he send me a flower?" asked Fredda.

"Well …" responded Alffo a bit uneasy, "Well, I didn't tell your grandpa that I told you about the flower ... I mean, the orchid, well … the message … y… you know what I mean. I managed to put your flower in the green house after you got the message, so he wouldn't get suspicious. I guess your grandpa doesn't know yet that you know about the talking flower, the message, you know what I mean," Alffo whispered.

"Yes, yes, I know what you mean." She thought, *If it wasn't for him, I would never have known about the message.*

"Besides, people only use this type of orchid for very important messages," Alffo continued whispering.

"Important messages?" Fredda whispered back.

"Important stuff, important things that people want to keep secret or don't want others to know about their business." He looked around, making sure nobody was near.

"Umm," Fredda pondered. She couldn't understand then why Grandpa Albert had sent her a message through a flower when he didn't want her to know about them. It didn't make any sense.

"Well, Fredda, I have to go."

"Wait, do you know why there are so many people outside?" asked Fredda.

"Don't you know about the festival?" Alffo sounded surprised.

"No, what festival?"

"The festival! The festival to celebrate Left-Handed People's Day. August 13th is International Lefthanders Day. Big day, big celebration, especially this year."

"Why is this year so special?"

"Because this year, the 13th will be on a Friday. Friday the 13th. Awesome, isn't it?" Alffo was all excited and he added, "Well, I have to go now. I'll see you around, Freddda. I got a job at Handless Pizzeria here in town, for the summer."

"Oh! That's great, Alffo. So, I'll see you around and thank you for bringing me my things."

"Welcome, bye then," returned Alffo already walking away.

"See ya," said Fredda, still thinking about the festival and her birthday. *I can't believe that Left-Handed People's Day and my birthday are on the same day! Weird how lefties, are celebrated here, but on The Right Side Maufrodezza and Numericoss hate me because I'm a lefty!*

Fredda tore open the envelope, almost ripping the letter in two pieces, and read aloud.

Dear Fredda,

Sorry about last time we saw each other. I had to run, and we did not have time to get to know each other better. There are still some things that I have to tell you, but as I said before, it is a bit complicated. I need some time to really have a long talk with you and tell you more.

However, I will be back. I am not sure yet when that may be. Perhaps, at the end of the summer.

Please, obey Mrs. Theoddora. She is really a lovely lady and doing me a great favor, as I already told you. I am well, don't worry about me. I hope you like the town, and I hope you have a wonderful vacation. I left you some money. It is with Mrs. Theoddora. Spend it wisely!

I love you,
Grandpa Albert

Fredda sat on the wide windowsill and looked down at the street below. She couldn't make any sense of almost anything that had happened to her in these last two days. Maybe the truth *is* complicated, as Grandpa Albert had told her. But she pulled her mind back. She focused on the fact that she wasn't in that awful school for a change, and on what a special birthday she would have with the festival being celebrated on the same day. '*Big day, big celebration!*', as Alffo had said.

Fredda stayed by the window for a while before she decided to start her day outside her bedroom. She opened her suitcase and laid out some of her fresh clothes. She had difficulty choosing, since ordinarily, she never wore anything other than her unpleasant uniform.

On the way to change, as she was passing the long mirror, she turned and her face stared back at her. Her reflection told her that she needed a shower and a brush for her messy hair. She reached up with her left hand to smooth her stray strands. As Fredda did this, she watched her image in the mirror raise her left arm too. But this was opposite of a mirror's illusion! Fredda frowned and tilted only her head to the left. Her mirror-self imitated her tilt exactly. The head of the girl in the mirror facing her also tilted her head to her left. Fredda brought her left hand up to scratch her nose. She gasped. The mirror was more than reflecting her! It was revealing her *true* self and urging her to use the dominant hand she was born with proudly.

This was unlike any other mirror that she had ever seen on The Right Side!

Then, Fredda caught an almost imperceptible ripple in the mirror. *Could the mirror be liquid?* She lifted her left hand and very carefully reached out her index finger toward it. She felt that something extraordinary was about to happen. Tentatively, she moved her finger closer … almost there … so close, and just then, someone knocked loudly on the door. Startled, Fredda jumped backward, her heart pounding. The knocking continued. Then someone called her name from the other side of the door.

Fredda waited another minute, took a deep breath, exhaled, and pulled it open. A blond girl bounced into the bedroom. Still flustered, it took Fredda a moment to realized that the blond girl was *Tildda*. Benn stood in the entrance with her.

"Fredda?" said Tildda. "I can't believe you're here! I just got here. I always think about you when I get here and how nice it would be to have you here with me! It's going to be a super summer now! Benn already told me about your grandpa. Isn't it wonderful that you have someone in your life after all?" Tildda was euphoric.

"Wait a minute! Why are you here? Why didn't you ever tell me about this place? I THOUGHT YOU WERE MY FRIEND, AND YET YOU NEVER TOLD ME ABOUT ELLIVNIOJ!" Fredda shouted at Tildda.

"I WANTED TO TELL YOU, ALWAYS!" Tildda shouted back at her. But Fredda didn't want to hear her friend's excuses. She continued yelling over Tildda's words.

"HOW CAN YOU BE MY FRIEND WHEN YOU HIDE THINGS FROM ME?" The shouting went on.

"I'M STILL YOUR FRIEND BUT …"

Benn interrupted by slamming the door and shouting even louder, "SHUT UP!" so loudly that probably the whole entire windmill could hear him.

"Sorry, girls, but you have to give it a break. There are things, Fredda, that you should know before going crazy on Tildda," Benn said with a straight face.

BUT SHE LIED TO ME!" exclaimed Fredda.

"I DID NOT!"

"CALM DOWN!" yelled Ben again.

Fredda sat down on the windowsill, her favorite place, and Tildda sat down on the second bed. Benn stood and rubbed his hands together, "Well …" and then another knock on the door.

Benn was closest, so he opened it and there was yet *another* surprise for her. It was Noell.

"Hi, Benn, your grandma told me that I could find you here with Tildda."

"YOU TOO?" shouted Fredda, "You also lied to me? What's going on here?"

"Fredda? What are you doing here?" Noell asked.

"I should ask you the same question, shouldn't I?"

"What did *I* do? Remember, my father's a lefty and we always come here for the festival," Noell finished, still confused that Fredda was there.

"AND YOU COULDN'T TELL ME AT SCHOOL THAT YOU COME HERE EVERY SUMMER? I THOUGHT BOTH OF YOU WERE MY FRIENDS!" Fredda was getting angrier and angrier. She stared at them, wishing someone would give her a straight answer for once.

It was Benn who spoke. "Well, as I was trying to tell you before, is that only the true left-handed person will remember what's going on here in Ellivnioj."

"What do you mean?" not quite understanding this whole conversation.

"What I'm trying to say is that Tildda and Noell are not lying to you, Fredda. They're telling you the truth."

"But, I still don't understand," even more aggravated by his lack of clarity.

"What I'm trying to tell you is, because Tildda and Noel are right-handed, when they cross over from this side to The Right Side, they won't remember anything whatsoever. But when they come here, to Ellivnioj, they can remember everything from The Right Side. Unless you are a *true* lefty, you'll not remember both sides. That's why this place is not known by all lefties, only by the true lefties. And believe me when I say not by *all* lefties, otherwise this place would be more likely the third most populated country in the world! Only true lefties can bring themselves here and also bring others like me, Tildda or Noell.

Fredda nodded tentatively, knit her brow and pursed her lips, but the explanation made some kind of sense. She said, "But you told me, Tildda, that you were going to France to see your grandma. And you, Noell, you told me that you were going to Egypt or some other place that I don't remember now, back in school."

"Yes, and I'm going to meet my father's mother in France. It's her favorite place in the world. But, I always come here to see my mother's mom before I go to France or any other place. My father is too busy to join us for the whole vacation, so I come here with my mother alone. Mom is an ambi like Benn."

"The same with me," said Noell. "I always come here with my parents and then we go someplace else after, before the summer is over."

"Oh! And by the way, Fredda, before you tell us that we didn't tell you this before, Tildda and I, we're cousins. My grandma, Theoddora, is her grandma also. Tildda will be sharing this room with you," completed Benn.

It was all too much for Fredda to comprehend at that moment. It was like there was a new life waiting for her to discover in Ellivnioj.

No one said a word for a long time. The only noise that could be heard was the blade from the windmill outside. But the silence was broken by another intruder. It was Blue who came from under the bed and jumped on Fredda's lap. She petted him and said, "Blue, are you hiding things from me too? What are you doing here?" Blue only purred.

Fredda considered everything - the school, her Grandpa Albert, Ellivnioj, the summer, her first vacation. So many questions to ask Grandpa Albert, and now Tildda and Noell!

The silence hovered over all of them. Finally, Tildda couldn't help herself, "Anyone hungry?"

"Starving," said Fredda, just like Olliver back in school. Everybody laughed.

"It's going to be a super summer this year!" said Tildda enthusiastically, "What are you doing in your pajamas? It's vacation time, Fredda! Free time! I thought it'd be a boring summer again here in Ellivnioj, but now that you're here with us, it's going to be *so* exciting!" Tildda jabbered on.

Noell and Benn went downstairs and waited for Fredda. Tildda stayed with her friend so she could, of course, ask her a bunch of questions. "So, tell me about your grandfather."

"There's not much to say. I don't really know him at all."

"Well, but aren't you happy that you have someone else in your life? I mean, a member of your family?"

"Well, I can't say that I'm not happy, as you see I'm here because of him, but at the same time I really can't wrap my mind around where he's been all these years," said Fredda, trying to figured out what to wear.

"Jail?"

"What?" said Fredda, dropping her new shirt on the floor.

"Jail, he was probably in jail," repeated Tildda.

Fredda's mouth dropped, and she couldn't bring it to close. *How could I not have thought about such a simple explanation? That was it! Grandpa Albert was too ashamed to tell me about jail. Instead, he told me all that stuff about trying to find my parents.*

Fredda didn't say a word to Tildda. She sped off to take a fast shower and to put on her new clothes.

The two of them then met with Noell and Benn at the diner. The diner was packed. However, Benn improvised an old wooden table and four wooden stools in a corner where they were surrounded by old books. Fredda had a chance to take a good look at them. She realized that they were for left-handed people. *The Lefties* as they were proudly called here.

Benn and Noell arranged the food on the table. Each one of them dove at it and began stuffing their faces.

Fredda, with her mouth full of mashed potato, asked them, "Can you tell me about the festival?"

"Ah, yes, the festival!" said Tildda thrilled. "The festival is to celebrate International Lefthanders Day." Fredda already knew about that. "And there's a lot to see, like the bicycle parade, the dance, art and food festival." Tildda shoved some pasta into her mouth.

"And the orchid festival at which they choose the most beautiful orchid," added Noell, opening his mouth so some beef stew could go in. He continued with a full mouth, "They say that the orchids have some kind of mysterious way of communicating with people."

Fredda stared. "What do you mean?"

"Well, they say that there are some orchids that can talk to you, that they can delivery some kind of private message when the sender doesn't want anybody else to know about its contents."

"But I've never seen one, yet. They say that it has to be a very rare orchid," said Benn looking at everybody. "It's only a legend."

Fredda was surprised that she actually knew something about the lefties that the three others didn't. She felt uneasy. Fredda thought about Grandpa Albert and why he hadn't told her the truth about the message. Maybe he had an important reason for not telling her. She felt that this moment wasn't the right one to tell them also, so she kept it to herself.

"Ah! Don't forget the draft beer festival, but this year there won't be alcoholic beer. There were too many drunken people last year after all the free beer. The mess was unbelievable!" chuckled Benn.

The loud chatter of the people in the packed diner and the clatter of plates and forks were so loud that the four of them could barely hear themselves.

Fredda scanned all the happy people talking, screaming, laughing and even singing songs to the tunes of a small upright piano on the other side of the diner. She smiled broadly.

"See that piano?" said Benn, "That's the first piano built for lefties. All the keys are in reverse. It's a very old piano."

Fredda thought, *So many things devised for lefties. It's incredible!*

"But I don't understand," said Fredda. "I mean, what do all these festivals have to do with the left-handed people."

"The legend said that Ellivnioj was a place founded by lefties when they were in great need of a place to escape to and save their lives. A desperate need." Benn sincerely looked into Fredda's eyes.

"Desperate need?" repeated Fredda.

"Yes, desperate need to be saved."

"Saved from what?"

"Not from what, but from whom?"

"*The righties*!" A light bulb went off in Fredda's head.

"Exactly! From the *righties*! No offense," said Benn to Tildda and Noell.

"From the *bad* righties," added Tildda.

"Yes, from the bad righties," repeated Noell.

"I'm still confused, Benn," said Fredda furrowing her brows, "Why don't the bad righties like us?"

"Because, Fredda, you're *different* and people don't like different. They think different is bad. Even me, in their eyes, I'm different being ambi."

"How did the lefties find this place?" asked Fredda

"Nobody exactly knows. The only thing that we do know is that they've found a great place to survive," said Benn smiling.

"But what does the festival have to do with the lefties?" Fredda asked again.

"Well, my grandmother always says that it's the simple things that make people happy - dancing, art, flowers, food, beer and even bicycles. These are the tools of our celebration. The festival is to honor lefties, a special day for them to celebrate their freedom from ridicule and their pride in being at their *best* as they *truly* are. Ellivnioj is a very simple place and its citizens want it to continue to be. People can come here to have fun and to have a great vacation, simply," finished Benn.

Before Fredda could ask any more questions, Mr. Theoddora, short, fat and balding, came out wearing his white hat and white apron to tell Benn, unfortunately, that he needed the table where they were having lunch because today was a crazy day at the diner.

The four of them finished eating and left the table. But before Fredda could go out and explore the town, she stopped at the kitchen and asked Mrs. Theoddora for money. The kitchen was a hot and busy place. Fredda saw at least three ladies scurrying around.

Mrs. Theoddora took an envelope from her apron, and gave Fredda some money and said, "Spend it wisely." Just like Grandpa Albert had said in his letter.

Tildda, Noell and Benn were already outside waiting for her. Benn had been released from kitchen duty after doing his chores to prepare for the day.

Benn and Noell were ready with their bicycles, but Tildda had none. Noell's bike looked sharp and new.

However, Benn's was an old, big model, not as sporty and fancy as Noell's.

"We're going to rent a bicycle for me at Mr. Bernno's shop. Would you like to rent one for yourself, Fredda?" asked Tildda.

Fredda nodded her head slowly, not really sure how she was going to handle a bike. She'd never had a chance to ride one.

They walked through the streets packed with people.

Today, Fredda was able to pay more attention to them. An old house, much older than the other houses and buildings around it, caught her eye. She stopped and Benn did, too. Tildda and Noell kept going.

Fredda read on a big plaque on top of a man-made cement stand: "Leonardo Da Vinci, Alexander the Great, Julius Ceasar, Joan of Arc, Beethoven, Michelangelo, Napoleon Bonaparte, Charlie Chaplin, Mahatma Gandhi, Henry Ford, Isaac Newton and Raphael Museum." The list continued on the other sides of the stand.

Fredda couldn't remember most of the things she had learned in her history classes, but for some reason she could remember some of these names not only from her history classes, but also from her art and music classes. But the name that she zeroed in on was Isaac Newton, the same person Mr. Numericoss compared her to when he described Fredda's distorted geometric figures.

"These are all very famous people, not only famous because they accomplished very important things, but they all have one other thing in common. They were all left-handed people, very famous left-handed people," said Benn proudly.

"Who was Isaac Newton?" asked Fredda.

"He was an English mathematician, astronomer, physicist, alchemist and much more I can't even remember at the moment," responded Benn, in one breath. "Why?"

That's why Numericoss used Mr. Newton's name when he was talking about my distorted geometric figure in his class.

"I was just wondering," responded Fredda.

Now it made sense. Now Fredda knew why Numericoss was so angry about Mr. Newton. Not only because he was a very famous mathematician but also because he was a lefty, a very important lefty.

"Hey, wait for us," called Fredda to Tildda.

It was still an intriguing place for Fredda, but it didn't seem as intriguing for the others. They were walking and talking and not paying attention to anything around them. Fredda, on the contrary, was absorbing everything like a sponge, anything she could put her eyes on.

They passed a music instrument store. The name of the place was Guittars for Lefties. They didn't go inside, but continued walking and passed the Handless Pizzeria, where Alffo worked. But Fredda couldn't see him because the restaurant was actually underground. They also passed Flora Florizeldda's Flower Shop, one of the most charming places in town. It was difficult to find a space to walk on the narrow sidewalk with so many people around them.

Finally, they arrived at Mr. Bernno's shop. It looked more like a barn than a bicycle shop. The two story building, painted dark gray with white shutters, was extremely narrow.

They went inside and Mr. Bernno, not looking at them because he was too occupied repairing a bike, said, "Yes, yes, yes, I'll be right with you."

Someone opened the door, and the bell above it tinkled. Fredda was so totally engrossed in the variety of organized bikes all over the place, even hanging from the ceiling, that she didn't take notice of who had walked in.

"Where's my bike, old man?" Fredda heard a bellowing voice coming from behind her.

"Where is it, old man?" She heard the voice again, coming closer.

She didn't recognize the voice, but for some reason it reminded her of school. As the four of them turned their heads to see who this person was, he stepped in front of them and said again rudely, "Where is my bike, old man?"

The boy was extremely handsome. He was a little taller than Benn with black shoulder length hair, dark eyes, and symmetrical features. His face was perfect, despite his remarkably thin red lips. Every piece of his clothing was black - black boots, black plants, black shirt, even black gloves.

He was accompanied by two others, another boy almost the same height as he, and a girl as tall as Tildda. Both of them were very light skinned and blond. The boy had short hair and the girl, long and silky like Tildda's. Both also wore dark clothes. And, they were so alike physically that they could be brother and sister.

Mr. Bernno picked up his head, and by the look on his face, you could see that trouble had arrived in his peaceful shop. He didn't say anything. He only pointed to a corner.

In the corner, was not only one, but three very expensive looking super new and sporty bikes. Even the bicycles were black, with shiny chrome rims and spokes. It reminded her of Grandpa Albert's old car - so shiny you could see your own reflection.

The boy and the other two went over to the corner. They each grabbed a bike and wheeled it back to Benn, examined the rest of them and the boy said arrogantly, "Look who's here. If it isn't the wishy-washy, Benn, with his rightie cousin and his little rightie friend. Wow, new friend, Benn?" referring to Fredda. "Another rightie or maybe an ambi like you? We know that you only like to hang out with *clumsy* people or *flip-flops* like yourself."

The other two with him only smirked at them. For a moment, Fredda's mind went back to her math class and even worse, the presence of the odious Maufrodezza. She decided not to say anything. However, she wasn't sure about Tildda, as Tildda couldn't restrain herself when she was provoked.

Fredda had no clue who this boy was or why he was talking to Benn like this or being rude to Mr. Bernno. Without saying any more, the boy and his two friends left Mr. Bernno's shop.

Benn didn't say a word. He only went to talk to Mr. Bernno. Fredda scooted over to Tildda and Noell. "Who's that boy?" whispered Fredda.

"His name is Evvos Sinisster. He's from the Sinisster family," responded Tildda uncomfortably.

"The Sinisster family?" repeated Fredda.

"Yes, the Sinisster family. The most powerful in this town and probably one of the most feared families around," Noell chimed in.

"Why are they powerful and feared, and why did he call Benn wishy-washy?"

"Well, the wishy-washy," said Noell, "is because Benn is ambi. They don't know if ambis are right or left-handed people. So they call them names like wishy-washy, you know … neither here nor there. I mean, the ambis who don't consider themselves lefties," Tildda continued, "Some of the ambis took the side of the left-handed and they're on the Sinissters' side. Along with the Sinissters, they hate the righties. That's why Evvos doesn't even look at me. Others just didn't take any side, like Benn, mom and our grandpa."

"About the powerful and feared," continued Noell, "well, they are extremely wealthy and well connected. That's what my father told me. And …"

Tildda continued, "They're very proud because every person in that family is left-handed, every single one. They only marry lefties and all of their children are lefties."

"Every single one?" said Fredda.

"Yes, everyone," responded Tildda.

"And who were the other two blonds?" asked Fredda.

"You mean the twins," Noell jumped in.

"They're Evvos Sinisster's cousins, Maggos Sinisster and Maggia Sinisster, and they frighten me. Even though they all are thirteen, they all look older, don't they? They actually remind me of Mrs. Maufrodezza," Tildda said terrified. "But even though he's from the Sinisster family, and he doesn't like people like me, isn't he handsome? I mean Evvos, of course."

Fredda thought, *Only Tildda could split a person into two different sides, inside the ugly, and outside the handsome.*

Benn came back to join them without saying a word about the incident. He told Tildda that Mr. Bernno had reserved a bicycle for her. Mrs. Theoddora had already asked Mr. Bernno to reserve one. She knew that this year there would be lots more people at Ellivnioj, because the 13th would be on a Friday.

Mr. Bernno pointed to where Tildda's bike was and Benn was the one all excited when he saw it, "Wow, the latest model, I can't believe it!" The bike was exactly the same one Evvos took with him, except for the color which was red. Fredda knew that probably Tildda's mother had paid for her bike. They were very wealthy.

"Well, Fredda, since all the bikes were reserved already, Mr. Bernno only had a very antique bicycle that he said you can use while you're here. He said that the model is so old that it wouldn't be right to charge you anything."

"Come, come, come with me, young lady." Mr. Bernno gestured with his left hand, showing Fredda the way. They all followed him to the back of his shop. Mr. Bernno opened the door. The room was tiny, dark and cold. He turned the lights on. There it was, a light pink bicycle. Actually, an extremely light pink bike.

Everything was pink, including the basket in front of the bike and something like a small iron seat in the back. The four of them made disapproving faces, but Mr. Bernno again told them that it was the only bike available at the moment.

"It's very …" said Fredda, and Tildda finished the sentence, "pink."

"It reminds me of …" said Fredda, and Tildda again continued Fredda's sentence, "the bow tie, the lace on the socks, and the number on the pocket of our uniform."

"Exactly!" completed Noell.

"We'll take it, Mr. Bernno," said Benn, "Pink will do. There's no other one for you to choose from, Fredda, and besides it's free. C'mon."

The pink bike creaked as Fredda pulled it out of the shop.

However, before they walked out the door, "Wait, wait, wait, young lady!" called Mr. Bernno, "Bring the bicycle back when you aren't using it anymore, would you?"

"Of course, Mr. Bernno. Thank you," responded Fredda and they left the shop.

If Fredda didn't know what a vacation was before she got there, now she did. The next few days she woke up late, ate lots of good food and walked around the town getting to know it better. Fredda loved her pink bike.

Benn taught her and Tildda how to ride their bikes. After many times falling to the ground and scratching her hands and knees, Fredda began to ride. Tildda wasn't so thrilled about the bike riding, but Fredda couldn't have enough of it. It was like the bike was a continuation of her body. The group rode down to the Crystal River, where the water was clear as crystal.

It was the first time Fredda had had the opportunity to make sand castles at the edge of a river. She didn't even know what a sand castle *was* before. She felt happy in Ellivnioj for the first time in her life, so happy that she could stay there forever. It was great to spend time outside school with her best friend, Tildda. Even Tildda looked more relaxed here, and wasn't so edgy.

Like life in general, nothing's perfect. They had been hiding themselves from Evvos Sinisster and his twin cousins. Benn said that it was better not to have any kind of confrontation. Actually in reality, what Benn was avoiding, was the humiliation that took place every time Evvos saw him. And humiliation was a very well-known subject to Fredda. She also thought it was a good idea to avoid confrontation.

But today, the town was extremely crowded, because it was the day before the big celebration for the lefties, and so they might not be able to avoid trouble.

And sure enough, unfortunately, Evvos and his gang were at the Handless Pizza where Fredda, Tildda, Benn and Noell were eating.

Evvos wasn't only accompanied by his cousins, Maggos and Maggia, but by two more teenagers. Even though the place was dim inside, Fredda could see them. They were all wearing dark clothes and sitting on the other side of the pizzeria.

"So, do you like the place, Fredda?" Benn asked her.

"Yes, I love it. It's very cozy."

People were shoulder to shoulder, eating at the closely packed wooden tables. There were old black and white pictures covering every wall, including on the low hanging ceiling. The clutter and crowds made the place look smaller than it actually was.

Fredda was accustomed to seeing only fancy rooms at school or at any other place the students visited on their school trips. The pizzeria was a real dump in comparison to International Academy.

Fredda could only imagine what Mrs. Maufrodezza would say if she saw this place! Fredda thought about what she had said in that horrible culinary class. Mrs. Maufrodezza noted that there are a lot of multimillion dollar deals done at a fine restaurant. Fredda pondered, *What kind of deals can be made in this place?*

A few minutes later, Alffo appeared to take their order.

"Hey! Hi, Fredda. What's it going to be, today?" he asked, very happy and ready to take the order with a little pad and pen in his left hand.

He was wearing a uniform, a white cook's hat, similar to the one Mr. Theoddora wore every day, and a red apron with the name Handless Pizzeria on it.

Tildda was the first to order. "I would like to have a small rightie with cheese only."

"Okay." Alffo jotted on the pad.

"The same for me, but pepperoni on the fingers," said Noell.

"Well, I'm going to have the small ambi with green peppers on the right, pepperoni on the left and ham on both sides," said Benn

That was a very strange order, Fredda thought.

"And for you, Fredda?" asked Alffo.

"Small and cheese all over," said Fredda not quite sure.

"Well, small lefty, right Fredda?" asked Alffo.

"I guess so," responded Fredda.

Fredda didn't understand what was really going on with the order, but decided not to ask any questions, as she was more concerned with Evvos' gang. Benn and Noell couldn't see them. They were facing Tildda and Fredda. But Fredda could see Evvos and his friends very well. Tildda, on the other hand, was more interested in the flyers spread on the table advertising all the Left-Handed People Day's events, and there were so many to choose from. The table looked a mess.

A few minutes later, the pizza was served and the shapes of the pizzas began to make sense. Benn got a small ambi, which meant two small pizzas with left and right hands united by the thumbs with green peppers on the right fingers, pepperoni on the left fingers and ham all over the two palms. Tildda got the right-hand shape with cheese only, while Noell got the right-hand with the pepperoni on the fingers and cheese on the palm. Fredda got hers with cheese melted onto a left-handed shaped pie.

They ate heartily. However, the girls couldn't finish theirs. Even the small size proved to be too much for them.

A few minutes later, a man approached the table. It was Mr. Segat, Noell's father. He said hello to Benn and Tildda. Then he looked at Fredda and said, "You must be Fredda Buttler, very nice to meet you." He extended his left hand, and Fredda took it.

"Very nice to meet you, sir."

"Sorry, Noell but we have to go now. I understand that you're having lots of fun these days, but your mother is waiting for us outside."

"Nice to see you all," said Mr. Segat and he left.

"We have to go to my parents' friends' house tonight. Oh! It's going to be so boring. And besides I have to dress up like a penguin. You know in a tuxedo." He shriveled up his face and shrugged his shoulders in resignation.

It had been such a great time so far. Fredda was relieved that Benn hadn't seen Evvos and his friends. But because happiness couldn't go on forever, Evvos appeared and walked towards Fredda's table. *He even walks arrogantly*, Fredda noticed.

Evvos and his gang stopped in front of Fredda's table.

"Judging by the pizza, we have a lefty at the table. So, finally Benn has a lefty friend. Am I right, Benn? But of course, I'm right! I may be left, but I'm always right," said Evvos in a superior tone.

"Yes, you are." Fredda responded sarcastically.

Evvos stared at Fredda for a moment. "Oh, spoken like a true fighter. She's braver than you, Benn. Of course, she's a lefty. What do you expect? Who are you? And what are you doing with these people? You should be ashamed to be seen with them."

"My name is Fredda," she said strongly.

"So, Fredda? Does Fredda have a last name or is it just, Fredda?' he asked condescendingly.

However, Fredda didn't respond to his question.

"Oh! Going to the concert, I see," said Evvos, looking at the flyer on the table, and he continued, "Trying to hide it under the place matt. I thought your grandma didn't allow you to go to that part of town, Benn, and you too, rightie," he finished, arrogantly looking at Tildda.

"What concert?" whispered Tildda looking at Fredda.

Fredda just shook her head.

Fredda knew that Benn wouldn't say anything back to Evvos because he didn't like confrontation. But, she wasn't so sure about Tildda.

But to Fredda's surprise, Tildda didn't say anything. She was probably admiring Evvos' good looks, or perhaps, she was so interested in the concert that she wasn't aware of what was really going on at the table.

Meanwhile, Alffo came from nowhere and stood there holding the bill and looking at all of them.

"I'll see you around, Wishy-Washy, perhaps tomorrow when a member of my family is going to win the flower contest again," said Evvos, haughtily as usual. He left with his party.

"Well, just to let you know, Mr. Segat already paid your bill," said Alffo smiling.

Tildda got hold of the flyer and she and Fredda read it. "Who are they?" asked Fredda.

"Oh! The LeftSide Band," responded Tildda. "They're great! Everybody's going to see them, I bet."

"Yes, everybody but *us*," said Benn under his breath.

"Wait a minute," said Fredda, "These two guys on the flyer, they look very familiar. But I've never heard about this band. Actually they look like …"

"Mr. Numericoss! Don't they?" said Tildda, laughing.

"Yes, they do, quite similar actually," said Fredda, now really studying the flyer.

"Because they are," Tildda giggled.

"What?" said Fredda confused.

"They're similar to Mr. Numericoss because they're his brothers. Not only are they his brothers, but they're also identical triplets."

"Are you kidding me, Tildda?"

"No, I'm deadly serious."

"But they look totally opposite from Mr. Numericoss. They have long hair and tattoos all over their bodies. They're wearing earrings and piercings," said Fredda, still staring at the flyer and not believing what she was seeing.

"Let me see it." Tildda grabbed the flyer from Fredda's hand. "Yes, Maxximus and Minnimus Numericoss, and they are lefties. They're great! We have to go to the concert. It's tomorrow night at the Darkkplace," said Tildda euphorically.

"Darkkplace?" asked Fredda.

"That's where things get a little bit difficult, because grandma won't let us go to the Darkkplace," said Benn, who up to that point was only observing the girls.

Alffo came back to the table to let them know that Evvos and his cousins were still hanging out at the front door and checking everyone who came out. "Maybe you guys should use the back door," said Alffo, watching the front door.

"No problem," said Benn, "We actually left our bikes in the back."

"Great, just follow me." Alffo led the way.

They passed through the extremely hot kitchen. The workers were so busy at the brick oven that they didn't even see them passing by.

Fredda tried to ask Tildda about the Darkkplace, but the place was too loud for them to talk.

Alffo showed them the way out, said goodbye and they were on their own. It was pitch black outside.

They heard a man screaming, "I DON'T KNOW!" But they couldn't pin point the location from where the voice was coming.

Benn put his finger over his mouth, letting the girls know not to talk or make any noise. They lowered themselves behind the garbage cans and some boxes and they stayed there for a moment.

They heard another voice. This time it was a different man's.

"Tell me where he is? Tell me where he is or I swear I'll rip your eyes out from your stinking face. You really stink, do you know that? How long has it been since you took a shower or brushed your yellow stinky teeth?"

"Oh! C'mon. Where is he?" another distinctive, raspy voice was asking the question now. "Answer my question, drunk man. You have mad eyes, do you know that?"

"I don't know. I don't know who you are talking about," responded the same man that was screaming before, with a tremulous voice.

"I know that voice!" Fredda whispered.

"Really?" Benn and Tildda questioned in whispers, too. "Who?"

"Uggo Schnapps!" snapped Fredda.

"Are you sure?" asked Tildda.

"Definitely! Mad eyes, yellowish teeth and stinky. Definitely, it's *him*!"

The door burst open. The same back door the three of them had used before. It was Alffo coming out, dragging a huge garbage bag and making a lot of noise.

"What are you still doing here?" he asked, looking at the three of them.

At the same moment, Fredda heard voices coming from the other side of the garbage cans, and footsteps like whoever was there was running away. But, she couldn't see much because it was too dark.

"What's going on?" asked Alffo.

No one answered his question.

Fredda, Tildda and Benn took off to find the man who Fredda definitely thought was Mr. Schnapps. Alffo dropped the huge garbage bag and ran after them.

They searched for a moment, trying to find him. Then, in the dark, they heard a moan coming from behind them. They all turned together to the location from which the noise came.

Alffo tip-toed toward it while the others followed. There was the old man sitting on the floor, holding his head, blood dripping from his brow.

"Is that you, Mr. Schnapps?" Alffo asked the man, "And what are you doing here? What happened to you?"

"I don't know, I don't know. Let me go, don't hit me anymore. I don't know," said Mr. Schnapps.

Mr. Schnapps raised his arms defensively.

"Oh! I think I'm going to throw up," said Tildda, "The smell plus the blood. Oh! He stinks so much. I'm definitely going to throw up," and she left them.

"No one's going to hit you, Mr. Schnapps. It's me, Alffo."

Mr. Schnapps started mumbling something that no one could understand.

"Oh! There we go, folks! He's in his mental mood swing again," said Alffo.

"Mental mood swing? What's that exactly?" asked Fredda, lost.

"He goes someplace else. I mean, it's like his mind goes away and he doesn't make any sense. I'm going to get some help inside," said Alffo. He hurried off.

"I'm going to check on Tildda," said Benn, "Fredda, stay here with him. I'll be right back."

Everyone left. Fredda was alone with Mr. Schnapps. She wasn't sure what to say or do. She decided to move away from him.

She started to walk, when Mr. Schnapps grabbed her left arm and said, "I know who they're after, those men. They are after your grandpa. They want something from him." Mr. Schnapps pointed to the sky. "The thing in the sky, the thing in the sky."

Fredda looked up at the cloudy night sky, but couldn't see anything, not even stars. And then, Mr. Schnapps stood up and ran away.

Fredda Buttler And The Left-Handed People

"Wait, Mr. Schnapps, please wait!" cried Fredda, but he disappeared into the black night. Fredda didn't understand anything at all.

Alffo came back with help. Benn came back with Tildda who stayed back warily.

"Where is he?" asked Benn

"Yes, where is he?" repeated Alffo.

"Gone. He took off, in a hurry. I couldn't do anything to stop him!" responded Fredda.

"Who cares? He's a loony anyway, actually a stinky loony," said Tildda.

"Let's go home. It's getting late," said Benn.

The trio jumped on their bikes and left. The streets were still packed with people, and they were very careful not to take any short cuts. They were afraid of the men who had hurt Mr. Schnapps.

It took them a while to get back home. They noticed, when they rode up to the Windmill Diner, that there was a delivery boy looking up at the address.

"Hello, excuse me. I'm looking for Ms. Buttler, Ms. Freddarika Buttler," said the young boy.

"I'm Freddarika Buttler."

"I have a delivery for you. Could you please sign here, Miss Buttler."

After signing the paper, the young boy gave Fredda a gorgeous purple orchid.

Fredda took the orchid from the boy's hands and said, "No card?"

"I'm afraid not, Miss Buttler."

"Who do you think sent you *this* flower, Fredda?" asked Tildda, who couldn't contain her curiosity.

"I have no idea."

"Oh! How could I forget!" Tildda blurted.

"What did you forget?" asked Benn, totally lost.

"Tomorrow is Fredda's birthday," Tildda said joyously.

"You mean her birthday is going to be the same day as the festival, August 13th?" Benn smiled.

Tildda just nodded her head and grinned.

However, Fredda stared at the purple orchid. Actually, her eyes were fixed on the curly leaf. She knew that someone was trying to tell her something. Fredda couldn't remember Alffo mentioning anything about purple when he had explained the meaning of the colors during their first meeting at Grandpa Albert's house.

They didn't use the main entrance. They had their bicycles, so they went to the back of the windmill. Benn helped Fredda with her bike and her flower.

As they were passing the greenhouse, Fredda took a glimpse. But, she couldn't see much because several bushes hid most of it from view. They used a back door to enter and the girls went straight to their bedroom while Benn went to tell his grandmother that they were back and that they had already eaten dinner. After that, Benn ran upstairs to join the girls. He wanted to know more about Fredda's birthday.

Benn knocked at their door. Tildda opened it, and to his alarm, Fredda was standing, seemingly hypnotized by the purple flower. The orchid was placed on the nightstand, and Tildda told Benn that Fredda had closed all the curtains and had not moved from her orchid vigil.

"Fredda? Are you okay?" asked Benn, now wondering why Fredda was so mesmerized by the flower.

Benn's voice brought Fredda out of her hypnotic state and she said, "It's not only a flower."

Tildda jumped in. "What do you mean, it's not only a flower?"

Benn crept closer to the orchid, while Tildda stayed close to Fredda.

"Do you remember when Noell told us about the messages in these flowers," said Fredda, still staring at it.

"Yes, but that's only stories, legends that people tell. Not really real. It's like books that we read when we were kids," said Tildda, putting her hand on her waist and pursing her lips.

"No, this isn't legend, Tildda. It's real."

"Oh! C'mon, Fredda."

"I'll show you that this is real. What's the message?" said Fredda confidently.

"What message?" asked Tildda.

"I'm not talking to you, Tildda."

The purple orchid seemed to sprout arms of green and plucked the curly leaf from its own stem. The arms seemed to unroll as if they were going to read from a scroll. A voice emerged from somewhere inside the flower, "This message is for Fredda and *only* Fredda. Meet me at Mrs. Flora Florizeldda's Flower Shop on the back flower patio, as soon as you can. Signed, Mr. Uggo Schnapps."

The leaf scroll disappeared in front of their eyes. Benn recoiled backwards so fast that he fell on the floor. Tildda froze. She couldn't believe what she had just seen.

Fredda tried to explain to Tildda and Benn that the color mattered. But they were still too puzzled by the orchid.

"Did you see that, Benn? A talking flower," said Tildda, still shaking. Benn nodded his head wordlessly.

After a while, Benn asked uncertainly, "Are you going to meet Mr. Uggo Schnapps?"

"I'm not sure yet."

CHAPTER 10

GOING RIGHT TO UNDERSTAND LEFT

Tildda was the one who broke the ice and said, "Why didn't you tell us about the orchid … the message? That you already knew what Noell was talking about the other day!"

"Would you have believed me if I'd told you about a talking flower?" said Fredda, staring at Tildda.

"Probably not."

"I figured," she was a bit annoyed with Tildda.

"C'mon girls, now is not the time to pick on each other," said Benn with his eyes still fixed on the flower.

"Anyway, why does Mr. Schnapps want to talk to you?" asked Tildda.

"He told me that the *bad* men are after Grandpa Albert before he ran away from us."

"I bet Fredda's grandpa's in big trouble! Maybe I can go with you to meet with Mr. Schnapps," said Benn.

"Really, Benn, would you go with me?"

"Of course."

"And if you think you two are going out there without me, think twice," said Tildda, with fisted hands on her waist like she was given them orders.

"Do we have any choice?" asked Fredda, looking at Benn.

"Nope."

"Ah! Very funny," said Tildda disapprovingly.

"Okay Tildda, you can come with us. But no throwing up again!" said Fredda.

Tildda touched base with her mother and assured her that she'd be in for the night. Benn's grandma was similarly informed. Tildda returned to the bedroom.

Benn told them to grab jackets because the temperature drops at night. He told them to meet him at the stairs while he was going to get a jacket for himself. The three of them were on the third floor, but they could hear people in the diner. They went one floor down, but it was too busy on the ground floor.

"We're never going to be able to pass the front or back door without anyone seeing us," Tildda whispered.

"You're right," replied Benn.

Benn remembered that the window in the stairwell led to a fire escape. Tildda complained, but she had no choice if she wanted to go with them.

They climbed downward until Tildda's jacket got caught on the iron stairs. Thankfully, Benn was able to help her to get free. Tildda looked up to see if Fredda was following, but to her disbelief, Fredda was still inside staring out at the greenhouse longingly.

"Are you coming, Fredda?" whispered Tildda.

Fredda only smiled at Tildda showing her beautiful dimples and whispered, "Wait, I'll be right back."

"Where's she going?" asked Benn. Tildda just threw her arms up and shrugged her shoulders.

A couple of minutes later, Fredda appeared, purple orchid in hand. She looked down to see if Tildda and Benn were there waiting for her. She managed to get down the fire stairs with the flower still in her arms.

"Why did you bring the flower with you?" asked Tildda.

"Well, I don't want anyone to know that I have this orchid. So I want to hide it in the greenhouse along with the other flowers."

"Ah! That's a great idea, Fredda," said Benn, taking the flower from her hand.

Benn went to place the orchid in the greenhouse while Fredda and Tildda waited for him. Upon his return, Fredda asked if he had had any trouble hiding the flower. He assured the girls of his success at blending the orchid with the other plants in the greenhouse.

Before leaving, Benn said, "Well, we can't use the main street. We should use the back streets and short cuts. This means we should go on foot rather than use our bikes."

"But aren't you afraid of the *bad* men, Benn?" asked Tildda.

"I don't think they're looking for *us*."

"Yes, I agree with Benn. I don't think they're looking for us," said Fredda.

And then, they left. Using every short cut Benn knew, and probably, unknowingly, trespassing upon many properties until reaching Flora Florizeldda's Flower Shop. They tried to get to the shop from the back, but the vegetation was too dense. The only way in was from the front.

As soon as the trio stepped in front of the shop, they were spotted by Evvos Sinisster and his two cousins, Maggos and Maggia Sinisster.

Fredda, Tildda and Benn didn't see them. Benn was the first to go into the shop, followed by Fredda and Tildda. Benn and Tildda had been in there many times before. It was Fredda's first.

Benn, leading, took them directly to the back patio. Meanwhile, Evvos and his two cousins parked their bikes outside Mrs. Florizeldda's shop and went in. Benn saw Mrs. Florizeldda, the owner of the shop, talking to a customer, but she didn't see them.

As Benn knew the shop well, it was easy for him not to get caught in the big maze of exotic flowers, bushes, plants and even trees out there. It was dark. They stopped walking and looked around for Mr. Schnapps.

Suddenly, Mr. Schnapps hobbled over, looking dreadful. He still had the blood on his forehead and an offensive smell that Tildda couldn't handle. She put her hand over her nose.

Fredda said, "Are you okay, Mr. Schnapps?"

He didn't answer. He only gestured with his left hand for them to follow.

They walked to a corner of the shop where the vegetation was so high that nobody could see them. Evvos and the twins were still searching the store for them.

"I don't have much time," said Mr. Schnapps. He seemed to be fairly stable and apparently almost normal.

"What do you mean, you don't have much time," said Fredda, staring into his eyes.

"It's complicated," responded Mr. Schnapps.

"Why does everything have to be so …" said Fredda angrily, and she paused, "*Complicated!* I wish someone would just explain about this whole complicated thing."

"The less you know, the better for you," said Mr. Schnapps.

"Oh! I actually don't *know anything!*" said Fredda. She wanted to ask a lot of questions, but Mr. Schnapps was in a hurry.

"Listen well, all of you," said Mr. Schnapps looking at Fredda. "I actually hoped to see you here alone, Fredda, but you brought your friends with you, I see. You're right to bring help. There are evil people chasing your grandpa. But he doesn't even have it … wh… what they're looking for," he stammered.

"It …? What do you mean … my Grandpa Albert doesn't have it?" asked Fredda, more confused than before.

"The, ah! The …" Mr. Schnapps paused, looked around, was going to say something, but hesitated, and then he squatted down and with his left index finger drew something on the floor.

Fredda moved next to him so that she could see what he was doing from the same angle as he. Benn also moved closer, but Tildda still holding her nose, decided not to join them.

"What is it?" asked Tildda impatiently.

"Do not say a word!" said Mr. Schnapps, looking around.

The drawing was of three boxes side by side. Mr. Schnapps finished by placing his left hand on the left box, his right hand over the right box and then both his hands on the middle box.

He lifted his head to the sky, opened his eyes, scratched his head, grinded his yellow teeth and pointed to the sky. "It's coming. You'll see, it's coming!"

"Oh! Not again. He's back in his loony phase," said Tildda, screwing up her face in disgust and continuing to hold her nose.

"The color is silver," said Mr. Schnapps. He wiped away the drawing from the ground with his hand and started moving away from the corner towards the thick vegetation.

There was noise coming from the shop. It sounded like there was more than one person talking.

Fredda decided to follow Mr. Schnapps. Benn went after her. Tildda had no choice but to follow.

Mr. Schnapps finally stopped in front of what seemed to be three gazebos - one on the left side, one in the middle and another one on the right side. He went mad at this point. He squeezed his neck with his hands and grunted.

"Hurry, we have no time to spare," said Mr. Schnapps.

"I don't understand," said Fredda, more confused than ever.

"Oh! I guess I didn't tell you. You have to go back to your great-aunt's house and get what I just drew for you. Just go into the middle gazebo. Hurry up, girl! You're the only person who can get it before the *bad* men put their hands on it. You have no more time to spare!" Mr. Schnapps looked up at the sky. He scrambled inside the left gazebo and he was gone.

The voices from the store got louder. Fredda didn't know what to do, but then decided to stand in front of the entrance to the middle gazebo. Benn followed her and Tildda after him.

"I don't understand anything," said Benn.

"Imagine me!" said Tildda, looking horrified.

The vegetation around the gazebo was high, Fredda, Benn and Tildda couldn't see anything other than the inside of the gazebo. However, the voices from inside the store sounded nearer.

"I'm not sure how I'm going to get back to the other side," said Fredda looking at Benn and Tildda.

"What do you mean?" said Tildda.

"Well, I came to this side with Grandpa Albert. I really don't know how to go back to the other side by myself. He never told me." Fredda's eyes were downcast and her voice trembled slightly.

"But I thought that you were a true left-hander?" asked Benn confused.

"What do you mean by that?" asked Fredda.

"Remember, I told you before that only true left-handed people can remember *both* sides, and only the true left-handed person can travel from The Right Side to The Left Side by themselves and vice versa," said Benn looking at Fredda.

"I came with Grandpa Albert, and he held my hand through the covered bridge. Wait a minute," said Fredda, concentrating, "Grandpa Albert let go of my hand, the last minute."

"What do you mean, he let go of your hand?" asked Tildda anxiously.

"I was afraid to go alone through the dark bridge, so Grandpa Albert told me he would go with me, and he held my hand, and we started walking through the darkness. But at the last minute, he let go and suddenly, we were here on this side," said Fredda.

"See, that's it!" said Benn.

"*It*? What do you mean by that?" replied Fredda.

"Don't you get it? You passed through the sides by yourself! You're really a *true* left-handed person," said Benn, all excited, " I can't believe that you're the real thing! I mean, well you know what I mean."

"No, Benn, it *can't* be," said Fredda.

"Why not?" Tildda chimed in.

The voices were much closer now. Now, they really had to decide quickly.

"Okay, let's go then," said Fredda.

"What do you mean, let's go? You know that I can't go to the other side. I mean, I agreed to come with you to meet Mr. Schnapps but not to go to the other side. I've never been to The Right Side. And besides, Grandma will kill me if she knows that I disobeyed her," said Benn, all nervous.

"We have no time to talk about this! There are people following us," Fredda urged.

Who's going to tell grandma, anyways? As far as she knows, we're in our bedrooms in the windmill. Don't be a chicken, Benn," said Tildda, winking at Fredda.

The voices were so close to them now, as if the voices could almost grab them. Fredda's heart sped up as her mind raced to find an escape from the dread that seemed to be following her. Instinctively, she turned and bolted into the middle gazebo. Once more, Benn followed her and Tildda after him.

Fredda clutched Benn's hand, Tildda grabbed Fredda's and Fredda stepped towards the middle of it.

Evvos, Maggos and Maggia had caught up in just enough time to see the three run into the gazebo. "We got em now!" Evvos eyes gleamed with triumph.

The Sinissters sprinted to the middle one, but to their surprise, it was empty. Maggia and Maggos checked the gazebo on the left and the one on the right. Evvos' face fell and then turned red with fury over losing them.

"So, what's it going to be Evvos?" asked Maggia.

Meanwhile, Fredda, Benn and Tildda, found themselves still standing there in the middle of the gazebo. It was night. Fredda wasn't sure what had happened. It seemed as if they hadn't gone anywhere.

"And who are *you*?" Benn asked Fredda.

"FREDDA?" yelled Tildda. "What am I doing here? I thought I was on my way to France with my parents. That's what I remember last. Where are we?"

"Well, if I'm not mistaken we're in the back of Mrs. Flora Florizeldda's Flower Shop," responded Fredda.

"And by the way, I'm Fredda." She said looking at Benn.

"Oh! Yeah, I think we are in the back of Mrs. Florizeldda's shop," said Benn. "But the noise? What is it?"

"Oh, please, don't you know about the noise? We're in the city and the city is always noisy," said Tildda.

Now, Fredda knew that she was back in The Right Side.

"Hurry," said Fredda, "We don't have much time. We have to go."

"Wait, go where?" asked Tildda, "and by the way, who are *you*?"

"Well, I guess, I have the same question for you, too," he responded.

"Oh boy, listen, I have no time to explain now. Can we go?" said Fredda.

"No!" said Benn and Tildda at the same time.

Fredda didn't know where to start. *How can I explain to Benn that he's no longer on the same side anymore? And what about Tildda? She's not where she thought she would be? This is crazy!*

Whatever Benn had told her about being a true left-hander was actually happening. She was the only one who could remember everything, and *she* was the one who had brought them to this side.

"Well, this is Tildda, and Tildda this is Benn. And I am Fredda, as I told you before. I know that this is kind of confusing, but we have to go to the teachers' quarters, on the other side of the street where the school is, and go to my great-aunt's old house and get something," she finished.

Tildda and Benn looked at each other, more baffled than before.

"ARE YOU OUT OF YOUR MIND? HAVE YOU COMPLETELY LOST IT?" Tildda screamed at Fredda.

"There's no school on the other side of the street. Actually there's a bakery on the other side of Mrs. Florizeldda's shop," said Benn, looking at Fredda.

"What?" said Tildda, "Where have you been? There's no bakery on the other side of this place." Fredda agreed.

"I'm going to show you that I'm right, girl!" Benn took off running. Fredda went after him. Tildda followed them.

Benn could run! He reached the front door of Mrs. Florizeldda's shop in a flash. Fredda, also running as fast as she could, and almost out of breath, yelled, "BENN,

PLEASE DON'T GO OUTSIDE. I NEED TO TALK TO YOU!"

Benn stopped, turned to Fredda and said, "I'm going home. It's probably late and Grandma is most likely worried about me."

Fredda thought for a moment and realized Benn remembered *some* things from The Left Side - Mrs. Florizeldda's shop, the bakery on the other side of the street and his grandma. But he couldn't remember Tildda or her. Tildda caught up with them.

"Oh! There you are," she said breathlessly.

Meanwhile, Benn opened the front door of the shop and stepped out.

"Hurry, we have to go after him," said Fredda to Tildda.

"I don't get it. Why is it so important to go after him?"

"You'll see," responded Fredda.

Fredda and Tildda rushed out the main door and almost crashed into Benn, who looked like a statue.

"Benn, are you okay?" asked Fredda, staring at him.

It took a while for Benn to respond.

"What *is* this place? Where *are* we?" he asked.

Tildda was about to say something, but was stopped by Fredda who said, "Don't say anything, Tildda, not now."

Tildda didn't understand what was going on, but listened.

Benn, on the other hand, was looking at everything! He felt overwhelmed as the sights and sounds of the city washed over him. Tall buildings, traffic lights, cars, buses, motorcycles, people on the sidewalks with their cell phones and other gadgets. His jaw went slack.

"Grandma always said that this side was different, but she never prepared me for *this*!"

Tildda looked at Fredda. Fredda just looked back at her and Tildda still didn't say a word. She just circled her finger near her temple to let Fredda know that she thought Benn was loony.

Fredda managed to get them all to the other side of the street where the school was located.

Meanwhile, on The Left Side, Evvos responded to Maggia's question, "We'll go after them!"

Evvos, Maggia and Maggos, placed themselves in the middle of the gazebo and a second later, they also were in The Right Side.

In no time, they were outside of Mrs. Florizeldda's shop. Their luck held and they saw Fredda, Tildda and Benn on the corner of the other side of the street.

"I'm so confused, Fredda," said Tildda, "Why do you have to go to your great-aunt's old house? And what am I doing here with you and your friend, Benn, beside me?" Benn was still so enrapt, he wasn't even paying attention to the girls.

"As I told you before, Tildda, I can't begin to explain what's going on at the moment. But I will. I promise you, I will," finished Fredda.

"Wait a minute," said Tildda, pointing her right finger at Fredda. "What are you doing outside school? You actually escaped! Oh! I can't believe that it took me so long to realize that you've escaped! And now you want to break more rules. DO YOU KNOW WHAT'S GOING TO HAPPEN TO YOU IF SOMEONE SEES YOU HERE, OUTSIDE?" Tildda was yelling now.

Fredda, didn't realize that she would have to explain to Tildda that she wasn't breaking any rules. And that in fact, she had permission to be out there for vacation with her grandpa. Out of the corner of her eye, Fredda saw Evvos, Maggia and Maggos.

"Oh, no! They're following us," said Fredda.

"Who?" asked Tildda.

"Benn?" said Fredda.

"Yes," he responded mesmerized by the traffic.

"Do you recognize those three people on the other side of the street?" The traffic was extremely heavy at that moment.

"The two blondes and the dark haired boy?" he asked.

"Yes," responded Fredda.

"No, I don't know them. I've never seen them in my life."

"We have to go," said Fredda. "Tildda! You have to help me get back inside the school. Can you help me? I really need to go back. I don't want to be expelled." Fredda thought this might get Tildda to go with her. She didn't think she'd have trouble with Benn.

"Oh! Finally you're making some sense!" said Tildda. "Yes, I can help get you back. I don't want you to get expelled. What would I do without you in there?"

They rapidly ran to the small side street, avoiding the main entrance of the school and the heavy traffic. The street was narrow and extremely dark. The wide tall, trees standing on both sides, threw eerie shadows with the street lights cast upon them. The three tried not to make any noise. They could see the guards inside the school gates.

Evvos and his cousins got stuck by the nonstop traffic, and they couldn't cross. This gave Fredda, Tildda and Benn some extra time.

They scurried around trying to find an entry point. It was almost impossible for someone to penetrate those walls surrounding the school. But they had to find a way, rapidly.

It seemed that the pressure to find an entrance fell on Fredda's shoulders. Benn still looked lost and Tildda looked scared.

At one point, Fredda stopped. Then, she retraced her steps. She walked back and forth on the same spot at least three times.

"What are you doing?" asked Tildda impatiently.

"Can you hear it?" asked Fredda.

"Hear what?

Benn piped up, "It's hollow, isn't it?"

"Yes, it is!" responded Fredda smiling, revealing her dimples.

"What's hollow?" asked Tildda, extremely annoyed.

"The sidewalk!" both Fredda and Benn said in unison.

Fredda stomped the ground with her left foot and Tildda heard the hollow sound. The three of them pushed aside the leaves covering the ground and they saw the metal plate covering the sidewalk.

Benn tried to open it. Fredda played look-out. However, it was awfully dark. Benn finally managed to pry off the cover. There were steps leading down into the blinding darkness.

"Let's go," said Fredda already descending.

"What?" said Tildda trembling.

Benn, still holding up the plate with his two arms, said, "I won't be able to hold it for too long. Get in there, now."

Tildda had the choice of going with them or being left on that dark street by herself. She chose to go. Fredda extended her left hand to help her friend and hastily crept downstairs slowly. They couldn't see anything.

Suddenly, the steps ended and they were on flat ground.

They saw a beam of light coming from above, a short distance in front of them. They approached the spotlight and they could see the impeccably uniformed guard passing above them. They were in! Now the difficult part was to find out *where* they were inside the school.

Fredda whispered, "We're under the main patio of the school."

"How do you know that?" asked Tildda softly, astonished.

"Look at the petals on the ground."

Tildda and Benn tilted their heads to see colorful petals spotting the ground.

"The main patio is the only place in school with such a variety of different flowers," finished Fredda.

"You must have a lot of free time on your hands," said Tildda rolling her eyes, "Where to now?"

Benn looked at them, still lost.

Fredda chose to go left. They went on silently. They knew the implications of getting caught. They walked for a while, Fredda always checking to see where they were heading. They followed the spotlights dotting the ground from above. Finally, she said, "It's here."

"Are you sure?" asked Tildda.

"Yes, I am," responded Fredda, firmly, "I can see the houses from here," as she looked through the grating. And there it was - the place Fredda hadn't been since that fateful day, when her Great-Aunt Annora was taken from there and never came back.

"Wait a minute!" said Tildda, rubbing her forehead. You were supposed to go to the dormitory, weren't you? And how are we going to get out of here? I mean …" Tildda studied Benn from top to bottom, examining his old clothes, "your friend, Benn, and I. And why are we here at the teachers' quarters? You've got to be kidding! You lied to me!"

"Yes, how am I going to go home from here? That place out there isn't home. I don't even know where I am! This is the other side. Isn't it, Fredda? The Right Side!" Benn's alarm was obvious.

"Yes, Benn, this is The Right Side," responded Fredda.

"You know that your friend, Benn, doesn't make any sense, don't you?" said Tildda, very aggravated, "And you're not making any sense either, Fredda."

"I know, Tildda. I would love to sit here and clear things up but it's complicated." Fredda sounded exactly like her Grandpa Albert or even more like Mr. Schnapps. She herself couldn't believe what she had just said to her best friend.

Maybe it is complicated for Grandpa Albert, and even for Mr. Schnnaps, to explain certain things! Now Fredda was in the same situation as Grandpa Albert and Mr. Schnapps, and it was too complicated to explain all these complicated events to the others.

"Okay, I have an idea, I'll go to my great-aunt's old house by myself and the two of you stay here and wait for me. Then we'll figure out how the two of you are going home."

"No!" Tildda and Benn chimed in together.

"There is no way I'm going to stay here alone with this crazy friend of yours," said Tildda, stomping her right foot on the ground.

"Oh! Like I want to stay here alone with you, either!" replied Benn.

"You two, please! Keep your voices down!"

"We go with you," Benn and Tildda said together.

They waited for a while to see if the guards would return. Together, they opened the metal grill. The two girls helped Benn go up first. Then Benn hoisted Fredda out, and the two of them pulled Tildda out from underground.

From where they were, they could see the teachers' houses lined up side by side. The two story brick houses were very old, dark and narrow, not as glamorous as the school was. Some houses had lights on and some were completely dark. Some teachers where there for summer vacation and others had gone.

"Where is it? What number are we looking for?" asked Tildda whispering.

"Number thirteen," Fredda whispered back.

"Over there," said Benn, "I can see number eleven."

"Good, let's go," said Fredda.

And the three of them moved quickly, hiding themselves behind the bushes on the dark, narrow street.

They waited again and they saw the guard passing by. They stayed motionless until he passed and then they crossed the street.

There stood number thirteen.

Five steps up and they were on the narrow porch in front of the double front door entrance.

"How are we going to get in?" asked Tildda impatiently. "Do you think someone is living in this house now that your great-aunt is gone?"

"Gone? Is your great-aunt dead?" asked Benn.

"No, my great-aunt is not dead," responded Fredda as she walked to the left porch corner, pulled up one of the old wooden planks from the floor, reached in and pulled out a small box. She opened it and took out a key. She opened the front door, put the key back in the little box, put the box back in the same spot, laid in the wooden plank, and continued, "My Great-Aunt Annora lives in a nursing home not far from here and she's not mentally well."

They snuck inside the house, looked around and saw no one there. Fredda locked the front door behind them. It was pitch black inside. She told them to stay put and wait for her. She remembered the inside of the house, and she vanished in the dark.

She came back a minute later with a tiny flashlight, closed the curtains, and swept the light around to see the place. The house was small and dusty. The living room had old fashioned furniture and books everywhere, well organized in book cases, like Grandpa Albert's house. There was a staircase to the right and a narrow corridor to the left leading to the back of the house.

"What are we looking for anyway?" asked Tildda, not wanting to touch anything.

"Yes, what are we looking for?" Benn questioned.

"Fredda, where do you think your Great-Aunt Annora would've hidden whatever we're looking for?" asked Tildda, looking around.

"Probably inside her room. It was the only place I wasn't allowed to go in the entire house. She used to lock the room all the time. I never understood why, but now I have a hunch," said Fredda.

They started up the stairs. On the way, they saw several old black and white pictures hanging on the wall. Tildda stopped in front of one of the photos and said, "Funny, this lady on the right side looks like my grandma."

"Let me see it," said Benn, "Ah! Impossible because this lady looks like *my* grandma."

"Yeah, that'll be the day when we're related!" said Tildda sarcastically looking at Benn.

"C'mon, we don't have time for this right now," said Fredda.

However, in the back of her mind she thought how funny this situation really was. Imagine if she were to tell them that they really *were* cousins!

They climbed upstairs. There was a bathroom in front of them and next to the bathroom door was a narrow staircase, most likely going to the attic. To their right was Fredda's old bedroom, and to their left, was Fredda's great-aunt's room. They went in. Fredda closed the curtains quickly.

The bedroom was small like the rest of the house. There was a bed, a nightstand on its right side with a small lamp on it, and a tiny desk with a chair under the window. There were more books organized in the corner on the floor next to the fireplace, an antique wardrobe, and next to it, a full length mirror extremely similar to the one in Fredda's room at Mrs. Theoddora's place.

Out of nowhere, Tildda said to Benn, "So, I know that you're not a student here at International Academy. Where do you go to school?"

"I don't go to any school," responded Benn.

"What?" said Tildda interested.

"Well, my grandma and grandpa teach me at home."

"Ah! Home schooling. I don't think I could do that, I mean, home schooling."

Fredda realized that she had never asked Benn anything about school. She assumed he went to school like her and Tildda.

"So again, what are we looking for?" asked Tildda.

Fredda Buttler And The Left-Handed People

But before Fredda could answer, they heard a noise from outside. Fredda peeked through the window and saw three guards standing in front of the house talking to each other. She turned the flashlight off. Then she heard a familiar voice.

"What is going on here?" It was Mr. Numericoss.

"Ah! Well, sir. We think we saw three children around house number thirteen."

"Boys, girls?" asked Numericoss.

"Two boys, one girl, sir."

Fredda thought, *It can't be us. We're two girls and one boy. It must be Evvos and his cousins. They're following us.*

"What is going on here?" another familiar voice, and this time it was Mrs. Maufrodezza.

"Some children broke in to the school area," answered Numericoss.

"One of ours?" Maufrodezza asked the guards.

"I don't believe so, madam."

"Oh, no! We're in serious trouble," said Tildda, looking awfully frightened.

"What's going on?" asked Benn.

"Mrs. Maufrodezza is the vice principal of this school and Mr. Numericoss is our math teacher," responded Fredda, not looking so brave now.

Tildda continued, "And they really don't like Fredda."

"You mean ... they *hate* me!"

"Let's go inside the house," said Numericoss to the guards.

"Wait a minute," said Maufrodezza to the guards. "I am in charge here, and I will tell you what to do. After all, I am the vice-principal of this prestigious school. And besides, Mr. Kaffona is not here at the present moment, as he is on vacation. This gives me the authority to be the person in charge here," finished Mrs. Maufrodezza, arrogantly looking at Numericoss.

He just looked back at her with the same arrogant eyes and said, "Well, then I guess you are not doing such a great job of protecting the school."

Maufrodezza looked only at the guards and ordered, "Guards! Go inside the house and check every possible place. Do not forget the attic or the basement. Bring me those rats."

"Yes, madam."

"We have to go! We can't stay here!" Tildda was horrified.

Fredda wracked her brain for a solution. They tried to go back to the staircase, but it was too late. The guards had broken one of the windows. The three of them could hear the guards inside the house now. They decided to go back to Fredda's great-aunt's bedroom and lock themselves in. It would just be a stall for time. The guards would probably break the door. They could hear the guards coming upstairs.

Out of the corner of Fredda's eye, she saw a flash of blue light coming from under the bed. Trepidatiously, she bent to look under and there was Blue, a tiny blue light shining from his leather collar.

"Blue!" said Fredda in panic. "What are you doing here?" she whispered.

Blue emerged purring and rubbed his body against Fredda's legs. The guards were right outside the door. Now everyone could hear them. Blue moved close to the mirror, looked at Fredda with his piercing golden eyes, purred one more time, jumped inside the mirror and disappeared. Fredda was astonished.

Only she had seen this happen because Tildda and Benn were too preoccupied with the door. The door knob turned, but the guards realized the door was locked from inside.

Fredda signaled Tildda and Benn to get away from the door. But they were frozen in fear. Fredda grabbed the two, and brought the three of them to the mirror. She leaned on it with Tildda and Benn in her arms. The only thing on her mind at that moment was that she would like to be in a safe place with her two friends and find what she was looking for. And within a second, just like Blue, they were gone.

A few seconds later, the guards crashed through the door, but saw no one inside. Only the tiny flashlight was visible on the floor.

The trio landed in a totally *new* place. Their landing pad seemed familiar only to Benn.

The round room was surrounded by several large windows. In the center of the room, stood a small square table with four small chairs. A full length antique mirror stood next to them in a corner.

"Where are we?" asked Tildda, impatient for answers as usual.

"We're in the attic of the windmill," said Benn. They could see the enormous blades passing by and making that whooshing noise that kept Fredda awake at night when she first got there.

"But something is really wrong with this place," said Benn, looking around.

"What do you mean *wrong*?" asked Tildda, also looking around. "You're right. I really don't remember this place at grandma's house, Benn."

"I mean, it's nice, nicer actually than the attic at grandma's place. I was in the attic a few days ago, went there to get some stuff for grandma, and it was a mess." Benn went to the window. "It's definitely not the same place," he said, looking outside.

"What do you mean, Benn?" said Fredda, also peering outside through the window.

"It seems like this place isn't as old as I remember. Even the outside. I mean, there are only a few stores and a few houses and empty spaces."

Tildda agreed with him. "We went back in time, didn't we?" asked Tildda seeming to put two and two together, glancing back and forth between them and the outside.

No one answered her question.

Fredda realized that now Tildda, Benn and she all knew each other and where they were. Fredda felt somewhat relieved.

They left the attic and went down a couple floors. They could hear voices coming from downstairs. They crept a few steps down between the second floor and the first. From where they were, they could see a big round table. There were six people sitting at it. They all appeared very young, probably in their early twenties. They were all dressed up and seemed to be celebrating some kind of special occasion.

"It can't be!" Fredda's mouth dropped open.

"What do you mean by that?' asked Tildda, already itching to know what was in her mind.

"That one with shoulder length hair, wearing wooden clogs is Grandpa Albert."

"What?" said Tildda in disbelief.

"And the young lady with him is Mrs. Lagarttus," Fredda finished.

"Are you kidding me?" said Tildda.

"Shhh! No, I'm not."

"She's gorgeous. I mean, was. Your Grandpa Albert wasn't bad either. Look at her dress! She always has so much style."

Fredda remembered the picture Blue had brought to her at Grandpa Albert's house. They were wearing the same clothes, but because the picture was black and white, Fredda hadn't been able to see the color of Mrs. Lagarttus' dress. It was an incredibly stunning royal blue.

"Wait a minute, that's Grandpa and Grandma," said Benn.

"Are you sure?" asked Fredda.

"Oh, my! I can't believe it! Yes, that's Grandma and Grandpa when they were young," said Tildda smiling broadly.

"But who are the other couple?" asked Fredda.

"I can't see them," said Benn.

"Neither can I," said Tildda.

The other couple was sitting with their backs to them.

Meanwhile, from the table they could hear Grandpa Albert toasting, "To my dear friends, Rutta and Vitello, I wish you both happiness and lots of love on this special day of your engagement."

The trio heard the clink of champagne glasses in celebration of Tildda and Benn's grandparents' engagement.

Then, Mrs. Theoddora and Mrs. Lagarttus took off to the kitchen, while the third lady got up from the table and went to play the piano. However, they couldn't see her face or the face of the young man who was with her.

The three young men remained at the table whispering to each other. Fredda, Tildda and Benn couldn't hear them anymore. Mr. Theoddora bent down and took a paper bag out from under the table. From inside the bag, he pulled out what seemed to be three silver boxes. The men glanced at them and then quickly put them inside the paper bag again.

Then Grandpa Albert turned around, took down a picture from the wall behind him, took a plank from the wall, placed the paper bag inside, put the plank back and hung the picture again. By this time, Mrs. Theoddora and Mrs. Lagarttus were back from the kitchen with heaping trays of food in their hands.

"That's it!" said Fredda. "The silver boxes were here all the time. We didn't have to go to The Right Side to find them."

"We should go now," said Benn.

"Wait, I want to see who the third couple is," said Fredda. But someone was coming from downstairs. They had no choice but to go upstairs to the attic.

"How are we going to get back home?" asked Tildda. "I mean we are home, but to the right time."

"Probably the same way we came in," said Fredda, looking at the mirror.

Fredda asked Tildda and Benn to give their hands to her. She also asked them to close their eyes and she did the same. She stepped forward into the mirror, thought about her cozy bed at the windmill and in no time, they were on the hard wood floors of the girl's room at Mrs. Theoddora's place.

Someone was knocking at the door and calling for Benn. Tildda grabbed a deck of cards nearby and sat back on the floor. Fredda hadn't even moved from the floor yet. Benn went to open the door.

It was Mrs. Theoddora. "Ah! There you are. I've been calling you but you didn't answer me," she said, without a breath, after having come three floors up.

"Sorry, I didn't hear you, Grandma," said Benn nervously.

"We were here … playing cards," finished Tildda.

"Ah! You need to get up early tomorrow to help your grandpa downstairs because I have to leave early," she said.

"Okay," said Benn, without arguing. "Oh! By the way, Grandma, could I clean the attic and make it a place for us to hang out?"

"Are you feeling all right, Benn?" asked his grandmother looking at him inquisitively.

"Yes, I am," he responded. "Why?"

"Because this is the first time in your entire life that you have ever asked me if you could clean something in this house without my having to beg you …" She smiled.

CHAPTER 11

LOVE SINISSTER

Next morning, as he had promised his grandmother, Benn got up early. Fredda and Tildda were still in bed. A commotion erupted outside the diner.

Fredda awoke and went to the window, but her body was heavy and she felt exhausted. Even more people were outside today than the day before. It seemed the disturbance from the street had moved inside the diner. The blades of the windmill passed by, as she tried to make sense of what was going on.

"Tildda," said Fredda. "Wake up! Something's going on downstairs."

Tildda didn't move. Fredda changed her clothes and tried to wake Tildda again. Finally, she stirred.

"Wake up, Tildda."

"Okay, okay, I'm up," said Tildda slowly opening her blue eyes.

"We have to go downstairs. Something's going on!"

Tildda rolled out of bed, not knowing exactly where she was. She felt like a truck had rolled over her. Sleepily she said, "The silver boxes ..."

Fredda's eyebrows lifted in surprise. She hadn't even been thinking about the boxes.

Tildda changed quickly and both of them went downstairs. As they were approaching the last step, they saw the round table, the same table they had seen last night when Mr. and Mrs. Theoddora had gotten engaged. On top on the table was a beautiful purple orchid, very similar to the orchid Mr. Uggo Schnapps had sent to Fredda. They stopped in their tracks and looked at each other worriedly.

With the noise from the diner in the background, Mrs. Theoddora sprang up in front of them seemingly out of nowhere. Fredda and Tildda stepped back.

"You two," she said. "Do not move." Pointing her left index finger at them, "Stay exactly where you are. I need to talk to you. By the way, you two look awful." And she went back into the kitchen.

For sure they were in trouble now.

"Where's Benn?" asked Tildda. "We need to talk to him."

A few seconds later, Mrs. Theoddora came from the kitchen, followed by Mr. Theoddora in his white cook's hat. Mrs. Theoddora had something in her hand.

However, Fredda couldn't see it very well. Mrs. Theoddora was trying to hide it from her. She stepped closer to Fredda. She sensed that something was about to happen. Everything that went on last night came back to her like a nightmare. She thought that Mrs. Theoddora was going to send her back to the other side. All these crazy horrible thoughts invaded her mind.

She saw Benn appear. Mr. Theoddora's helpers from the kitchen, Mrs. D'Rof, and others who she didn't even know, were approaching her. Then, Mrs. Theoddora stepped aside. There stood Mr. Theoddora and Noell holding a beautiful cake alit with candles. Everybody began singing *Happy Birthday* to her.

Taken aback by all this, Fredda thought she was going to faint. Tildda was the first to hug her friend and wish her a happy birthday. "Now it's official, you're thirteen."

Benn came up to Fredda and wished her a happy birthday, followed by everyone who was there. She had totally forgotten that it was her birthday, as well as a special day to be celebrated - International Day For The Left-Handed People.

While Mrs. Theoddora was cutting the cake, guests dropped their colorfully wrapped gifts for Fredda on the table. Fredda crooked her finger at Benn signaling that she wanted to talk to him over by the staircase.

He approached Fredda and Tildda. Fredda asked, "Why is the purple orchid on the table?"

"You're not going to believe this, but Grandma took the flower from the greenhouse, brought it to the contest, you know the one where they choose the most exotic and striking orchid, and guess what?"

"She won!" responded Tildda excitedly.

"Yep, she did. She's been trying to win the contest for the past thirteen years, but a member of the Sinisster family always gets the first prize. Grandma's extremely happy."

"Oh! So, all the noise coming from the outside was about that?" asked Fredda.

"Yes, all her friends, neighbors and people who know Grandma came here to congratulate her," said Benn.

Fredda Buttler And The Left-Handed People

"And what does she win? I mean, is there any reward?" asked Fredda.

"Well, other than the prestige and the tickets to go see the ballet tonight, and the blue ribbon that's placed at the entrance of the diner, I don't think she gets anything else."

Fredda tilted her head to see the entrance. There, upon a pedestal standing at the entrance, was the first place blue ribbon.

"Here, Fredda, your cake. I cut a piece for you." Mrs. Theoddora smiled. "Oh! You should have seen the Sinissters family's faces at the moment the judges told us who got first place!" She talked on and on about the contest.

After they finished eating the cake and heard the story about the first place win over and over, Tildda, Benn and Noell helped Fredda take her presents to her bedroom.

Alone, now they could talk.

"How're you feeling, Benn?" asked Fredda.

"Since yesterday, after all that, I feel really tired. I mean, my body *and* my mind."

"Tildda and I, we feel the same."

It should have been a joyous occasion for Fredda. She had never gotten so many presents in all her life. There were all those people there celebrating her birthday. But it seemed that now, it wasn't so important.

"What's going on?" asked Noell. "Aren't you going to open your presents, Fredda?"

"Well, not now, Noell. We have other stuff to discuss," said Tildda, as bossy as usual.

"Well, aren't you going to tell me what's going on?"

The three of them whispered at the same time, "It's complicated!"

They explained every detail about their adventure the evening before to Noell. They left out nothing, including the purple orchid and how today the flower ended up receiving first place. Noell's face was unmoving. His jaw hung open like he was watching a horror movie. His blue eyes widened as he followed their lips. When they finished telling their story, Noell said, "And I was wearing that stupid tuxedo and had to be on my best behavior at that stupid dinner with my parents, while you guys were having so much fun! No fair!"

"Yes, but it wasn't all fun, Noell. I was scared," said Tildda, "And if we had gotten caught in action at school or even worse gotten stuck in the past? Imagine me in the past? I couldn't live in that time knowing that the future is so much better. And now we know so much more. Maybe we're in danger like your Grandpa Albert or even like Mr. Schnapps," said Tildda, horrified.

"All right," said Fredda, "We can't say anything to anyone about last night. Not even to Mr. Schnapps. If we see him again we're going to tell him that we didn't go to my great-aunt's house, okay?"

"But, what about Evvos, Maggia and Maggos Sinisster?" asked Benn apprehensively.

"Well, I don't know yet. We deal with them later," said Fredda, also troubled.

"We went to so much trouble to learn about these silver boxes last night, and yet we don't know much about them at all. And, what if Mr. Schnapps was only using us to get to those boxes! He should've told us why we need them. I think what we did last night was really stupid!"

Sometimes, Tildda didn't make any sense, but she had a point now. Fredda thought about what Tildda had just said. She wasn't really sure why they had followed Mr.

Schnapps orders either. Fredda's mind was working overtime, *What if it's true that Mr. Schnapps was only using us?*

"So, what are we going to do now?" asked Benn, waiting for an answer.

"Well, I think we should remove the boxes from the diner, if they're there, and hide them in another place," said Fredda.

"And how are we going to get in and check on the silver boxes?" asked Tildda.

"We can't do it now!" responded Benn.

"Then, when?" asked Fredda, also nervous. Noell stood around listening.

"Well, Grandma's going to close part of the diner today and reopen it around 2:00 this afternoon. You know, because of the bicycle parade. And the area where the round table is located is the area that's going to be closed. I'm supposed to check all the tables and sweep the floors. So I can check and see if I can find something in that hiding spot," Benn whispered.

"And if you get them, where're we going to hide them?" asked Fredda.

"I have an idea," said Benn, "Maybe we can put it in the attic. I already asked Grandma if we can clean the room and make a place for us."

"Oh! That's a great idea, Benn," said Fredda.

A little more relaxed now, Fredda finally opened her presents. She received lots of clothes and shoes. Just what she needed! She envisioned herself in her new wardrobe instead of that ridiculous uniform. She also received a present from Grandpa Albert. It was a wrist watch, and of course, it had all the numbers in reverse like the big clock at the bicycle station.

Fredda put it on her right wrist. It was her first watch. It was nice to know that Grandpa Albert remembered her birthday. There was a note inside the box, but Fredda didn't want to read it in front of everybody, so she put it in her pocket.

They all went up to the attic. The place was a mess like Benn had said. It looked like a dusty old junk shop filled with discarded and stored items – old chairs, lots of boxes, books, small tables, old clothes, umbrellas, pictures and more.

They didn't even know where to start. Tildda looked at the place disgustedly. She didn't want to touch anything. But they opened all the windows first and little by little the four of them made progress. The place started shaping up.

Benn told them that he had to do his chores downstairs. They looked at him nervously. Neither of them said a word. They knew Benn would be looking for the silver boxes. Fredda, Tildda and Noell continued cleaning, putting their energy into something better than just waiting anxiously for Benn.

About an hour later, Benn came upstairs and brought a carton with him. He placed it on the small wooden table in the center of the room, looked around and said, "Wow! This place looks great. Now we have a place to hang out."

"Did you get the silver boxes?" Fredda whispered.

"Yes, I got them. It was quite easy. Nobody was there. And besides, everybody is too busy today with so many things happening."

Fredda stepped over to the table and looked down at the carton. She lifted its top and peeked inside. There sat the bag they had seen being placed inside the wall last night.

Fredda Buttler And The Left-Handed People

Carefully, she opened it and pulled out its contents. Sure enough, there were the three silver boxes. She placed them on the small wooden table. The three silver boxes were exactly like Mr. Schnapps had drawn them - all of them with hands imprinted on their tops. One with the left hand, one with the right hand and another one with both hands imprinted on their lids. Fredda stared down at them.

Finally, restless, Tildda asked, "Aren't you going to open them?"

Fredda grabbed the one with the left hand imprinted on it, studied the box, tried to pull the top off, but the lid didn't move. She thought for a moment and placed her left hand on top of the left hand imprinted on the box.

Tildda's eyes fixed on the silver box expecting something to happen, but the attempt was in vain. She couldn't. Fredda put the box down. She tried the other boxes, but nothing happened. She couldn't open them either.

"Oh! Great," said Tildda. "We went through so much for nothing."

"Let's just forget about it for now. Okay? Let's find a place to hide them," said Fredda extremely disappointed.

They hid them behind some of the many piles of books in the attic. The group continued cleaning the rest of the room with their disappointment hanging in the air.

After they finished organizing, they sat down on the two old ragged but comfortable couches. The room looked awesome.

"Oh! I just remembered, grandma and grandpa are going to the theater tonight to see the ballet. This is our only chance to go to see the LeftSide Band!" said Tildda, wild with excitement.

"Well, I don't think it's such a good idea," replied Benn.

"After all I went through last night, I think I deserve it. I'm going," said Tildda imposing herself. "And besides, my mother is going to the theater with grandma and grandpa."

"I've never seen a concert in my entire life," said Fredda, smiling at Tildda.

"Me neither," said Noell.

Loud noise drifted up from outside, like the chaos this morning. They ran toward the windows. They'd been working so intensely that they hadn't realized that it was time for the bicycle parade.

They bolted from the attic to the first floor and got caught by Mr. Theoddora who told them that running wasn't allowed in the windmill. It reminded Fredda of International Academy. They calmly walked outside. However, once out there they were all totally enthused again.

The parade was unbelievably colorful and packed.

Finally, the quartet found a place to enjoy it. They watched Mr. Bernno on his latest tricycle. It was amazing to see the variety.

Other familiar faces showed up, but this time not so pleasant. It was Evvos Sinisster, his cousins, and more members of his family. Evvos's eyes locked on Fredda's. He gave her a long gleaming stare and then smiled, but Fredda knew it was a dangerous one.

Her memory went back to school, when she had thought Attos Azzar was the worst thing that had ever happened to her. But, she knew the moment she had laid eyes on Evvos Sinisster, Attos was no match whatsoever. There was something evil about Evvos.

Fredda Buttler And The Left-Handed People

Fredda broke the stare, and scanned the people with him. "Who is that old man?" she asked Benn.

"Ah! That's Mr. Morbiddus and his wife, Mrs. Avidda Sinisster. They're Evvos' grandparents. That one is Mr. Trevvous and his wife, Mrs. Almma Sinisster, Evvos' parents. And the girl, is Ophellia Sinisster, Evvos' little sister." Ophellia was about eleven years old. "The ones on the opposite side are Mr. Ceuss and Mrs. Manddra Sinisster, Maggos' and Maggia's parents. And the ones in the middle are Mr. Mauss and his wife, Mrs. Solitudde Sinisster, Faddus' and Fadda's parents." Fredda remembered seeing them at the Handless Pizzeria with Evvos, Maggos and Maggia once. "Mr. Trevvous, Ceuss and Mauss are Mr. Morbiddus Sinisster's sons," finished Benn.

It was a tradition for the Sinisster family to join the bicycle parade. You could tell who belonged to the family by blood. Most of them seemed to have dark beady eyes, thin lips and were long and lanky. They all wore dark colored clothes and looked extremely morbid.

After the parade, the group headed back to the diner. They realized they hadn't eaten since morning. The only thing they had in their stomachs was Fredda's birthday cake.

As they approached the entrance of the windmill, another tumult was rising in front of the diner. It was Mrs. Matrakka, yelling. On the opposite side was Mrs. Camerron, her twin sister, holding her husband's arm. Right in front of the four of them was Mr. and Mrs. Theoddora. And Mrs. Theoddora held a large glass of champagne, as she had been celebrating the accomplishment of her first place win since early morning. The twin sisters shouted at each other as loudly as they could.

"YOU STOLE HIM FROM ME!" said Mrs. Matrakka loud and clear.

"I DID NOT!" Mrs. Camerron yelled right back at her. "HE LOVES ME, NOT YOU!"

"I CAN'T BELIEVE YOU BROUGHT HER HERE! SHE'S NOT EVEN ONE OF US!" shouted Mrs. Matrakka to Mr. Camerron.

After a while of screeching at each other, things calmed down. They all disbanded and walked away.

"Ah! Isn't love beautiful! Cheers! TO LOVE!" said tipsy Mrs. Theoddora, drinking her champagne.

"What was that all about, Grandma?" asked Tildda

"Love is such a beautiful thing, don't you think?" she said, putting her arms around Tildda walking inside the diner with her. Fredda, Benn and Noell followed.

"Why were they screaming at each other?" asked Tildda.

"Oh! My dear, it is all about love, that's it, love. MORE CHAMPAGNE!" screamed Mrs. Theoddora to her workers in the kitchen. "Well, I'll tell you the story about Mrs. Matrakka and Mrs. Camerron," she continued, as she headed toward the big round table. The same big round table they had cake at this morning, and the same table the three of them had seen when they were in the past.

Mrs. Theoddora sat down, Tildda sat next to her. Fredda sat on the opposite side. Benn and Noell sat with them. By this time, they had even forgotten about food, as the story that Mrs. Theoddora was about to tell seemed more interesting.

"Well, this is what happened. When the twin sisters were very young, they were very pretty and, as you know, totally alike." Mrs. Theoddora laughed giddily, "I know I should not laugh, but I can't help myself. HA, HA, HA. So, Mrs. Matrakka met this handsome man …"

One of the workers came from the kitchen with a bottle of champagne. Mrs. Theoddora grabbed the whole bottle and plunked it down on the table. She drank a little more and continued, "Mrs. Herta Matrakka fell in love for the first time. She felt she had found the love of her life. They had a date to go to a dance party given by one of his friends. But, Mrs. Matrakka fell ill and couldn't attend with him. Her love went along with some of his pals. Hilda happened to have been invited to the same party.

Not knowing who Mrs. Matrakka was seeing at that time, Hilda, her sister, found herself attracted to a young man she had met there. This young man was Mr. Camerron and when he saw Hilda, he thought that it was Herta. He was surprised when he found out that Herta had a twin sister. She hadn't ever told him. It turned out Mr. Camerron's attraction to Hilda was mutual. Even though you couldn't not tell them apart, there was something special in Hilda that he had not seen in Herta. Their love grew. Oh my, oh my … when Mrs. Matrakka found out that they were seeing each other, she almost killed her sister with a sharp knife. Mrs. Matrakka never forgave her for stealing her man."

Mrs. Theoddora took another sip and said, "Love is a strange thing, my dear. You can die for it or you can kill for it."

Now Fredda understood why Mrs. Matrakka hated her twin sister.

Mrs. Theoddora went on, "But Mrs. Matrakka was not the only person who lost the love of her life. So did your Grandpa Albert, Fredda." Another sip of champagne slid down Mrs. Theoddora's throat. "Your grandpa, my dear, was a knock out in his time. Don't tell my husband I said that. He's very jealous. Well, where was I? Oh yes, your Grandpa Albert was engaged to Lotta Lagarttus."

Fredda's jaw dropped.

"I believe she's one of your teachers at school. Well, they were engaged and ready to get married, when *boom*. First, Albert's mother, your great-grandmother, Fredda, tore and burned all the invitations for the wedding. She didn't approve of the marriage because she thought it would be difficult for Albert to marry a rightie. Lotta never forgave her for doing such a horrible thing.

So, they had to postpone the wedding day. And then, Albert met Adelle, your grandmother. Oh! She had beautiful dimples like you, Fredda. They fell in love with each other the moment they saw each other. The rest is history. It was Mrs. Lerddus who introduced Adelle to your Grandpa Albert. Guerdda and Adelle were friends since they were young, like you and Tildda."

Fredda thought for a moment, *Mrs. Lagarttus was very rude to Mrs. Lerddus at Grandpa Albert's house. No wonder Mrs. Lagarttus dislikes Mrs. Lerddus so much.*

Mrs. Theoddora kept talking, "Oh! I've a photograph around here somewhere." She looked above their heads to see if she could find the picture on the wall. Sure enough, she found it. "It's behind you Benn, that one," she pointed to it.

Benn took the picture from the wall and handed it to Mrs. Theoddora. "Here we are, on my engagement day, at the theater. Albert and Lotta, my handsome husband-to-be and me. And oh! How could I forget about them?" She pointed to the couple in the picture and said, "Mr. Uggo Schnapps and your great-aunt, Annora, Fredda."

Fredda took a good look at the picture. Tildda tilted the picture in her direction. Benn stood up to see it. The three looked at each other, but no words were said because they knew that they couldn't discuss anything in front of Mrs. Theoddora. They also knew that was the couple who they hadn't recognized last night. They let her finish her story.

"Oh, it's a shame. They were so in love and they were such a beautiful couple, until that fateful day when he lost his mind. He was such an intelligent man, and she also such an intelligent woman. Together they really formed a spectacular mind. They had all their lives ahead of them."

They were very quiet up to this point and then Tildda, who could no longer contain her curiosity asked, "Grandma, how exactly did Mr. Schnapps lose his mind?"

Mrs. Theoddora thought for a moment and said, "Nobody exactly knows what happened to him."

They knew she wasn't telling them the truth.

Mrs. Theoddora took a look at the picture one more time and said, "Only your grandpa and I made it. We got married and we stayed married until this day. Look at my wedding band," and she displayed the gold band on her left finger and said, "I never take it from my finger. It's bad luck if you do, you know."

"Mrs. Theoddora, why do people wear their wedding bands on the fourth finger of the left hand?" asked Fredda.

"Well they say that it is related to the vena amoris, meaning vein of love. The legend says that there is a vein that runs from the heart directly to the fourth finger of the left hand. But if you ask me, it's because it's the correct hand, of course!"

"Are you happy being married to grandpa for so many years, Grandma?" asked Tildda.

"Oh! Yes, I'm very happy. I made the right choice." And another sip of champagne went down her throat.

"Anyone hungry?" asked Mrs. Theoddora.

"Starving," said Noell. Up to that point he had sat and only observed them.

"Doesn't your father feed you, boy? You look so skinny. We'll have to fatten you up! We have food here, lots of food," said Mrs. Theoddora totally inebriated. "I think I need to take a nap. Benn, would you please help your grandpa for a while?"

"Yes, Grandma. I will."

They all left the table. Benn told the girls to go upstairs to the attic, while he and Noell would go to the kitchen to get food and bring it up so they could be alone to talk.

The girls started upstairs, but on the way up, Fredda put her hand in her pocket and remembered that she hadn't read the note Grandpa Albert had sent her. She told Tildda she had to go to the bathroom and she'd be there shortly.

In the bathroom, Fredda unfolded the note and read it to herself:

Dear Fredda,

I am sorry for not being able be there with you on your 13th birthday, but I love you very much and Happy Birthday to you. I hope you like the watch.

P.S. - Please stay away from Mr. Uggo Schnapps. I know he has been trying to contact you. You know he has not been well for a long time. He has a very disturbed mind.

Love,
Grandpa Albert

Fredda ran to the attic. Benn and Noell weren't there yet. A moment later, they arrived with some food. Benn ran downstairs one more time to get the rest.

They discussed the picture over the meal. Fredda also showed them the note from Grandpa Albert. Now, for sure, they knew that Mr. Schnapps was trying to get to the silver boxes.

"So, what're we going to do?" asked Tildda.

"Nothing, we don't have to do anything," responded Fredda. "Let's stick with what we had said before. If we see him, we're going to tell him that we don't have the silver boxes. That's it."

They all agreed. Benn had to leave them again to help his grandpa downstairs. Tildda told him that if he wanted to go the concert tonight he should meet them outside where the bicycles were parked after grandma, grandpa and her mother were gone.

"Okay, I'll think about it," and then he left.

Fredda sat on the windowsill. Tildda and Noell joined her. It was a great spot to look down at the busy street.

Nothing was said for a long time. They could see the blade from the windmill circling in front of them.

Normally, it was Tildda who always broke the ice. But this time, it was Fredda who asked a question. "What happened to Benn's parents?"

"What?" asked Tildda.

"Benn's parents ... Where are they? I mean, I didn't want to ask him about it. You know how I feel when anyone asks me about my parents."

"Oh! I keep forgetting that you don't know some of the stuff about this side. Nobody knows exactly what happened to my mother's sister and her husband. Grandma said that one day they left the house and just never came back home, like they vanished."

"You mean they disappeared?"

"Yes, something like that. But, I think Grandma knows more about it and chooses not to tell us."

"But they aren't dead, are they?" said Fredda.

"We don't know."

Fredda leaned her head on the windowpane. The blade continued its turning. She seemed lost in thought.

Tildda finally broke the silence. "What is it, Fredda?"

She took her time to answer. "Well, when my grandpa came to see me at school, he didn't have any answers about my parents either."

"What do you mean?"

Fredda related the whole story Grandpa Albert had told her about her parents, and how it came to be that he didn't know about having a granddaughter.

When Fredda finished, Tildda said, "So, that means that your parents aren't dead. They may be alive."

"Exactly! That's why I need to talk to Grandpa Albert. But he was in such a hurry last time I saw him. He's always running from something or someone."

"And Mr. Schnapps told you that the *bad* men were after him."

"And now that you told me that Benn's parents also disappeared, it makes me wonder. Do you know when his parents vanished?"

"When he was a baby, I guess. I don't talk to him about this subject. Benn never talks to anyone about it, never."

"Yes, you're right. Benn doesn't like to talk about his parents," said Noell, who had been very quiet.

Fredda thought, *And neither do I.*

Noell added, "And by the way, I have to go now. I have to think about what I'm going to say to my parents about tonight. You know, the concert. I wanna go. I don't wanna miss anything anymore!" And he left.

Fredda and Tildda stayed in the attic for the rest of the afternoon observing the party downstairs. The weather was great. It was a beautiful sunny day. They even had a chance to see the dancers dancing on a wooden stage outside next to the windmill.

The outside stage was created for the people who couldn't pay to go to the theater. It was wonderful! From where Fredda and Tildda watched, they really had the best seat in the house.

Fredda's birthday day was her best birthday ever.

She looked at the time on her new watch and saw that time had passed quickly. It was almost time for Mrs. Theoddora, her husband and Mrs. D'Rof to go to the theater. Fredda and Tildda saw a yellow bicycle taxi come to pick them up.

"Let's go. We're going to have so much fun," Tildda bubbled animatedly.

Unexpectedly, not only Noell, but Benn, were waiting for them downstairs. Tildda smiled and winked at Benn. Then, they mounted their bikes and rode away.

It was almost dusk when they arrived at the Darkkplace, which was not far from the windmill. None of them had ever been there before. Now, Fredda could understand why it was called the Darkkplace. It seemed that life had been drained from it and that included its color.

The only color Fredda could see was the orange and red of the fire torches illuminating the narrow streets. In the wake of that dim light, she could see outlines of people walking toward the concert. Most of the lifeless gray buildings in the area were abandoned.

They continued walking and suddenly Fredda stopped. She turned her head to the left and froze. The street that she looked down seemed like a long, dark and slithering snake crawling toward the abandoned house at the end of it. Tall black wisteria trees lined both sides of the street with their Medusa-like branches arching over it. She shivered. She sensed sheer agony coming from that street.

"What *is* this place?" said Fredda horrified.

Noell looked petrified.

"You mean this street?" said Benn.

"Yes, what is it?"

It was Tildda who decided to tell Fredda. She also looked terrified. Even though it was her first time at the Darkkplace, she knew the story very well.

"Well, the story about this street is a very famous one. The street used to be called Palm Street, but now it's called Black Wisteria Street. Frederikk Sinisster was its owner and of the old house you see at the end of it also.

Frederikk was in love with Mella Cattarina. Frederikk's father never approved of Sinisster marrying a rightie, never. It would be a disgrace to the family. So Mella's mother pushed her to marry Jullious and continuously preached, 'Jullious is a good man'. Mella also needed someone to help with her sick mother. She felt she had no choice but to marry Jullious because she knew that Frederikk's family would never allow her to marry the love of her life. So, with a broken heart, she consented to marry Jullious, the baker. They say that Mella remained in love with Federikk all her life, even though she married Jullious.

After the wedding, Frederikk went somewhat insane with anger and guilt over losing Mella to the baker. He chopped down all the beautiful palms, fifty seven, and he planted the black wisteria instead. The street used to be magnificent, alive and green. Now it's sad, morbid and dark. Nothing grows between the trees. Not even the birds come to this street. They say if you enter this street, you'll get trapped like Frederikk was, trapped in the darkness.

Frederikk never loved anyone else but Mella and he died old, single and in despair. After that, this place attracted horrifyingly bad energy to it, and people started moving their businesses to different locations. And it ended up like you see it now."

Fredda, Benn and Noell were dumbfounded.

"Okay, let's get going! We're going to be late for the concert," said Tildda.

They continued walking on the main street, joining the increasing number of young people headed for the concert. Fredda saw a few small stores along the way.

They passed a shop window and the sign said, Let Me Read Your Future.

Fredda looked inside through the glass store front, and she saw an extremely old rail thin woman with long gray hair down to her waist. The woman sat on a chair at a tiny wooden table, pen in each hand, both writing on the piece of paper in front of her. Fredda was fascinated by what she was seeing. The ancient looking lady could write with both hands at the same time!

Fredda detoured into the place. Everything looked ancient, just like the lady. Now close to her, she could see that not only was the lady writing with both hands at the same time, but also from right to left. It was amazing.

The old woman smiled at her. It would've been better if she hadn't. She had only two teeth hanging from her upper gums. Fredda was somewhat shocked. She had never seen a person with no teeth or almost no teeth.

It took a few seconds for her to recover. Tildda covered her mouth with her hands. Noell looked like he was going to throw up. Benn was the only one who seemed to be okay.

The old lady put aside the paper that she had been writing on and started writing again on a fresh piece. She wrote with great speed with both hands. When she was done, she folded the piece of paper and handed it with both hands to Fredda. Fredda extended her left arm and took it from her.

The woman looked at her, and then looked at the red dish that was lying on the wooden table. Fredda saw that there was some money in it. She realized what the woman wanted, reached into her pocket and put some money into it.

Then the ragged lady said in a raspy voice, "Only open it when you need it most, and you'll need it soon. You'll feel the need." It was eerie. Then she shooed them out.

They literally ran out of the place almost breaking the door.

Fredda still had the folded paper in her hand but stashed it away in her pocket.

"What was that all about?" asked Noell.

"Can we have some fun now?" said Tildda, annoyed.

They ran on. They didn't stop anywhere else, until they finally reached the shabby building which looked as if had once been a theater. There were people selling tickets outside. They bought tickets for themselves.

The entrance was only a big open arch in the wall. They walked through, and to their astonishment, found themselves standing in only a shell of a building with the sky and the stars as its roof.

"AWESOME!" yelled Tildda.

The first note could be heard from the stage, and then, the young crowd went wild as the music surged. Fredda was shocked. She had no idea a rock concert would be like this. She looked around and saw teenagers screaming, dancing, singing and laughing uninhibitedly.

A familiar face jumped in front of them. It was Allfo dancing in discombobulated movements.

"HI THERE, FREDDA!" yelled Allfo over the music. He continued dancing, although he was somewhat uncoordinated.

Tildda was the first of their group to start dancing and pushed Fredda to do the same. Fredda didn't know exactly what to do. She had never danced before, especially to this kind of music.

Like everything else that's good doesn't last forever, so went the concert. They had spent the last two hours having fun and a wonderful experience. They walked out of the old building heading directly to where they had left their bicycles.

Fredda looked at the time on her new watch. She figured that they'd be home way before Tildda and Benn's grandparents, and also Tildda's mom. Everything was going according to their plans.

However, when they were nearing their bikes, Fredda saw Evvos Sinisster, and this time he was accompanied not only by his cousins, Maggos and Maggia, but also by his other two cousins, Faddus and Fadda.

"Look who's here," said Evvos threateningly. "I want to know what you were doing in that school of yours? And why did you bring the wishy-washy boy and the rightie with you? Brought another right-hander with you today?" Evvos was referring to Noell. And the cousins started laughing.

"It isn't any of your business what I do or don't!" Fredda answered bravely.

Tildda was surprised at Fredda's brashness.

Evvos smiled at Fredda slyly. She knew he was not to be trusted.

"FREDDA!" yelled Tildda, "Let's go, now!"

Tildda, Benn and Noell were already on their bikes and took off. A few seconds behind them, Fredda reached her bike and left the scene. The five Sinissters were right behind her. She pedaled as fast as she could, but her bicycle was such an old model, no match for the Sinissters! They would catch her at any moment. Fredda lost sight of her friends.

And unluckily for her, there was a fork in the road. She had to make a quick decision where to go, and unfortunately, she decided to go right, which turned out to be private property, and the wrong direction.

Tildda was close enough to get a glimpse of Fredda going the wrong way. She told the boys to stop riding.

"Fredda, went in the wrong direction! We have to go back and help her," said Tildda almost out of breath.

"Okay! Let's go," said Noell already turning back.

"NOT YOU, NOELL!" shouted Tildda. "Only Benn and I. Go home and don't tell anybody what's going on."

"But …"

"GO NOW, FAST, NOELL!" Tildda shouted again.

"Okay." Noell knew he couldn't contradict Tildda, especially now that she was so nervous and about to explode.

"Let's go, Tildda. Fredda biked on to Mr. Morbiddus Sinisster's property, Evvos's grandfather's house," said Benn.

Benn and Tildda pedaled back speedily.

Meanwhile, Fredda found herself going uphill and her legs gave up on her. She got off her pink bike, and started pulling the bike up hill. She reached a point where the road ended right before it turned into what seemed to be an endless abyss. A horrifying thought that she could have fallen into it, never to be seen again, flooded her brain.

Fredda was defenseless and trapped with nowhere to go. All she could do was to stand there and watch the five Sinissters approaching.

"Look who's here, trespassing. This is private property. Don't you know?" said Evvos, smirking. "Not so brave now, Fredda Buttler. Yes, I did my homework about you and your family."

Fredda saw Benn and Tildda riding toward her, but she didn't know exactly what to do or what to expect.

"Oh! Look, your friends, also trespassing. But I'm more interested in you, Fredda Buttler. How dare you come to this side after all that your parents did to my family?"

Evvos stepped forward. The other Sinisster members did as well. Fredda stepped backward and brought her bicycle closer to her, between them. She couldn't move any further back, otherwise, she would tumble into the deep dark hole.

Evvos continued, "And how dare you step foot onto a Sinisster property!"

"I just want to leave, and I don't understand what you're talking about," responded Fredda, sweating now.

"Why did you go to The Right Side?" asked Evvos losing patience.

"Leave her alone," said Tildda tremulously.

"Shut up, rightie. My business is with Buttler, not with you or that wishy-washy. You think that we're bad people, don't you?"

"Yes, I think you can be bad if you want to be," answered Fredda. She could feel the sweat rolling down her face.

"You're more like us than you know, Fredda Buttler."

"I'm not like you or your family. My mother and father had nothing to do with you. And I would like to go now."

"I'm surprised, I don't think she knows," said Evvos smiling sardonically.

"Know what?"

"You really *don't* know. I can't believe it. They kept this secret from you," said Evvos arrogantly and he shot a deadly look toward her.

"What secret?"

"Your mother broke the tradition of our family when she married your father. YOUR RIGHTIE FATHER!" shouted Evvos.

"YOU'RE LYING!" Fredda shouted back at him with her already big brown eyes growing even bigger.

Tildda's hand flew to her mouth. Benn stood there not knowing what to say. This was news to them.

"Your mother was a Sinisster, but not anymore. And you're not welcome here," he finished condescendingly. They heard a dog barking not very far from them.

"Let's go," ordered Evvos, "It must be Uncle's Ceuss' dog and it's a horrible creature." The Sinissters' biked off hurriedly.

Fredda didn't have time to move before the black dog showed up. The humungous Rottweiler bared his sharp fangs and snarled at a shivering in fear Fredda.

Right behind the fierce-looking dog, stood a man dressed in black. Benn and Tildda, at this point, couldn't do anything to help, but were still in viewing distance of her.

"Sic the trespasser!" Evvos's uncle commanded his dog, and then, he just walked away.

A scream welled up in Tildda, but Benn reached out and covered her mouth to stop it. He was afraid Evvos' uncle might come back for them.

Saliva dripped from the huge dog's vicious mouth. And then, the monstrous canine lunged for Fredda. She instinctively jumped back, forgetting the emptiness behind her. In horror, she began to plunge into the abyss, still holding on to her bicycle with all her strength.

Tildda screamed again, stepping forward to run to Fredda. But Benn wrapped his arms around her, pulling her back. He was afraid that Tildda would fall into the abyss as well. Their eyes were wide in grief and horror. They stood helpless as things seemed to happen in slow motion.

Fredda's pink bicycle began morphing in front of their eyes. At first the shape was unrecognizable. Fredda gasped as she felt its shape shift. It seemed to just hang there in the emptiness with Fredda atop it. Although it seemed like hours, within a few moments, the transformation was complete. There, beneath Fredda, carrying her on its back, was a giant pink dragon with huge pink wings spread wide soaring her to safety. Tildda and Benn were stone still, their jaws dropped open.

The dragon descended gracefully in an empty lot near the windmill. As quickly as it had before, it transformed back into Fredda's bicycle.

Fredda wasn't sure if she had just experienced an hallucination, but she realized that she was safe for the moment. Shaking about the news of her mother, trembling with the thought that she herself could have died, and astonished with the transformation, she didn't exactly know what to feel anymore. She needed the truth – complicated or not.

So, Fredda sped away heading for the windmill. She leaned her bike against it and bolted inside. Mr. and Mrs. Theoddora, Mr. and Mrs. Segat, Noell's parents, and Mrs. D'Rof, were already back from the theater. Fredda went straight to Mrs. Theoddora and almost breathless, she challenged, "Tell me, tell me that my mother is not from that horrible family!"

"What are you talking about? What happened to you? Look at you? Look at your clothes all dirty, Fredda!" said Mrs. Theoddora concerned.

"Tell me, Mrs. Theoddora, tell me, that my mother is *not* from the Sinisster family?"

"Who told you that?

"Evvos Sinisster."

"Oh! That boy's just trouble!"

Mrs. Theoddora looked deeply at Fredda, pulled up a chair, and sat down, and said, "I'm sorry, Fredda, but I'm not going to lie to you, dear. Yes, your mother *is* from the

Sinisster family. She is the sister of Ceuss, Trevvous, and Mauss Sinisster. But she was very different from them. She was a lovely lady."

Fredda gasped in shock. Her eyes blinked in disbelief. After a moment, she turned and ran toward her room. But on the way up, she decided to go back and ask more questions to get the truthful answers she thought she deserved. But then, she heard Mrs. Theoddora still talking. All she could think about was what Evvos had told her. Hiding behind the staircase, Fredda listened.

"Poor Fredda! She had to learn about her mother from that horrible boy!"

"Roma Sinisster was such a lovely soul. Her name backwards means Amor, which is love. And that was what she was, a loving woman," said Mr. Theoddora, sighing.

"Yes, Amor. Love Sinisster," finished Mrs. Theoddora.

The group just sat silently and stared ahead with sadness in their eyes.

CHAPTER 12

THE REAL DARKKPLACE

   Fredda hurried to her room. She slammed the door so violently that it could be heard downstairs. She was monumentally angry. Her overwhelming emotions wanted to burst from her core.
   She had always thought that her parents were nice loving people. But now she knew that her mother belonged to the Sinisster family. This made her a Sinisster also. Not by last name, but by *blood*. Evvos and his cousins were her own family. Hate filled her mind.
   Meanwhile, Benn and Tildda arrived in the kitchen. Mrs. Theoddora angrily ran over, stopped them and asked where they had been.
   "Where's Fredda?" Tildda asked preoccupied.

"She's upstairs!" responded her grandpa. Tildda breathed deeply.

"Where have the two of you been?" asked Mrs. Theoddora pointing her index finger at them.

"Fredda came home extremely upset because that miserable boy, Evvos, told her about her mother," said Mr. Theoddora before Benn or Tildda could respond to her question.

"Is that true, Grandma about Fredda's mother?" asked Tildda nervously.

"You didn't answer my question yet, young lady!" said Mrs. Theoddora even more upset now.

"Well, Grandma, we were riding our bikes here around the streets, when Evvos and his cousins saw us. Then they came after us and ..." Tildda was afraid that Benn would say something about where they really had gone, she continued, "... so Fredda fell down and that was when Evvos had the chance to tell her that her mother is from the ... Sinisster Family. Is it true, Grandma?"

Once more, Mrs. Theoddora sat down and took a deep breath and said, "Yes, Fredda's mother *was* from the Sinisster family. She was Mr. Morbiddus' daughter. But she was so unlike the rest of the family. She was such a wonderful woman.

Tildda thought, *If Fredda's mother was Mrs. Morbiddus daughter's then that makes Evvos, Fredda's cousin.*

"Why didn't anybody tell her about her mother?" asked Tildda frowning.

"Because it's for her great-aunt or her grandfather to tell her the truth. This is a family matter, not gossip. This is a very delicate subject. And I bet you, that terrible boy just told her in a horrible way."

Benn was the first to run upstairs. Tildda followed, even though Mrs. Theoddora was yelling at them not to disturb Fredda.

They didn't even knock at Fredda's door. They just burst in. Fredda sat on the windowsill. She was holding the note that the lady, who wrote with both hands, gave to her. The paper was still folded. She looked as if she had been crying

"Oh! We were so worried about you, Fredda!" said Tildda near tears herself.

"You almost died out there, tonight!" said Benn nervously. "If it wasn't for that … pink dragon …" continued Benn having trouble believing he had really seen one.

Fredda didn't say a word. Her eyes fixed on the folded note. It was silent for a while. The only noise was the blade passing by. And then Fredda said, "How do you feel about me now that you know I'm a Sinisster?"

"You're not a Sinisster, Fredda. You're not anything like them," said Tildda firmly.

"You're totally different from them, Fredda. I know Evvos and his cousins. I grew up around them," Benn completed.

Fredda was obsessed with the piece of paper. She didn't comment about what Tildda and Benn had just said to her.

"I feel it," said Fredda.

"Feel what?" asked Tildda.

"Remember what the old ugly lady said? You'll feel it," responded Fredda with her eyes fixed and even more obsessed with the paper in her hand.

"No, you're angry. It's different!" said Benn.

Fredda Buttler And The Left-Handed People

Suddenly, the paper started moving by itself. Fredda startled, dropped the note on the windowsill. The paper unfolded itself. Fredda was terrified, but stood up and went closer to see what was written on it.

"I can't read it. It seems that it's written in another language."

"Let me see it." Benn moved closer. "Yes, it seems that it *is* written in another language."

All of a sudden, the paper moved again and glued itself to the windowpane.

Benn tried carefully to unglue the paper from the glass, but the only thing he was able to do was to pull a corner down from the window.

"Wait, wait, Benn. I can read it." Fredda was able to read it from the reflection in the glass.

"I should have known! The old lady wrote from right to left! She writes using mirror scripts. Leonardo Da Vinci used to write using this technique."

"Shouldn't we use the mirror then?" asked Tildda.

"Not mirrors in *this* town. All mirrors here reflect your true self. It wouldn't work," responded Benn.

"Hurry, Tildda, get a pen and something to write on. I'm going to read it …" said Fredda.

Tildda grabbed a pen from the drawer, but couldn't find any paper. She grabbed a book from the shelves and said, "I'm ready."

Fredda looked at the writing and started reading, "Number thirteen is your lucky number but a number of trouble. Thirteen will give you entrance to a new world, but a dangerous one. There you will get answers to your questions. Only the strong will survive this treacherous place. It will change your life forever. The magnificent become sad, the alive become morbid and the green becomes black. Silver is your color tonight."

The note disappeared in front of their eyes.

Nothing was said until, Tildda exclaimed, "She's talking about Black Wisteria Street!"

"And how do you know *that*?" asked Fredda.

"The street used to be magnificent, alive and green, now it's sad, morbid and dark. It's the only thing I know very well about this town. It's such a tragic love story," said Tildda frowning. "But there are fifty seven horrible trees on that street, not thirteen."

"It doesn't matter," said Fredda sitting down again on the windowsill and looking outside. "It doesn't really matter anymore!"

"Why not?" asked Benn.

"Because I already know about my parents! And it's all that matters to me!" responded Fredda still looking outside.

"And just because your mother came from the Sinisster family, you think you know her?" said Benn walking toward Fredda. "You've never had the opportunity to look into her eyes. You never talked to her. You don't even know who she is. How can you judge her without even knowing her? I'd give anything to see my parents, who disappeared a long time ago. I wouldn't care if my mother was from the Sinisster family. I would at least give her a chance without judging her. But I guess you're okay because you really don't care about her anymore!"

They locked eyes. She could see the pain in his. The same pain she had felt so many times when she thought about her parents.

"I do care! I do care! It's just that I'm so angry that she's from that treacherous family!"

"It's not her fault that she was born into that family! You're letting your anger take over the love that you have for her. Don't do that to yourself, Fredda!"

Tildda stood there and didn't say a word. She'd never seen Benn talk about his parents in such a deeply emotional way. Actually, he had never talked to anyone about his parents. It was a subject that Tildda knew very well not to ask any questions about.

In silence, they stood still for a while in the room. Not even Tildda, who disliked silence, said a word.

After a while, Fredda said, "Benn? You said that your parents disappeared. When did they disappear?"

"Well, I was a baby. I really don't remember. Why?"

"When I first met Grandpa Albert at school I asked him about my parents. I thought they were dead. But he said that he couldn't answer because he didn't know where they were either. He said that they had disappeared. Like your parents. I was also a baby when they vanished and my great-aunt took care of me."

"Do you think that they disappeared at the same time?" asked Benn looking at Fredda's big brown eyes.

"No, my father disappeared first, and then I was born.

After that my mother set off to find him and Grandpa Albert, and then she also disappeared."

Tildda was amazed how Benn, for the first time, as far as she could remember, was talking about his parents. It seemed that Fredda and Benn had something very personal to share about their lives.

"Maybe we should talk to your grandma about my parents and your parents. Maybe she knows something."

"Grandma never talks about them. This is a very painful subject to her. She won't say anything. Even if she knows something," responded Benn, gazing out the window. Once more the blade passed in front of them.

Fredda took the book from Tildda's hand. The book in which Tildda had written the words in the note. She tore the page out of the book and said, "It says here that I'll get answers to my questions. Silver is my color tonight."

"Wait, hold it. I'll be right back," said Benn excitedly and he ran out the door. Fredda looked at Tildda. Tildda just shook her head and shrugged her shoulders.

A few minutes later, Benn was back with a backpack in his hand. He opened it and said, "Silver is your color tonight." He had the three silver boxes with him.

"Do you think that the strange toothless lady was talking about these boxes?" asked Fredda. Tildda frowned.

"I don't know but these boxes are the only silver things I see."

"So, you think that we should go to Black Wisteria Street with them?" asked Fredda.

"Oh! No! I don't think that's a good idea," said Tildda worried.

"What time is it anyway?" asked Benn.

Fredda checked her right wrist so she could see the time, but only now realized that she didn't have her watch anymore. She had probably lost it when she fell earlier. It was the first birthday present she had gotten from her grandpa and she had lost it so soon. She was despondent.

"It's 11:25," responded Benn looking at the clock on the wall, and he continued, "probably Grandma, Grandpa and your mother went to bed. We should go! As the old lady said … Silver is your color tonight. We have to go before midnight."

"Are you two out of your mind? Have you lost it completely? You almost died tonight, Fredda! And you Benn ... I understand that you don't have your parents and you two have something in common, but this is too crazy! That's a horrid street. Nobody goes there during the day, so imagine at night! And besides, you know what they say about the street. If you enter, you'll get trapped in the darkness like Frederikk was."

"I know, Tildda, but I also need some answers to my questions. It's not only about my parents or Fredda's parents," he paused and looked at Tildda, "What about the others who also vanished?"

"Vanished? Who else vanished?" asked Fredda surprised.

"I keep forgetting that you don't know much about this side," said Benn now looking at Fredda.

"Not only had our parents disappeared, but other people did too. There was a time that it wasn't safe to be on this side. But we don't know much about it because no one talks about it. It seems that everybody is afraid to say anything about that period of time. Grandma said that we should always live in the present. Forget about the past because it's too hurtful. And she said not to think about the future."

Fredda thought for a moment and remembered, "When I crossed for the first time to this side, Grandpa Albert told me ... 'Always think about the future. Pay attention to the present and never forget the past, *never*!'"

"I think what your grandpa said makes more sense, way more sense," said Benn.

"Let's go, Benn," said Fredda folding the page of the book and putting it in her pocket.

Once again, Tildda had a decision to make – stay home or go with them. The safe way was staying home, but her curiosity outweighed her need for safety. She joined them.

It was around 11:30 p.m., technically, still Fredda's birthday. She and her friends had already had quite a full day of adventure, but her need to know more about her family and the others who had disappeared burned inside her.

They crept downstairs. It was very quiet. It seemed that everyone had gone. They hopped on their bicycles and left. They got to the Darkkplace quickly. Benn had used the back streets to get them there.

"I still think this is a bad, bad idea!" said Tildda nervously. She looked around and was barely able to see them in the blackness.

"Nobody told you to come with us!" said Benn irritated with Tildda's nagging. At the same time, he took out two small flashlights from his backpack. He gave the second one to Fredda.

It was pitch dark, until the flashlights snapped on.

They were at the entrance of that beastly street. Benn took the lead. Fredda followed him and Tildda was close behind. It seemed that life had vanished from this place and only deep agony had replaced it. They walked on, trying to avoid touching the dreadful black wisterias. But they couldn't avoid their roots. The roots crept out of the ground like they also wanted to leave this place.

"What're we looking for?" asked Tildda impatiently, being careful not to be far from Fredda and Benn.

"We don't know yet!" responded Fredda looking around for some clue.

"You don't even know what you're looking for, do you?" said Tildda panicking.

"TILDDA!" shouted Benn, "If you aren't going to help, please be quiet," said Benn, beaming the flashlight in her face.

They were too far in for Tildda to change her mind now and go back. Actually, they weren't far from the Frederikk's old eerie house either.

Suddenly, someone emerged from the darkness. Tildda screamed so loudly that her voice echoed throughout the spooky street. Benn shot the light on the intruder's face.

To their surprise, it was Mr. Schnapps.

"What are you all doing here in this dreadful place?"

Mr. Schnapps looked awful, even worse than the previous time they had seen him. His eyes bulged as if they were about to pop out from their sockets. His smell was unbearable to Tildda, who moved away from him, holding her nose.

"Doesn't he ever take a shower or brush his teeth?" said Tildda in a nasal voice.

"Not now, Tildda," said Fredda.

"But it's true."

"And what are you doing here, Mr. Schnapps?" asked Fredda calmly.

"I was following you three, of course," he said shifting his eyes all over instead of looking at them.

"Why are you following us?" asked Benn.

"IT'S COMING!" Mr. Schnapps screamed and he shook his head like he wanted to disjoint it from his neck.

"How could such an old bum have been a teacher?" asked Tildda still holding her nose.

"Remember, Tildda, before Mr. Schnapps had his mental confusion problem, he was a very intelligent man.

Maybe a genius like my great-aunt," responded Fredda frowning.

"Hard to believe!" replied Tildda.

Mr. Schnapps started again, holding his head and grinding his yellow teeth and screaming, "IT'S GOING TO START AGAIN, ALL OVER AGAIN! THE BATTLE, BAD TIMES, CONFLICT …" he paused, "THE TWO SIDES, BAD TIMES AGAIN."

"He doesn't make any sense as always," said Tildda tremulously, "Let's get out of this creepy place, please!"

The wind suddenly started to pick up, and began to push against them. The branches of the trees swayed wildly. Fredda saw a bright light coming from behind the old house. Mr. Schnapps warned them not to look at it. He told them to cover their eyes. Fredda put both hands over her eyes and stood there in panic, not knowing what would happen next.

But it was unavoidable. Her fingers started spreading slowly, against her will, until her big brown eyes weren't covered anymore. There it was! The most beautiful thing Fredda had ever seen in her entire life. It was monumental and hypnotizing. Fredda was mesmerized by the size of the brilliant full moon. It was a huge vibrantly yellow bright ball devouring the horizon and part of the sky. She had never seen a moon this size. While the moon was growing, Fredda looked at Tildda, Benn and Mr. Schnapps, their hands still covering their eyes. The wind was building.

Mr. Schnapps spoke in a clear voice and with his thoughts well organized. "They call it the Darkkmoon because it brings darkness to your mind and soul, especially to your soul. If you stare at the moon too long you may lose your soul. Others have such a strong soul that instead, they end up losing their minds." And with that he ran away. Fredda saw him fall a couple of times and then disappear into the darkness.

Fredda's attention was then drawn to shapes of glowing hands which seemed to be floating slightly in front of the trunks of some of the black wisterias. From where she was standing, she counted six trees on her left side and six trees on her right. She noticed on her right that three of the wisterias beamed glowing marks. She moved closer to them. Floating in front of the wisteria on her left, was a single glowing left hand. Suspended in front of the tree on her right, a single right hand glimmered. The one in the middle was a twin wisteria and in front of it shimmered both right and left hands.

She thought, *That's it! Six plus six is twelve. Twelve plus one with the twin tree makes thirteen.* And her thoughts continued, *Fifty seven is five plus seven which is twelve plus the twin makes it thirteen. How could I have computed so quickly? I'm not even good at math!*

Fredda neared the wisteria toward her left and she noticed a square the same size as the silver boxes right behind the glowing hand. The reflection of the moon's light had enabled her to see them. She got hold of Benn's backpack, and removed the boxes from it. Carefully, she placed each silver box in its corresponding square carved into each of the three trees. They each fit perfectly!

Just then, the roots of the trees began to move. Fredda ordered Tildda and Benn to open their eyes without looking at the moon, but to watch out for the squirming roots on the ground.

She had to think of something fast to get them out of this hideous place. The roots started creeping in their direction. Fredda stood paralyzed in front of the wisteria with the left mark on it.

"DO SOMETHING," shouted Tildda, "THESE CREEPING ROOTS ARE GOING TO TRAP US!" Sweat dripped off Fredda, and she had no idea what to do.

"THINK FAST!" shouted Tildda again, while the roots were closer and closer seeking to surround them.

Suddenly, it occurred to Fredda. She shouted to Benn, "BENN, CHANGE PLACES WITH TILDDA." Fredda knew that Tildda was desperate and wouldn't listen to her.

"What?"

"Benn, *you* get in front of the mark with the two hands and put Tildda in front of the last one, with the right hand," Fredda ordered again.

Benn didn't understand why, but just nodded his head anyway, and grabbed Tildda.

"Tildda! You have to go in front of that tree. The one with the right hand glowing on it."

"WHY?" shouted Tildda, holding Benn so tightly that he could barely move.

"FAST! MOVE FAST, YOU TWO!" shouted Fredda.

"C'MON! TILDDA," yelled Benn, "WE HAVE TO GO! NOW!"

Benn started moving toward his right with Tildda glued to him. Finally, he got her to the right spot. Now Benn had to get back to the middle one. The wind blew even stronger than before and the roots tried to wrap around his legs. But, Benn was faster than the roots. He managed to get to the middle spot.

Fredda Buttler And The Left-Handed People

"PUT YOUR HAND OVER THE GLOWING HAND!" screamed Fredda to Tildda, "BENN, YOU HAVE TO USE BOTH YOUR HANDS!"

But at the same time Fredda and Tildda placed their hand over the marks, a huge branch from the wisteria grabbed Benn's waist. He didn't have time to do anything more than embrace the tree with both his arms and fight for his life. The branch squeezed his thin waist and tried to pull him from the trunk.

"I CAN'T HOLD IT ANY LONGER!" yelled Benn trying to hold tight to the tree. His hands were slippery and the ferocious branch was ungluing him from the trunk little by little.

"HELP, HELP, SOMEONE HELP!" Tildda shouted in vain.

When the vicious branch had almost detached Benn from its trunk, he swung his body forward with all the power left in him. He stretched just enough for both hands to meet their marks.

Fredda and Tildda screamed his name at the same time, "BENN!"

The three fell instantaneously to the ground, their hearts still beating ferociously. It took a few moments for them to even recognize where they had landed. The gusting wind was gone, the huge moon was replaced by a normal sized one and there were stars in the sky. The black wisterias were gone and they were surrounded by giant palm trees. There was an impressively stunning house at the end of the street. They stood up and looked around.

"It's magnificent!" said Tildda.

"Alive," said Fredda.

"And green," finished Benn.

"And who are the three of you?" A voice arose from behind and startled them.

They all turned together. There stood a creature the likes of which they had never seen. It had long, lanky frog legs, a short squat body with a head that was a combination of a frog and a rat. Fredda thought, *Maybe more like a rat. But it doesn't have a tail. Maybe it looks more like a frog.* Fredda couldn't make up her mind. It was half their size and wore something like dark shorts and held a long wooden stick. For some reason, Fredda didn't find it frightening. There was something almost endearing about the creature.

Fredda wanted to ask what it *was* exactly. She always got so distracted by people's appearances. And now, she was distracted by something like a strange animal who could talk.

Even though Tildda was beginning to panic, she still proceeded to ask, "And w… what are you, exactly?"

The creature looked at her from head to toe and said, "And what are *you*, exactly?"

Fredda wanted to laugh but held it in.

"I'm a human, of course!" said Tildda firmly. "And you?"

"And just because you are a human, you think that you are prettier than me?" the creature questioned Tildda with his strange face.

Again, Fredda wanted to chuckle but decided not to.

"Where are we anyway?" asked Benn looking around.

They heard a sound coming from a place nearby.

"What is it?" asked Tildda holding Fredda's hand.

"It sounds like some kind of animal, maybe a dog or a wolf," said Benn.

"Like a werewolf?" asked Tildda quickly, "You know … full moon, werewolf …"

The creature just shook its head and said, "Werewolf? Where have you been? I bet this is a story from The Right Side. What does the full moon have to do with werewolves?"

Suddenly, a huge palm frond snapped off from its giant trunk and landed right on the creature's head with a loud thud. The poor creature fell to the cobblestone, out cold.

Fredda jumped. "Do you think he is dead?"

Tildda chastised Fredda, "Great! And now, what are we going to do? I told you it wasn't a good idea to come to this street."

Fredda and Benn paid no attention to her whining. They were more interested in getting away from this place.

"Well, if this is the same street as Black Wisteria Street, and Mr. Frederikk Sinisster's house is that way …" started Benn.

"Then, Ellivnioj is that way," said Fredda pointing in the opposite direction. They looked at each other and began walking. Tildda followed.

"Not so fast," a high pitched voice came from behind them. The three of them stopped immediately.

"And who are *you* now?" asked Tildda surprised.

"I call myself Oolliy."

The creature looked like the other one, but younger and a little shorter.

"What are you and is he dead?" asked Fredda.

"No, he is not dead, only unconscious. He is the Keeper Of The Paths."

"Keeper Of The Paths?" The three of them questioned in unison.

"Yes, he keeps the rules of the paths, of course! And makes sure that everyone follows the path they choose."

"What do you mean by *the rules of the path*?" asked Tildda almost nose to nose with the creature.

"Well, you three are, I assume, left, right and ambidextrous, correct?

They nodded their heads confused. "How could you know that?" Tildda asked.

"That's why you were allowed to come here! That's the first rule. Here are the three of you together – a lefty, a righty and an ambidextrous person. This is the combination that opens the lock to this dimension. A limbo from which you must choose your path as the others before you."

"The others? What do you mean by *the others*?" asked Fredda staring at Oolliy.

"The others who came here before you, and you and you," said Oolliy pointing to each of them.

"Are the others dead?" asked Fredda abruptly, "I mean the others who disappeared?"

"No, not dead, only trapped in that dimension," said Oolliy pointing to the right path toward Frederikk Sinisster's house with his frog-like legs ending with long brown nails.

"You mean if we decide to go to the right, we would be able to be with the others, but not able to come back?" Fredda asked the creature, trying to understand these rules.

"Going to the right does not guarantee that you are going to be in the same dimension with the others. You *may* find them, but not for sure. And, yes, you will not be able to come back. You will be trapped like the others who disappeared."

"And what will happen if we take the left path toward Ellivnioj. That's Ellivnioj, isn't it?" Fredda pointed to the left.

Oolliy stared at her with his frog-rat eyes and said, "Oh! That path? No one has ever taken it before."

"Why not?" said Fredda demanding an answer.

"Because if you cross over to that side, you would be able to free every person who is trapped, every person who ever disappeared but …"

"But what?"

"But you would also close off all the passages from The Left Side to The Right Side and there would be no more Right Side only The Left Side."

"What do you mean no more Right Side?" asked Fredda nervously.

"It means that they would no longer exist," responded Oolliy stretching his neck toward Fredda. She leaned away.

"And only the one who is a true lefty can take this path," said Oolliy looking toward the left one.

"Only the true leftie?" asked Fredda.

"Yes, only the true lefty can unlock this path. Otherwise, one can be trapped in an infinite loop of time."

"Is there another way?" asked Benn.

"Oh! Yes, there is a third way. You can go back to the same place from which you came. Not to the left, not to the right but to the middle. You'll need the keys that is hanging on those palm trees," he pointed to the trees. Fredda, Tildda and Benn could see three silver objects hanging on the palms.

"Place the chain around your neck like a necklace. Place the key in the center of your hand, your true hand.

For the ambidextrous one, place the key in between both your hands and you will be in the same place you came from in no time."

"You mean with the vicious roots?" said Tildda already panicking again. Ooliiy just smiled with his mouth full of huge pointy teeth.

Fredda thought, *If it's so easy to destroy The Right Side, why hasn't any member of the Sinisster family, who hates the righties, ever chosen this path?*

"Because the Sinissters don't have anyone over there. And also, one must love another enough to be willing to possibly risk their lives to save from there. To choose this path, your purpose must be to save, not only to destroy," said Oolliy to Fredda. Fredda was baffled by the creature's knowledge of her thoughts.

Fredda contemplated, *So if the Sinissters didn't have anyone over there, it means that everyone who disappeared first were righties, like my father. Then, Grandpa went after him and my mother went after them.* "How did all these people disappear in the first place, Oolliy?"

The creature just stared at Fredda.

"How did they disappear?" She asked him again.

Oolliy approached Fredda closely and whispered in her ear and said, "I cannot say, as I am not the Keeper Of The Paths."

Fredda was disappointed. Trying to figure things out for herself, she asked, "Benn, what about your parents? Were they lefties, righties or ambi?"

"Righties both of them. Why?"

"Because I think all the righties disappeared first and then the lefties went after them to try to help and they also vanished."

"I don't even have a choice. Since I'm ambi, I can't go there anyway," Benn considered sadly.

"So, it seems the best thing we can do is to take the middle path. Let's go then," said Tildda anxiously, already moving to get her key. Benn followed her.

Tildda and Benn reached up and each grabbed their key. It wasn't exactly the shape of a key. It looked more like a pendant. Tildda reached for the one with the imprint of a right hand and Benn the one with both hands on it. They looked around, and at first, didn't see Fredda. Then they saw her still standing next to Oolliy, her eyes fixed on the left path.

"You've gotta' be kidding me, Fredda!" Tildda was angry. "Do you even know how many people live in The Right Side?"

Fredda didn't say a word, her eyes still beaming toward the left path.

"Approximately, six point eight billion people live in The Right Side," said Benn.

"BILLIONS?" repeated Tildda astonished.

"Yes, billions." Benn continued, "And don't forget, the majority of true lefties are still in Ellivnioj celebrating the festivals. They won't be affected by Fredda's decision.

But Fredda just remained where she was, staring toward the left without even responding. In her mind, she was back in school burning with humiliation at Maufrodezza and Numericoss' hurtful words. Fredda's thoughts whirled in her head. Now was her chance to be free from those who detested lefties. She'd also, like other children, be with the parents who loved her and for whom she longed. Benn would be able to look into his mother's eyes for the first time. Maybe she and Benn wouldn't have to feel the pain anymore.

It seemed that some magnetic pull was drawing her to the left path. Now her heart was filled with hate only. Tildda called Fredda again, but she was in her own world. Fredda started walking forward to the left path silently. Tildda shouted Fredda's name but she just kept walking as if she was in a trance.

"She's not coming back, Tildda," said Benn holding her face and looking into her frightened blue eyes.

"But it will be billions of people who will be extinguished! How could she do that? Could *you* do something like that to save your parents?"

"If I could take that path, I'm not sure myself if I could resist the temptation of bringing my parents back." Benn held Tildda's hand, stopping her from chasing after Fredda. "We need to go now. It's her choice to make."

They looked away and held their pendants. Tears stung Tildda's eyes as she turned to look at Fredda one more time. Instantaneously, Benn and Tildda vanished.

They reappeared on that wretched Black Wisteria Street. The roots were still, but as soon as Benn's foot moved, the roots started crawling toward them again. Tildda yelled at the roots as if they were going to listen to her.

Benn saw his backpack and the three silver boxes that had been left behind not far from him. He lunged for it and stuffed the silver boxes inside.

Suddenly, they heard a startling pop and a form appeared in front of them. Tildda screamed and Benn gasped.

"FREDDA!" shouted Tildda.

"Hi guys, I couldn't do it. Sorry, Benn, I just couldn't do it. I know that you'd like to see your parents as much I'd like to see mine. But I couldn't. Whatever this fight is between the lefties and the righties, I can't just save one side and allow the other to be destroyed. I can't do that to billions of people."

"WE HAVE TO GET OUT OF HERE!" shouted Tildda.

"This way toward Frederikk Sinisster's house. We'll be safe there," said Fredda already sprinting. Tildda and Benn followed her, but not without fighting against the vicious roots. They reached the rotten iron gate, opened it, and headed toward the front door as the roots chased after them.

"Do you think this is a good idea?" asked Tildda breathless.

"Nothing seems to be a good idea tonight, Tildda. But we have no other choice," said Benn following Fredda.

Fredda opened the old creaky front door. They hurried inside and to their amazement, they landed on the still safe ground that led to Black Wisteria Street.

Still lying there, they lifted their heads and saw the same moon they usually saw at night overhead. Not even the bright light from the full moon could bring any life to that horrible place.

"It's like we never even moved from here," said Tildda perplexed.

"But we did," said Fredda holding her silver pendant with the imprint of a left hand on it.

Tildda walked toward Fredda and said, "I'm so happy you're back ... By the way, Fredda, how did you know that the house would be safe?"

"Oolliy told me."

"Oh! That creature!" said Tildda grinding her teeth.

Benn checked to see if he still had the silver boxes in his backpack. All three boxes were there.

Benn looked deeply at Fredda's bright brown eyes and said, "I'm glad you decided to come back."

Exhausted physically and emotionally, they trekked back to the windmill. Fredda told them that she'd like to return the silver boxes to their original place. Tildda and Benn agreed.

They placed the silver boxes back from where Benn had gotten them. Without any more to say, they went to bed.

CHAPTER 13

YOU GOT IT ALL WRONG!

It was the end of her incredible summer vacation. But for Fredda it was the beginning of a new life. The trip to Ellivnioj meant joining a world she had never known. She had been unaware that both her parents and Benn's might be alive. Fredda felt renewed hope that someday, somehow, she would be reunited with them.

Tildda had left a few days earlier to be with her other grandma in Paris. Noell was off with his parents to resume their vacation elsewhere. He was beyond disappointed that he had missed every opportunity to do amazing things like Fredda, Tildda and Benn had done this summer.

Fredda packed her small suitcase, walked toward the window and took a look once more at Ellivnioj. The town was quiet and calm after so many days of parties.

Benn came upstairs to help Fredda with her suitcase. Both of them looked into each other's eyes not really knowing what to say or do.

After a moment, Fredda said, "I'd love to stay here. I feel that this place and the people are the family I've never had."

But she couldn't stay, as Mrs. Theoddora reminded her, "It is your grandfather's decision. He wants you to go back to school."

She kissed Benn's cheek. Blushing, she quickly turned and ran downstairs. As she was descending, she said, with her voice slightly trembling, "Please, don't forget my suitcase."

Benn stood there shocked. He touched his face to feel her kiss and then he smiled.

She said goodbye to Mr. and Mrs. Theoddora and thanked them for being so welcoming. Mrs. Theoddora embraced her warmly. She was about to leave with Mr. Gattus when she saw Mr. Bernno.

He was wearing his helmet and goggles, looking more likely to fly off rather than give them a ride to the bicycle station.

"Oh! Mr. Bernno, thank you very much for letting me borrow the pink …" and she paused, "… bicycle! I asked Benn to give it back to you."

"Oh! Yes, yes, yes … It's old, but it gives you quite a ride, don't you think?" He winked.

Fredda frowned. She wasn't sure if he knew the truth about the pink bicycle or if he was just kidding around. She heard the whooshing sound of the blades above them and said, "Yes, great riding, Mr. Bernno."

She stepped into the yellow bicycle taxi with Mr. Gattus and they left. The main street was serene now. The ride back to the bicycle station was quick and Mr. Gattus was quiet.

At the bicycle station, Fredda realized she had totally forgotten about the forbidden words.

"Mr. Gattus," asked Fredda, "What happens if you say any forbidden word?"

"You'd bring a curse upon yourself, Fredda," Mr. Gattus warned.

Fredda thought, *It seems like he knows what he's talking about! But did he just say c-u-r-s-e? Wasn't that word written on the wall ... .*

And then he distracted her with, "Shall we go?"

They walked together over the covered bridge. Halfway between the two sides, Fredda already longing to be back, couldn't help but turn to look back at The Left Side. She saw the lovely dense green vegetation.

She looked up at Mr. Gattus and then slowly looked toward The Right Side. Darkness began to descend, but straight ahead she could still make out Mrs. Matrakka's form.

"Hi, Fredda, did you have a good vacation?"

"Yes, I did. Mrs. Matrakka. Where's Grandpa Albert?" Fredda looked around.

"Oh! I thought Mr. Gattus had already told you."

"Well, Mrs. Matrakka, Fredda didn't ask me about Mr. Buttler."

"Oh! I see ... Well, Fredda your grandfather isn't here. He couldn't come to meet you."

"Who's going to take me back to school? I thought he had to take me back, you know about the rules and regulations."

"Tomorrow Mr. Gattus is going to take you back to school. Your grandfather already arranged everything."

With grave disappointment, Fredda walked silently along with Mrs. Matrakka and Mr. Gattus back to Grandpa Albert's house.

Dinner was served early. She wanted to be alone, so it was a good excuse for her to go to her bedroom early too. Depressed, because Grandpa Albert wasn't there, she plopped on her bed and just sat. She was about to drag herself up to get ready for sleep when Blue entered the bedroom.

"Oh! There you are! I haven't seen you for a long time, Blue. And by the way, thank you for saving me, Tildda and Benn from Mrs. Maufrodezza and Mr. Numericoss. I owe you one."

Blue purred, got himself comfortable on Fredda's bed, as he always did, laid on his back almost like a human with his arms straight next to his sleek gray body, his back legs semi-open, and fell asleep.

"I really wonder about you, Blue." Fredda stroked him affectionately and smiled slightly.

Next morning, Mr. Gattus drove Fredda to school. They were almost there when he stopped the car. The back door swung open and there stood Grandpa Albert. Fredda gasped. He hurried into the back with her.

"GRANDPA ALBERT!" Fredda shouted, delighted, "I thought you couldn't come." He smiled as usual.

"Hello, Fredda. Sorry! I did not mean to scare you. *I* have to bring you back to school. You know very well about the rules and regulation, don't you?" He smiled again with a mischievous gleam in his eyes. She smiled back at him.

Fredda Buttler And The Left-Handed People

Fredda could see the iron gates of school from where they were, "Grandpa Albert … . Do I really have to go back to this school? Can't you find me another one?"

"Fredda, perhaps another time when I have more time on my hands. Sorry, but I'm in a hurry, as usual." She knew that he was taking a risk in coming. His eyes darted around the street as they spoke. Fredda followed their path but saw nothing.

"This is a great school! You have good friends here and more importantly, you're safe," as they were passing through the gates, Grandpa Albert continued, "Look at the guards - best in town!"

"Not everybody likes me in here."

It seemed that Grandpa Albert knew exactly what Fredda was trying to tell him about people not liking her and said, "My dear, Fredda, tolerance is something that, we, the lefties, have to learn on The Right Side. You have to tolerate the inconvenience of being left-handed. But imagine if the right side was the opposite. Imagine if the world was *leftie*! What would the right-handed people have to do to overcome *their* inconveniences? We're not abnormal or handicapped, Fredda. We're only *different* and *different* doesn't mean *bad*. There are good and bad in each of us. Don't forget that. You should be proud of who you are. I love being left-handed. It makes me feel special. It doesn't matter if you're left-handed, right-handed or even ambidextrous, what matters is *who* you are."

"Sir, we must go now," said Mr. Gattus apprehensively.

Grandpa Albert held up his left index finger, gesturing to Mr. Gattus that he needed at least another minute with Fredda. Then he said, "Sorry, Fredda, for not being there for you when you found out about your mother. I'd like to have been the one to tell you."

Fredda didn't look at him. Her eyes were fixed outside the car window.

"I know it is difficult for you, but it is also difficult for me. For all of us. Just remember what I said to you when you first saw her picture. She was a lovely lady and made your father very happy. And he, too, made her very happy. As your mother used to say, 'At the end of the day, we are people and we have the same basic needs as all other humans. No matter where we are in the world, we are only people.'"

Grandpa Albert hugged Fredda goodbye and waved to Mr. Kaffona who was wearing his ridiculous orange plaid suit. This meant that Mrs. Cellestin wasn't back from the hospital yet.

Mr. Gattus opened the door for her. The guards took her suitcase and they quickly left. Fredda was glad that Grandpa Albert didn't mention anything about the Darkkplace.

"Have you had a good summer vacation, Miss Buttler?" asked Mr. Kaffona.

Fredda only nodded her head and kept her eyes on the black car. She knew that she might not see Grandpa Albert for a long time. Actually, she wasn't sure if she was going to see him ever again.

Fredda arrived at school a couple of days before everybody else. The school was still empty, so she would have time to think about everything that she had gone through on The Left Side. Fredda still hadn't had the time to really get to know her grandfather.

She avoided any contact with Mrs. Lagarttus but she was very interested in talking to Mrs. Lerddus, who hadn't made herself very visible. Fredda didn't feel like doing much. She spent most of her time in her bedroom, ruminating.

Two days later, it was still early morning, when the door burst open and Tildda entered the bedroom like a rocket, talking non-stop.

"Oh! Summer vacation is over! I've so much to tell you, Fredda … I really missed you … France was delightful as usual!"

Fredda, still sleepy, thought, *If I could tell you about my summer vacation you wouldn't believe it.*

"What are you doing in bed, Fredda? I already talked to Olliver and Noell. C'mon let's have breakfast together," said Tildda opening the curtains and letting light flood the room.

"Mm, breakfast sounds good," said Fredda, barely seeing Tildda in the blinding sunlight.

Tildda left and told Fredda to meet her in the main garden.

Fredda walked through the spectacular garden in the middle of school. She could see the huge half-moon window of Mr. Kaffona's new office, when Tildda popped up in front of her with a broad smile.

"You scared me, Tildda," said Fredda. Then she saw the silver pendant that Tildda was wearing, "Where did you get this pendant?"

"Oh! I have no idea. It just appeared in my suitcase when I got to France. It's beautiful, isn't it? Not sure what the right hand stands for. And actually every time I look at it, it reminds me of this dream I had. Oh! Let me tell you about my dream. I guess it was a dream, actually seemed more like a nightmare." She paused and continued, "It couldn't be reality …" she pondered, really questioning herself.

Tildda told Fredda about the dream. In it she, Fredda and this person, Benn, were in the back of Mrs. Florizeldda's Flower Shop. Tildda went on and on about her vivid dream.

"Do you know anyone named Benn?"

Fredda just stood there shocked by the lack of Tildda's memory and wasn't sure how to respond, so she countered, "I actually have something to tell you …"

"Don't tell me that you found a way to escape!"

"Better!"

"What do you mean by better?"

"I have a grandfather."

"WHAT?" shouted Tildda excitedly. "Why didn't you tell me before?"

"Well, you didn't give me a chance!"

"Oh! Look, the boys are here. Wait, don't move, stay here. I'll get Olliver and Noell and then you can tell us all about your grandpa. This is terrific, Fredda!"

Fredda sat on a wooden bench while waiting for Tildda, who was shouting the boys' names. It was a magnificent garden. The sun was shining brightly on her face. It was already a hot day, but Fredda knew that it was the end of the summer. Suddenly, she heard a voice coming from underground, whispering her name. The voice startled her.

"Fredda! Fredda!" It was a familiar voice.

"Is that … you, Grandpa Albert?"

"Yes, Fredda. It's me."

"What are you doing down there?"

"Well, I had to come back to talk to you. I really shouldn't be here, but I had to come and talk to you in person. I know about you and your friends ..." he paused, "... That you went to Black Wisteria Street. I spoke to Mr. Schnapps. That is the reason I had to come back. The first thing I need to tell you is that you should not attempt to try to find your parents, Fredda. It is too dangerous. I almost died trying to find them myself. I beg you, I beg you not to go after them."

Fredda understood, at that point, that Grandpa Albert knew she could go to the other side by herself. He had tested it when they first crossed the bridge to Ellivnioj.

"You must promise me that you are not going to go after them!"

Fredda didn't want to answer because she knew she couldn't be sure that she wouldn't go.

He asked her again.

"Promise me!"

Hesitantly, she said, "Okay, I promise."

She was itching to ask him more questions about Ellivnioj and she was even more interested in why her parents, Benn's parents and the others had disappeared. She knew that she might not see him again. She had already realized the danger he was talking about.
She knew that at any moment Grandpa would tell her that he had to go in a hurry as usual.

She remembered what Mr. Schnapps said in his moment of mental instability, *IT'S GOING TO START AGAIN. ALL OVER AGAIN. THE BATTLE, BAD TIMES, CONFLICT ... THE TWO SIDES, BAD TIMES AGAIN.*

So she mustered up the courage and asked him, "Why do they fight, Grandpa? I mean why do the right-handed people hate us so much? It's going to start again, all over again. The battle between the righties and the lefties. Is it true, Grandpa?"

"Oh, no, no Fredda, you've got it all wrong!" Yes, yes, there *is* going to be a battle. But a battle between our own kind. The lefties, of course. The lefties against the lefties. It is not a fight between the lefties against the righties. It is a fight between the *bad* lefties, who want to destroy all righties and the *good* lefties, who want to save them! I'm proud of you, Fredda, for not taking the left path and destroying the righties. But yes, this battle has been going on for many, many centuries. And my dear, Fredda," Grandpa Albert paused, "It has just begun again!"

"WHAT?" shouted Fredda completely confused by what she was hearing.

"I know, I know. I probably confused you more, instead of explaining what this battle is about. Discrimination against the lefties is one of the deepest prejudices that exists. We appear to others as clumsy or uncoordinated or even handicapped because everything is made for righties. But even with all the discrimination against our kind, it gives us no right to destroy them. That would make us just like them! It's wrong for any side to destroy the other. No matter what happened in the past, no matter if we suffered at their hands, it's just not right! It only takes *one* to make a difference, Fredda, only one."

Fredda thought for a moment about the path she had almost taken, in a moment of hate for the righties, and of course, to save her parents and the others. She could've done such major damage.

"We can live in harmony, Fredda, if we can only accept people the way they are."

"So, you never hated the righties? You never had anyone hating you because you're leftie?"

"Oh! Fredda, there will *always* be a reason to hate. But I believe every single leftie has had their moment of dislike or even hate for the righties at some point in their lives. It is inevitable. But how could I, my dear? How can any parent hate their children or force their children to be right-handed. How could I hate your father, my only son?"

Fredda thought about Evvos Sinisster and how he hated her only because her father was a rightie even though she's a leftie.

"How can you hate people only because they're different? Do you ever think about Tildda as a rightie or does Tildda think about you as a leftie? Or do you just think about Tildda as your friend?"

Fredda had never thought about Tildda in that way. The only way she ever thought about Tildda was as her best friend.

"I really have to go now ... Fredda, just remember ... I love you very much. Don't you ever forget that."

Fredda knew that he had to go and she knew that he had made a great effort to come to see her. "I love you too, Grandpa Albert." Fredda smiled and her beautiful dimples appeared.

Fredda saw Tildda coming back with the boys. She had so much to live for after this summer. She wasn't alone anymore. Her parents might be alive, somewhere. She had a grandpa who loved her very much. She had her grandpa's friends, who also loved her and were there for her. She also had a new friend, Benn, on The Left Side. There was Noell and Olliver. And she had Tildda. They were inseparable.

And in the end, what was left was *love*.

ABOUT THE AUTHOR

C. R. MANSKE believes that life without left-handed people wouldn't be right. To find out where the author was born – hold up your mirror and look at the word – ELLIVNIOJ. This city is located in the south of Brazil. She now lives in Fort Lauderdale, Florida.

Made in the USA
Charleston, SC
25 October 2012